Advance Praise for

Lady in the Window

"Maryann Ridini Spencer lends her talented pen to a sweeping tale that is sure to involve the heart."

—Debbie Macomber

#1 *New York Times* best-selling author

"*Lady in the Window* is an inspiring and inspirational story; a perfect remedy for the stresses we all experience, and as soothing as an ocean sunset.

Maryann Ridini Spencer writes beautifully with great insight into the human heart. This is a story that will stay with you for a long time."

—Nelson DeMille

#1 *New York Times* best-selling author

"Grab your beach towel, a passion fruit ice tea, and Maryann Ridini Spencer's *Lady in the Window* for an afternoon of magic, mystery, and tropical romance. Afterward, you'll be searching the Internet for Kauai real estate."

—Suzy Spencer

Author of *Secret Sex Lives: A Year on the Fringes of American Sexuality*

"Who knew sweet and spooky went together so well? An easy, breezy summer read that has me wanting to pack a bag and move to Hawaii and fall in love all over again."

—David J. Burke

Award-winning executive producer, screenwriter, and film and television director

"The moment Kate Grace steps on Hawaiian soil, she can feel the magical mana (spirit) created in a land where people live 'The Way of Aloha,' honoring and protecting our human ohana (family) and the natural environment. The Aloha spirit comes alive in this passionate story about family and the bonds of love which never die but surround us always, as is the gift of a beautiful, fragrant lei, which will never be forgotten . . . *He lei poina'ole.*"

—Danny Akaka, Jr.

Hawaiian Cultural Practitioner and Director of Cultural Affairs at Mauna Lani Bay Hotel & Bungalows

"An exquisite and heartening page turner offering hope, inspiration, and a touch of heavenly magic that takes the reader on a young woman's journey of self-discovery and purpose after faced with some life altering circumstances—loss, betrayal, and the death of a beloved family member. You won't be able to put it down."

—Rev. Maria Felipe

Speaker, Spiritual Leader, and author of *Live Your Happy*™

"An intriguing, beautifully woven story of great loss and heartbreak and the hope and healing inspired by life's miracles and magical surprises that will soothe anyone who has experienced grief and wondered if there is any hope for their future."

—Barbara A. Berg, L.C.S.W.

Grief Counselor and Psychotherapist,
Author of *How to Escape the No-Win Trap*

Lady In The Window

a novel

Maryann Ridini Spencer

SelectBooks, Inc.
New York

Lady in the Window is a work of fiction. Names, characters, and events and incidents are products of the author's imagination or are used factitiously Any resemblance to actual persons, living or dead, is entirely coincidental.

This edition published by SelectBooks, Inc.
For information address SelectBooks, Inc., New York, New York.

First Edition

ISBN 978-1-59079-407-4

Library of Congress Cataloging-in-Publication Data

Names: Spencer, Maryann Ridini, author.
Title: Lady in the window : a novel / Maryann Ridini Spencer.
Description: First edition. | New York : SelectBooks, Inc., [2017]
Identifiers: LCCN 2016028849 | ISBN 9781590794074 (hardcover : acid-free paper)
Subjects: LCSH: Life change events--Fiction. | Self-realization in women--Fiction.
Classification: LCC PS3619.P4655 L33 2017 | DDC 813/.6--dc23 LC record available at https://lccn.loc.gov/2016028849

Book design by Janice Benight

Manufactured in the United States of America
10 9 8 7 6 5 4 3 2 1

For my husband and soul mate,
Dr. Christopher Scott Spencer,
and my dear parents,
Dr. Leonard and Kathleen Ridini

A Mother's Love

A Mother's love is Eternal,

A place of warmth and light,

A devoted beacon that shines forever bright,

Guiding her children through the dark and perilous night.

Whether present or distant,

In this world or the next,

Her love is constant, never ceasing,

Like the endless tide of waves that kiss the ocean's shore,

A mother's love influences our Now and Forever,

And the best of our lives, in all our endeavors.

Acknowledgments

MAHALO TO MY OHANA: My husband Scott, my stepchildren Candy, Izabelle, Logan, and Liam; my parents Len and Kathleen and my grandparents Mary and Leo Ridini, Theresa and Leo Murphy, and Anna and William White; my brother Len and his spouse, Carol, and their daughters Jennifer and Kim; my brother Steven and his spouse, Michael; my brother Chris and his spouse, Kristina, and their children Carley, Dylan, and Michaela; my brother David and his spouse, Jill, and their children Lexi, Jake, and Olivia; and my sister Kathy Treiber and her husband, Fred, and their son Max; Uncle Mike and Auntie Jo, Auntie Pat and Uncle George, Uncle Leo and Auntie Jeannene, Uncle Ritchie and Auntie Caroline, Uncle Jimmy and Auntie Franny, Uncle Bill and Aunt Mary, and all my great aunts and uncles and cousins for their love, inspiration, and encouragement; friends Marcia Wiesenfeld, Maxine Picard, Emmy Davis, Gale Dorion, Tina Slutzky, Kathy Sutherland, Andrea and Brian Lievens, Barbara and George Adams, Stephanie Taylor, Merry Aronson, Nick Ellison, Jane Mullen, John Farahi, Rebecca Fearing, Shelley Hofberg, Frank Lunn, Natasha Lubin, Jim and Soodabeh Babcock, for their beautiful friendship and support; my ohana book team: Agent Bill Gladstone, publisher Kenzi Sugihara, Nancy Sugihara (managing editor), Kenichi Sugihara (marketing director), and Molly Stern (editor) at SelectBooks; my book editor Trudi Roth for the pleasure of working together; to Danny Akaka, Jr., for assisting with the Hawaiian translations in *Lady in the Window*; and to my City of Ventura ohana: Luke Kirouff, Nancy Broschart, Ray Olson, Joe Yahner, Courtney Lindberg, Jill Santos, Christine Wied, Tobie Mitchell, Lars Davenport, Richard Guzman, Shana Epstein, Craig Jones, Debra Martinez, and Diane de Mailly for their friendship, professionalism, and "greening" my days.

Prologue

Hanalei, Kauai

Present Day

A balmy, gentle breeze rolls off the nearby azure ocean and makes its way through the towering palms lining Weke Road. Studded with picturesque homes, from simple beach cottages to lavish mansions, the street ends at Kauai's breathtakingly beautiful, otherworldly Hanalei Pier. Birds chirp in unison, breaking the morning's stillness as if to greet one another with a cheerful "*aloha.*"

In the second-floor window of a charming white cottage nestled in the heart of Weke Road stands the lady. She looks down at the street below, catching sight of the pretty, thirty-year-old Kate Grace, who is deep in thought as she walks in front of the home, pebbles crunching underneath her feet as she kicks a stone here and there with the rim of her sandals.

The tropical breeze gingerly caresses Kate's shoulder-length auburn hair, and every so often, she eyes the white cottage, an inviting plantation style bungalow with a large, roofed lanai and a welcoming pathway of gray pavers leading up to a pastel blue front door. The two lush plumeria trees that stand on each side of the front entryway with their blooms of fragrant, velvety white blossoms and sunburst yellow centers seem to beckon her in.

Suddenly Kate stops her pacing. Overcome with sadness, she breaks into deep, guttural sobs, quickly covering her mouth with one hand and her heart with the other, as if trying to repress the outpouring of emotions. Head in her hands, she collapses forward on the hood of her rented PT Cruiser.

The lady in the window, her eyes now wide with wonder and concern, feels a sudden stab of empathetic pain for the girl, and grabs hold of her heart in the same fashion.

The lady watches as Kate's tears flow unrelenting. With an urgent desire to ease this young woman's sorrow as any mother would want to do for her own daughter, the lady moves her hand from over her heart, and places it on the windowpane. Spreading her fingers wide, and with a will powered by the Divine, a sudden burst of compassionate energy flows from the depths of the lady's soul, through the tips of her fingers, and sears through the glass to the ground below, where it surrounds Kate like a pair of loving arms.

Kate immediately feels an overwhelming sense of warmth and comfort, and as abruptly as they started, her tears stop. The pain dissipates. A light switch has turned from on to off. Puzzled by her change of mood, Kate stands still for a moment to relish the comforting sensation before wiping the wet tears from her cheeks and taking in a few deep, cleansing breaths.

The respite doesn't last long, as Kate, realizing that her realtor will be pulling up any minute, glances at her watch. She then digs deep into the large straw bag slung over her shoulder, and pulls out a compact. As she looks into the mirror to assess the damage and make the necessary makeup repairs, she notices some movement—a darkened figure in the cottage's second-story window.

Is someone home?

"Hello! Hello!" Kate yells, waving. Walking onto the stone pathway, she calls out again. "Excuse me, hello! Is anyone home?"

There's no one home. She decides the sun must be playing tricks on her eyes. After all, the realtor told her the house has been empty for some time. Kate shakes her head, chuckling to herself as she deposits the compact back into her bag.

Leaning with her back against the PT Cruiser, she stares up at the vacant window. As she does, Kate feels another curious surge—a warm, tingling sensation on her bare arms. She hugs herself, reveling in the feeling. Her face, stained with tears just a moment ago, is now bright with a smile. The lady looks down at Kate and smiles broadly in return. Several minutes later, Kate's realtor, Elaine Harrison, pulls up in her white Mercedes convertible.

"Aloha, Kate!" Elaine, an attractive woman of forty-two, dressed in a smart floral capri pant set, embraces Kate with genuine affection.

"Mahalo, for coming," replies Kate using the Hawaiian word for thank you.

"But of course, daahling," says Elaine. Originally from London, her sophisticated British lilt is evident from the lovely, gentle rising and falling of her voice. "Come, let me show you the lay of the land."

Kate's mouth drops open as she enters the cottage. It's much more than she bargained for—so warm, with casually elegant décor right out of the pages of a magazine. But the outward appearance alone isn't what grabs Kate; it's the aura of the home, which fills her with a comforting sense of joy, as if the house is enveloping her in a wave of loving light.

"What a happy place!" Kate exclaims with delight, as she walks in circles around the open room.

"Oh, it has a wonderful *mana*!" replies Elaine. "'Mana' is a spiritual energy or force that encompasses a person, place, or thing."

"Yes, yes, it does," says Kate, a thrill running up and down her spine. Leave it to Elaine to summon precisely the right word to express the inexplicable way the cottage makes her feel.

Upstairs the lady chuckles and silently echoes the sentiment, "A wonderful mana indeed."

Part One

A NEW DOOR OPENS

Manhattan, Long Island, and Hawaii

1

Five Months Earlier

Sitting at her massive redwood desk in the impressive Madison Avenue offices of *New York View Magazine*, Kate pecks away at her computer's keyboard composing the last bit of copy for her upcoming cover story, "A Wine Lover's Tour of the North Fork Vineyards." Every so often, she gazes up at the television, volume set to low, which sits at the center of the mahogany hutch directly in front of her.

On the screen famous talk show host Olivia Larkin, a vivacious forty-two-year-old black woman, interviews a group of stunning, bare-chested male hula dancers on the lawn in front of her spectacular waterfront home in Kauai.

One of the dancers, with bulging muscles, silky black hair pulled back in a ponytail, and a devastatingly gorgeous smile, demonstrates several smooth, sexy dance moves, which Olivia attempts to repeat . . . to no avail. To help her, the Polynesian hunk places one hand on each of Olivia's hips and proceeds to gently move her body from side to side. The action, just too overtly sexual for Olivia to take seriously, causes her to burst out in an explosive wave of infectious laughter.

"Oh my God!" Kate can't help but yelp in amusement.

"What've you got going on here?" asks a bemused Cindy Maroni as she pops her head into Kate's open office door. Cindy is a well-dressed fortysomething woman with a slightly pudgy frame, who is both Kate's BFF and the magazine's fashion editor. "Got your lover boy stashed away somewhere in here or something?"

"Yup. Jason's chained under the desk . . . where he belongs."

"Sounds like fun," quips Cindy. "Say, I've heard of playing music while you write, but watching TV?"

"I usually don't, but I heard Olivia Larkin is doing a week of shows on location from her estate in Kauai. I just had to get a peek."

"Well, it looks like you're getting more than a peek. Those men are hot and the locale sure beats her New York studio any day!"

"Did you file your story yet?" asks Kate.

"Of course—would I be slinking around the office if I hadn't? The gang is going to P. J. Clarke's for drinks with Jasmine to celebrate her engagement. Wanna come? That is, of course, unless you're meeting your *lov-ah,*" Cindy says with a bat of her eyelashes. "Don't worry though, if it's one thing I understand, it's a better offer."

"You're incorrigible!" says Kate, laughing.

"That's what you love about me."

"Absolutely. And I'm in—Jason's on a business trip so there's no better offer."

"Again? Well, his loss, our gain. All work and no play will make Kate a very dull girl, and we certainly can't have any of that."

P. J. Clarke's is hopping. The bar and surrounding tables overflow with the usual under-forty professionals in tailored suits, laughing and drinking. In a corner table away from the bustling crowd, Kate and Cindy ogle their coworker Jasmine's three-carat engagement ring.

"That is some rock!" exclaims Cindy.

"It's beautiful, Jaz," adds Kate.

"Clive slipped it onto my finger as we were gazing at the sun setting over Maui," beams Jasmine. "It was so romantic."

"I bet," Cindy says, rolling her eyes and mocking Jasmine's dramatic delivery.

"I'm really happy for you," Kate says, playfully kicking Cindy's foot under the table for her bad behavior.

"Have you planned the date?" asks Cindy, heeding Kate's prompt to act with decorum.

"In the early fall when all the leaves are turning," Jasmine answers without missing a beat. "Probably somewhere out on Long Island. I love that time of year, and after all, why wait, right?"

"Dig in, ladies. No need to hold back in front of moi!" trills *New York View's* dapper, pencil-thin arts and entertainment editor, Henry Weinberg, as he peers at them through his chunky designer glasses and sets a large dish of crab cakes down on the cocktail table.

"Oh, don't worry. We won't," exclaims Cindy as she plunks her fork into the mound of crab cake appetizer topped with avocado puree.

"Yummmmmy! Almost as good as sex!" she squeals. "But don't tell my husband I said that."

Kate chuckles and takes a sip of her Chardonnay.

"You got that right," Henry adds in a low, suggestive voice as he eyes a handsome young stud at the end of the bar.

"Planning your next victim?" fires Cindy as she follows Henry's unabashed stare.

"I beg your pardon. You know I'm a one-man *woman*," retorts Henry.

"Oh really?" laughs Jasmine. "Then why do I hear you talking about a new man in your life all the time?"

"Seriously. You get more action than Kate here, and she really *is* a one-man *woman*," adds Cindy.

"Yes, but perhaps Kate shouldn't be," Henry says with a playful frown.

"What's that supposed to mean?" asks Kate.

"Kate, sweetie—we're all friends here, so let's level. How long have you been dating Jason now, five years?"

Kate nods.

"You always said you'd never go beyond dating a year without a rock in sight. When you met Jason, you said he was on the same page. Cut to five years later and . . . bubkes, nada, nil, nunca. But Jasmine, on the other hand, our dry, but of course very talented business editor friend, who cavorts more with balance sheets than bedsheets—no offense, sweetie—has it all locked up in under a year with her man."

Jasmine shrugs innocently, taking a sip of her wine. Kate decides to let the comment slide.

"You know, I heard on Dr. Phil once that most women over forty have a better chance of being run over by a truck than of getting married," Cindy says, a mouth full of crab cake.

"That's from an old *Newsweek* article," corrects Jasmine. "The saying is actually, 'a woman over forty has a better chance of being killed by a terrorist than of getting married.'"

"Oh, well, whatever," says Cindy, as she waves her hand in dismissal.

"And this obnoxious fact is supposed to have something to do with me?" asks Kate, none too pleased. "Anyway, don't make me older than I am—I'll remind you all that I'm *only* thirty!"

"Ticktock, ticktock," Henry mutters, not exactly under his breath.

"I heard that!"

"So, what gives?" asks Jasmine in earnest.

Kate scrunches up her nose. "It'll happen. We've talked about it a number of times, and Jason always says he wants to. He wouldn't lead me on. He knows how important marriage and family are to me. Non-negotiable, period."

"Well, glad to hear it. And I don't mean to be hard on you Kate, because you know I'm crazy about you," says Henry gently. "But hasn't it always been you that's brought up the 'M' word?"

"And I repeat," adds Cindy, "a woman over forty has a better chance of being killed . . ."

"Geez Cindy, whose side are you on?"

"Now, now girls," Henry chides. Seeing an opportunity for a joke to lighten the mood, Henry plucks the olives out of his martini and places them on either side of his cheeks, á la Marlon Brando in *The Godfather.*

"Is this guy gonna deliver the goods, or do we have to send someone to break his legs?"

While Cindy and Jasmine laugh at Henry's imitation, Kate musters a tight smile and feigns amusement. Her thoughts meanwhile focus on the elephant in the room and her growing impatience with Jason's lack of commitment.

"Love you, honey," says Kate's father Glen, a handsome seventy-five-year-old man with a head of thick white hair, chiseled features, and an air of sophistication.

"I love you soooo much, sweetie," adds Kate's mother Catherine, a slight, elegant woman seven years her husband's junior. "To the moon and beyond. God bless. Smooch, smooch."

"Love you too, to the moon and beyond," Kate says, blowing back kisses into her cell phone as she lays sprawled out on the living room sofa of Jason's hip Battery Park City apartment, dressed in comfortable black yoga pants and a black jersey scoop neck top. She clicks off FaceTime and sets the device down on the nearby coffee table, trading it for the real estate section of *The New York Times.*

Smooth jazz plays on the stereo as Kate peruses the listings, dreaming of a future home for her and Jason. Sally, a black and brown striped tabby, sits curled up in a contented ball next to her on the plush leather sofa in the modern, monochromatic black and white apartment with sweeping New York City skyline views. Kate strokes Sally's back tenderly.

"I know technically you're Jason's cat, but since he's out of town so much lately, and I've become the designated cat sitter, we've become best buds, haven't we, Sally?" asks Kate. Hearing her name, Sally's ears perk up and she lifts her head before turning on her back so Kate will rub her tummy.

"Yeah, see, that's what I'm talkin' about," Kate chuckles. "I've been thinking about what might be a good opening to get Jason to talk about marriage again. Maybe after my parents' upcoming fiftieth anniversary and vow renewal?"

"Meooooow," Sally agrees, wriggling her tiny body this way and that, commanding more attention.

"OK, I'll take that as a yes," Kate laughs.

Kate loves her career, and she relishes the thought of being a wife and mother someday just as much. While there will certainly be some sacrifices to make, why not try to have it all? It'll take a little juggling, but it will surely work out in the end. Her mother did it. A stay-at-home mom until the kids were all off at school, she made her way back into the workforce in her forties to become a top real estate agent, then branch manager in Long Island.

Even though Kate's biological clock is now ticking, she was never in a rush to fulfill a certain deadline. Growing up, and in her twenties, it was all about school, doing well, and honing her skills as a wordsmith in order to pursue her lifelong passion as a writer. In the Grace household, it was always understood that all the children—Kate and her older siblings, Carla, now forty-two, and Derek, now forty-five—would go to college.

Kate appreciates the fact that she's got great role models, and her desire to follow in their footsteps is real and strong. Like her mom, Kate excelled in English at school, was a good seamstress, loved to cook and entertain, and had an eye for interior design. Ditto for her sister. Derek, on the other hand, was his father's son, excelling in team sports, business, and financial matters. He rarely had to study to get A's, and getting into Columbia University had been a piece of cake.

Her parents, married almost fifty years to date, and her deceased grandparents, the Italian Grammy and Gramps, on her mother's side, and the Irish Nana and Grandda, her father's parents, all married for love. They had remained devoted partners for fifty-five and sixty-five years respectively, until they passed. Family and longevity matter to Kate and all of her near and dear. Kate believes her vision for a productive career and a happy married life is reachable, and she also feels she has found that life with Jason. There's just one little hitch for the moment—the marriage part.

Not a problem, Kate thinks as she strokes Sally's belly. *This too shall pass. It'll work itself out.*

Almost on cue, Kate's cell phone, which plays a tropical beat, begins to jump around the coffee table.

Jason.

"Hey, hon, where are you? I thought you'd be home by now."

"I got delayed in Chicago—sorry, babe."

Kate groans, moving Sally off her lap to stand up, then begins to pace around the room.

"Sorry. I'll be home tomorrow morning, K?" Jason says in a playful little boy voice.

"OK," sighs Kate, dejected. "What time shall I make the dinner reservations for then?"

"Reservations?"

"For tomorrow night."

The awkward silence on the other end of the phone is deafening.

"To celebrate our first date. Remember?" Kate says to dead air.

No response.

"Hello . . . Earth to Jason. We talked about it when we had dinner with your clients at Nobu, remember?"

"Oh, yeah!" Jason replies, making a quick recovery. "Sorry, babe. Make it for seven o'clock."

"OK, will do. Love you."

"Love you too, babe, kisses. Give you a ring at work when I get in."

The line is dead even before she hangs up. Kate plops back down on the couch and Sally, seeing her sitter's empty lap, climbs back in for a cuddle—now needed by both parties.

"Well, sweetie poo, it's just me and you again."

Kate fidgets anxiously as she sits in the plush burgundy leather chair facing the large mahogany desk of her editor, Edward Alexander. Medium height and build, with strong features, thick grey hair, and steel blue eyes, Edward is a strikingly handsome, charismatic man of sixty-eight with a commanding presence, yet a kind, solicitous demeanor.

The custom-made wooden bookshelves that line his office are filled with antique finds and first editions. Behind his desk, in front of the bay window with a water view, are beautiful shots of Edward's family—his wife Meredith, sons Jared and James, and daughter Elizabeth. Kate loves looking at Edward's family smiling at her from their various European travels, relaxing on glistening beaches in Hawaii, and sailing their yacht in the Peconic Bay.

What a dream life, Kate thinks. *Ralph Lauren advertisements come to life. And if anyone deserves it, it's definitely Edward.*

A self-made man and devoted husband and father, he's worked hard as the founder of *New York View Magazine* and has reaped the benefits of his labors after thirty years as editor and publisher. Kate is grateful to Edward, as he has been like a second father to her, taking her under his wing when she was fresh out of journalism school. They work exceptionally well together, thanks to their mutual appreciation of and passion for art, good food, design, and the written word. Kate has diligently worked her way up the ranks of the magazine to land as head feature writer and editor for the esteemed publication.

This is my dream job, she thinks. She never loses sight of how lucky she is.

Edward sits on the corner of his desk facing Kate. "Your cover story on the North Fork vineyards is phenomenal."

"Thank you, Edward. That means a lot coming from you."

"It's fierce out there in editorial land, and the Internet and social media have only made it tougher. As you know, we always have to be on our toes and think outside of the box just to keep ahead of the curve," Edward begins. "Now that we have some new travel and hospitality advertisers joining us for our print pub and the online version of the magazine, I'd like to expand some of the features we do to include regular stories on places outside of New York, in locations that are important to our advertisers."

"OK, so what are we talking?" asks Kate.

"For example, give readers a taste of the local flavor of a particular place, the landscapes and architecture, the food, the restaurants, the arts. Perhaps we'll cover an important local event, interview key personalities at their places of work or in their homes, and so on."

"Sounds good to me, Edward. Where are you thinking we should cover first out of the gates?"

"Well, to begin with," Edward starts, then takes a couple of seconds for a dramatic pause, "how about the Hawaiian Islands?"

"What?" Kate's mouth drops open, her eyes sparkling.

"That's exactly how I thought you'd react."

"And you've been keeping this from me?" Kate playfully accuses.

"I just told you now. I had to make sure all the contracts were signed, sealed, and delivered."

"This is awesome."

"You're preaching to the choir. I know how much you love the place. The first assignment is in Kauai. Think you can handle it?"

"Kauai?" Kate cries out excitedly. "Seriously?"

"I'm sending you to do a cover story feature on Olivia Larkin."

"That's so funny! I just saw her show the other day that she taped at her home in Hawaii."

"Great, so you're a step ahead."

"How did you get Olivia?" Kate asks, barely containing her excitement.

"Her publicist, Connie Martin, called me, and we got to talking. I mentioned that we landed several Hawaiian Islands-based travel and hospitality accounts, and she told me Olivia was there for the next month taping some shows at her home in Princeville, Kauai. One thing led to another and, well, you know the rest. It's a good fit, a win-win all around, don't you think?"

"Absolutely," Kate enthuses.

"I figure we'll do a cover story featuring Olivia in her favorite tropical paradise. Maybe you could take in some of the local color with her, shadow her doing whatever it is she likes to do, as long as it includes some of our new accounts, of course. That way she can promote her pet projects while we get a cover story our advertisers like and that people are interested in reading about. What do you say?"

"You had me at Kauai."

"Yeah, a dream assignment," Edward chuckles. "So pack your bags, young lady. I'd like you to go right after your parents' fiftieth anniversary party. Just check in with Martha in travel, and she'll make all the necessary arrangements."

Edward scribbles on a piece of paper and hands it to Kate. "Here's Connie's cell number so you can touch base with her about coordinating the activities with Olivia."

"I really appreciate this, Edward. I promise to do you proud."

A WEEK BEFORE the celebration of Kate's parents' fiftieth wedding anniversary, Kate and her sister convince their mother to go shopping for a new bridal outfit. Afterward they celebrate their find over a "girl's lunch" at Long Island's historic Jedediah Hawkins Inn in Riverhead. Sitting on the inn's oversized outdoor veranda while they snack on tomato and basil bruschetta and cod cake appetizers, the women laugh and chat as they leisurely nurse glasses of iced tea.

The inn and restaurant, situated on twenty-two acres of beautiful, meticulous land where they grow the outrageously fresh food for farm-to-table dining, is adorned with a plethora of lush green foliage and perennial flowering gardens overflowing with pink, purple, and white hydrangeas, a charming gazebo, and a pond. The structure, originally built in 1863 in the Italianate style popular at the time, has been recently restored to a comforting blend of traditional and contemporary design.

"You really like the dress?" asks Catherine.

"Mom, you're a knockout in it," Carla reassures her.

"I don't look silly wearing white?" Catherine frets.

"You look beautiful, Mom!" says Kate. "I can't believe you were thinking about wearing the blue dress you wore to Lucas's first communion. It was nice, but—"

"I like that dress! It's beautiful," Catherine protests defensively.

"It is, Mom," Carla agrees. "It was perfect for my son's communion, but for fifty years, you needed something really special. Something that says, WOW!"

"I have to admit, wearing it, I do feel like a young bride again."

"So you should!" Kate exclaims, smiling broadly.

"You girls are really something. I love you both so much, you know?"

"We know, to the moon and beyond, we love you that way, too, Mom," says Carla.

"And I'm so proud of you both," adds Catherine. "And speaking of proud—Kate, you must be so excited to interview Olivia Larkin, and in Kauai no less. She's really quite a lady. An amazing humanitarian and a true women's advocate."

"All your hard work is really paying off, Sis," Carla agrees.

"Thanks guys. I'm feeling really blessed in so many ways."

"I hope you're planning to take some vacation time while you're over there," Carla says pointedly, knowing her sister's workaholic tendencies.

"You really should, dear," agrees Catherine. "You never take a break. It will do you good." Catherine reaches for Kate's hand and holds it, then takes Carla's in her other, little tears forming at the corner of her eyes.

"Mom, are you crying?" asks Carla.

"Tears of joy, sweetie. Today has been such a special day," Catherine sniffs as she dabs at her eyes.

"Mom, tell us again about the night you met Daddy," Kate requests. While Kate has heard the tale probably over a hundred times, it never gets old for her.

"Well, in my day, young men and women used to go to dances. That's how many people met their husbands and wives back then. Your father was with one of his buddies, and to tell you the truth, I didn't even know he was interested in me. I thought he was checking out my friend Nancy. Later, she told me that your dad asked her for *my number.*"

"But didn't another man give you a promise ring?" asks Kate.

Catherine blushes. "Yes. I didn't go to the dance intending to meet someone—I was only accompanying Nancy because she asked me, and I had nothing else going on that night."

"Tsk, tsk, Mommy," Carla playfully chides, "What made you go out with Daddy if you were engaged to another man?"

"A promise ring back then was the promise of an engagement, not quite as serious as an engagement ring, but of course I knew what was coming. Brian, my intended, was out of town, doing his obligatory two years in the service," says Catherine. "While he was away, I guess I had time to really think about our future, and truthfully, I couldn't imagine what life would be like with Brian. He was a nice enough guy, but when I really thought about it, I wasn't in love with him. As soon as I met your father, something inside me told me I had to go out with him. So we went to church and then for an ice-cream cone."

"To church?" Carla asks. She always likes to chide her mother about this particular part of the story.

"It wasn't a date. We went as friends," Catherine explains. "Afterward, when your father bought me an ice-cream cone, I realized my feelings were more than just friendly."

"An ice-cream cone?" laughs Kate. "Wow, sounds like Dad really pulled out all the stops to sweep you off your feet."

The ladies share a good laugh.

"Things were a lot different then," says Catherine. "Very sweet, simple, and innocent. Like I said, I had an overwhelming sense that I should go out with your father, even just once. I can't tell you why I felt that way, I just did. And it was that one non-date that wound up sealing my fate."

"And then what?" asks Kate.

"After that first time, I knew," smiles Catherine. "But I told your dad I couldn't see him for a few weeks, that I had some things to sort out with Brian, who was coming home for a few days on leave. Your dad was upset, but he waited. My plan was to give Brian back the promise ring, and as nicely as possible to let him know that I was no longer interested in moving forward with him."

"How did you know Dad was the one so soon after you met?" asks Kate.

"Like I said, I can't explain it, I just knew," Catherine responds, remembering clearly how she felt. "It was like I had known your father for years. He felt like home to me, as if there was no question that we belonged with each other. I just couldn't imagine life without him. Your father told me later that he felt the same way."

"Frank and I felt like that when we met," says Carla, "Although it took a while for the timing to get to 'I do.' How about you Kate, did you feel that Jason was 'the one' when you first got together?"

"I don't know if 'the one' popped into my head," answers Kate, thinking back, "but I did know he was really special and that I was very attracted to him. It took a few months of dating casually, though, before we decided to be exclusive. And of course we're both committed to getting married and having a family."

"Well, he is a very handsome and successful guy," Catherine says. "I can see how you would be attracted to him."

"Any normal red-blooded American girl would be. That and the fact that he's so charming, not to mention a Yalie," Carla teases as she winks at her sister.

"So, sweetheart, you mentioned that Jason and you talked about marriage and family, but that was a while ago. Have you discussed any more about the future?" asks Catherine. "Not that there's any rush," she adds, not wanting to appear judgmental.

Kate sips her iced tea as she ponders her mother's question. "We haven't recently, but I'm sure we will. I do love him, Mom."

"My wish for both of you girls is just to be happy," says Catherine. "To see you both living the lives you desire, with the loves of your life. Carla, I know you've found that, and Kate, I'm confident it will happen for you. Just remember to always follow your heart, whatever you do. When in doubt, or if you ever need assistance, ask God and the angels for guidance, and they will never steer you wrong."

"Let's toast to us," Carla says, lifting her glass of iced tea. "And to Mom and Dad's fiftieth!"

"You may now kiss the bride," the priest says as he blesses Catherine and Glen with the sign of the cross.

The bride and groom stand on the steps of the Centerport Yacht Club, a private members only venue located on Long Island's North Shore. A slice of Gold Coast architecture built some seventy years ago, the club sits on the inlet of Centerport Harbor, not far from the forty-three-acre Vanderbilt mansion (now a museum) on Little Neck Road. To passersby, the club appears to be just another stately New England home. Sailboats docked in the inlet sway in the gentle wind, in full view of the blue sky and white powder puff clouds. It's a picture-perfect day to renew vows in such a romantic setting.

"Don't Mom and Dad make a gorgeous couple?" asks Derek. Kate's brother is a handsome man with the demeanor and looks of a young Tom Hanks.

The crowd bursts out in another round of applause to acknowledge the couple that looks more in love today than they were fifty years ago when they first said, "I do."

"I'd like to make a toast to Mom and Dad," announces Derek. "Waitresses are coming around with glasses of champagne, so all those twenty-one and over, take one please."

Derek looks at his two pretty teenage daughters standing beside him and his attractive wife Julie. His daughter, Dawn, the eldest of the girls, is dark like him. Ashley is fair, and resembles her mother.

"You girls can each have a sip of your mom's champagne, but otherwise it's soda or iced tea, got it?"

"Long Island iced tea?" quips Dawn. Ashley chuckles.

"Ha, ha, ha," says Derek sarcastic.

Two young children burst forward through the crowd of adults: Carla's son, eight-year-old Lucas, followed by a family friend's daughter, Emma, a little girl of six. Emma fiddles with her cranberry silk dress. Her head is a mass of flowing brown curls. She looks at Derek with a large expectant grin.

"Yes, my sweet, what can I do for you?" Derek smiles, unable to resist the charming little dear.

"We want to toast, too," squeals Emma.

"Yeah!" Lucas scrunches his nose and yells happily.

"You two, how can I resist?" Derek shakes his head at the children, and then turns to a waitress who's passing by.

"Miss, would you mind getting these two young people Shirley Temples with at least three cherries each?" he says, winking at the young pair. The waitress gives a playful thumb-up, and scoots off to the bar.

Everyone is dressed to impress for the joyous event. Glen and all the men present look handsome in their suits and ties. Kate and Carla wear dark purple satin, knee length dresses with sheer black stockings and fashionable pumps, and Catherine's stunning cocktail-length antique white gown with sheer sleeves and a scooped-neck bodice showcases a pretty teardrop diamond necklace—her anniversary gift from Glen.

Jason, looking very *GQ* in his fitted Armani suit, stands next to Kate, his arm draped around her waist.

"Are you nervous?" he whispers in her ear.

"A little," says Kate. "I'm usually behind the scenes. I'm not used to being in front of a crowd like this."

"Well, it's for a good cause," smiles Jason.

"Mom and Dad," Derek begins, now that everyone appears to have a glass of something in their hand. "Carla, Kate, and I would like to say a little something to you both on this momentous occasion. For my part, I want you to know how grateful I am to have you as parents. You've given your children and your grandchildren such a wonderful example to emulate. The selfless love you have for each other, your devotion, your caring, your understanding . . . and perhaps most importantly, your commitment to family. You've always been there for your children, you've sacrificed for us, guided us, taught us, and loved us through thick and thin, when we were good, and when we were bad. Actually, were we ever bad?" he says, looking to Kate and Carla.

Laughter rises from the crowd.

"Mom and Dad, we toast you in celebration of your fifty years together, and we hope we are all around to celebrate the next fifty! Here's to you!" Derek cheers, raising his glass high.

"Here, here!" cries one guest.

"Alla famiglia!" another shouts.

"Erin go Bragh!" screams a contingent of Irish cousins.

Derek puts an arm around Carla as she begins her toast.

"Mom, Dad, ditto what Derek just said," starts Carla. "One of the greatest gifts you have given to your children is your unconditional love, and that started with your unconditional love for each other. In this day and age, when divorce runs rampant, and when people give up rather than work on solutions together, I'm glad that you showed us how rewarding persistence, forgiveness, and open communication can be. I'd also like to thank you for your guidance. Growing up, you took the time with Derek, Kate, and me to help us explore our talents, tap into our desires, and get on our respective paths to achieve those goals. You made us believe that we could do whatever we set out to accomplish, and inspired us to make this world a better place than it was when we came into it. We love you, Mom and Dad, God bless," says Carla, lifting her champagne glass.

The crowd toasts and cheers, taking another sip of their champagne.

With Carla on one side of Derek, Kate moves to the other. She nervously unfolds the piece of paper in her hand.

"Since I've been labeled the writer in the family, and also since I'm not so good at speaking extemporaneously, I wrote down a little poem that expresses what I want to say to you today, Mom and Dad. I speak for myself, but I also include Derek and Carla in this, too.

"To our parents on their anniversary;
We love you more than words can say,
And we wouldn't want it any other way.
Your love is a hearth,
A haven,
A place to come home to,
To celebrate,
To appreciate,
To enjoy and enfold;
Creating a family that means more than gold.
Your love is the sun that lights up the sky,
Providing solace, guidance, and comfort when things go awry.

Like a wave of warm breezes when times grow cold,
Your love and encouraging words never grow old.
As children, by nature, we grow self-focused, unaware,
As adults we see more clearly, just how much you truly care.
We are blessed by our Creator,
To share and to hold,
Our family together, in a Divine fold.
Through the years and beyond, we'll remain together,
Nothing can separate us now . . . not ever.
You, our parents, love so deeply, so honestly true,
Yes, that which you have given,
Now comes back to you.
Thank you,
Thank you,
Thank you,
For everything you do,
Have done,
And continue to do.
Our dear, dear parents, we so love you."

A well of applause fills the air.

"Bravo!"

"Congratulations!"

"Alla famiglia!" the crowd cheers once again.

"Come on inside everyone," says Derek, waving happily.

The crowd begins to make their way up through the Club's massive glass entryway. Some linger a bit behind to congratulate the bride and groom.

"Let's do what the Grace family does best," Derek continues. "Let's *paaarty!*"

Later that evening, as the anniversary festivities conclude, a few party stragglers sit enjoying cocktails on the massive veranda. It's a spectacularly clear night, and the lights from the surrounding homes and boats reflect off the still waters. In a private corner, Kate and Jason sit opposite one another on large wicker chairs, a coffee table with a bowl of cashews between them.

"That's really great about your cover story Kate," says Jason, sipping his Merlot. "But I'm sorry, I don't think I can make it to Kauai. My schedule has me traveling."

"Again?" moans Kate. "I was hoping we could have some real R & R time together. It's so beautiful, romantic, and restful; plus the hotel would be completely comped by the magazine and advertisers."

"I said I'm sorry."

"Well, you know," Kate's wheels were turning, "maybe I could look into changing the dates. I'm good as long as I file a few months ahead of production."

"Kate, I just can't," Jason says firmly. "I have to keep myself open and available."

Kate, now dejected and annoyed, doesn't know what to do, so she picks some cashews out of the bowl and begins anxiously eating them, one after another.

"Kate, please stop. It is what it is."

"Fine. I just wanted us to have a nice vacation, that's all."

In the deafening silence that follows, Kate's thoughts turn to the conversation she had with her work associates at P. J. Clarke's. Henry's question about Jason and her getting married repeats over and over in her mind. And she can't help but chew on Cindy's remark about how a woman over forty has a better chance of being killed by a terrorist than of getting married. Before the voices echoing in her head can get the best of her, Kate reaches across the table and touches the top of Jason's hand.

"Jason, you know Jasmine from my office?"

"Yeah."

"She and Clive got engaged. Their wedding is in the fall."

"Good for them," Jason says, a touch of bitterness in his voice. He doesn't like where this is going.

Kate takes a sip of wine for fortification, then asks with all the moxie she can muster, "Have you thought more about us?"

"What do you mean?"

"Getting engaged, married?" Kate tries her best to sound casual.

"I don't know if we should be talking about this right now."

"Why not? It's actually the perfect time—we just witnessed a beautiful, joyous event celebrating fifty years of marriage and togetherness. As you'll remember, when we met we told each other that's what we wanted for our future."

"We did, but I still am not seeing why we have to discuss this right now."

"Because it's five years later, that's why. I just want to know if we're still on the same page, that's all."

Silence.

"Are we?" asks Kate.

Jason wiggles uncomfortably and takes another sip of his wine. Kate waits patiently for an answer, even though her stomach's starting to tighten.

Finally, to break the unbearable silence, Kate adds, "It's OK, please just tell me what you're feeling, whatever it is. I need to know the truth."

"Let's just talk about this later. Why upset a nice evening?"

Kate feels a clenching in her heart.

"I'm sorry if you find talking about this uncomfortable."

"It's not that," says Jason, exasperation in his voice. "Look, it's just that, well, why do we need the piece of paper? Aren't we beyond all that?"

Kate's mouth becomes suddenly dry. Her head begins to hurt. She wants to cry, to scream. She also wants to speak, but suddenly the right words evade her. Her mind immediately turns to the advice given in all those dating and relationship books that sit on her bedroom shelf.

Stay calm. Don't get angry. State your feelings and desires, but don't nag. Wait for an answer.

"Our life, when we are together, is wonderful," Kate replies slowly and deliberately. "You know how important family is to me, and why marriage is a nonnegotiable. You led me to believe it was important to you too, and that we were on that path. We've also talked about this before, and I've given you plenty of time to sort through your thoughts. After five years of dating, we know everything there is to know about each other. If this isn't what you want, Jason, I just need to know."

Kate practically bites off the inside of her lip waiting for Jason to speak.

"Well, I'm going to need some more time to think about it," says Jason, finally breaking the icy silence between them.

Rather than crumble, Kate suddenly feels a surge of energy accompanied by a deep knowing of how to react to him. Where this instinct is coming from, she isn't exactly sure, but she goes with it.

"You've had five years, Jason. If you need more time to think about it though, take it. I'll be in Kauai and you'll be doing whatever's on your schedule. We can settle things when I get back."

"What do you mean, 'settle'? You mean there's a possibility things would change between us if we don't get engaged?" asks Jason.

"Yes, until we're both on the same page, that's about the size of it."

"Heard anything more from Jason?" asks Cindy as she watches Kate pack.

Kate's bedroom is straight from the pages of *Elle Decor*, an eclectic mix of antique and contemporary. The creamy beige walls, topped with well-appointed crown molding, are adorned with beautifully framed paintings of colorful tropical flowers and seaside landscapes. A large king-size bed in the center of the room with a dark mahogany headboard and an elegant white comforter invites Cindy to sink into its gorgeous yet comfortably soft decorative pillows—which she does appreciatively.

To each side of the bed sit matching antique nightstands and lamps that Kate found for a steal in SoHo. On the right wall is a large bay window with floor to ceiling satin drapes. Opposite the window is the perfect place for Kate to read and write—an oversized loveseat upholstered in a beige, blue, pink, and green floral patterned fabric with a matching ottoman for her to prop up her feet or set down a pot of tea. On the wall facing the bed is a magnificent hand-carved French Country armoire, also one of Kate's bargain finds.

"Jason called to tell me where he was and that he hoped I had a smooth flight to Kauai. He says he's really going to see what he can do to join me, but again, schedule permitting," says Kate, with a note of hope in her voice as she folds a shirt before placing it into the suitcase on her bed. "I take it as a good sign, since he knows our next conversation is an important one. I don't want to get my hopes up too high just in case he can't make it for whatever reason, though."

"Good. Just go with the flow and enjoy yourself. You deserve it," Cindy says.

"Do you really think I did the right thing?" asks Kate.

"Are you kidding me? You should have put Jason's feet to the fire a long time ago. Now you'll know what he's really made of—and if he's the man for you. It's not like you haven't talked about this before. I'm so proud of you for standing up for yourself."

"I hope it's going to be OK. I don't know what I'll do if he doesn't come around."

"Don't worry about that right now," Cindy assures her in a comforting tone. "You'll be fine no matter what happens. You're gorgeous, talented, and have never had a problem getting a date. Just sit back and let him do all the work."

"That's what my mom said."

"Smart lady. So, take our advice and go to Kauai, do your story, have a great time, and get some R & R. Just remember, if you get too bored talking to interesting people, enjoying the lodgings, dining at five-star restaurants, and drinking in those fabulous sunset views, I'm only a phone call and an airline ticket away," laughs Cindy.

THE NEXT MORNING, Kate arrives at JFK airport, ready for her ten-hour flight to Hawaii. Her arrival at Kauai's Lihue Airport at 4:00 p.m., six hours behind New York, was intentionally planned in order to give her enough time to enjoy a late afternoon dip in the hotel's infinity pool, followed by a leisurely dinner. Kate is grateful that she's flying first class—one of the perks of the assignment—as her seat reclines into a bed, and theoretically, she's able to sleep. Still, Kate finds herself only able to doze for short periods of time, as thoughts of Jason keep replaying over and over in her head.

What will their future be? Where is he at this very moment? Is he thinking of her? While she doesn't know the answers to those questions from Jason's perspective, she has been thinking about her boyfriend nonstop in the days since their last conversation at her parents' anniversary party. Eventually Kate decides to watch a few movies to help pass the time, and also to force her to stop obsessing over Jason.

As the plane travels farther away from the US mainland and gets closer to Kauai, a strange but welcome calm seems to permeate Kate's being. As the third movie ends, Kate's thoughts turn not to Jason, but to the adventure that awaits her, especially the upcoming interview with Olivia Larkin.

Kate watches from the plane's window as it makes its descent into Lihue airport. The lush green tropical foliage is breathtaking, as is the aquamarine water surrounding Kauai. When the plane touches down on the runway, all the passengers, including Kate, immediately break into enthusiastic applause.

"Aloha," says a female voice over the airplane's PA system. "We hope you enjoy your stay in the Garden Isle. Please stay seated until your seat lights are turned off, indicating that it's safe to move around. Your luggage can be picked up at Carousel B."

The moment Kate exits the plane via a metal staircase that deposits her on the tarmac, she feels a warm, wet wind on her face and a flash of welcoming sunlight. Gorgeous distant mountain views dominate one side of her view, and the expansive ocean occupies the other. She feels her skin tingle and her stomach jump with excitement. The sensation is unlike any other, and one that she has only experienced in these islands. Her last visit, two years ago, was to Maui. She's also traveled to the Big Island, Oahu, Molokai, and Lanai. However, Kauai, the oldest and northernmost island in the Hawaiian Island chain, is unexplored territory for her. From everything she has ever read or been told, it promises to be a most magical, prehistoric place, having been born from an ocean floor volcanic eruption some six million years ago.

Just beyond the open-air terminal, beautifully constructed of dark wood with colorful murals depicting ocean scenes and garden landscapes, Kate sees rows of swaying palm trees, burnt orange ginger plants, and colorful flowering trees lining the airport's main road. A light breeze with the sweet scent of fragrant blooms sweeps through the terminal.

"Aloha," a pretty Polynesian woman with an effervescent smile greets Kate.

The woman, wearing a flowing white dress, sports a burst of flowers behind her right ear and several fresh, floral leis around her neck and on one arm. The leis, some made with purple and white orchids, and others made with sweet-smelling plumerias with velvety petals of white and deep golden yellow centers, call to Kate.

"How much?" Kate inquires.

"Fifteen each, two for twenty-five," replies the woman.

"I'll take one of the plumeria leis please," says Kate.

The woman places the lei around Kate's neck and looks directly into her eyes.

"E pili mau nā pōmaika'i me 'oe," she says in her native tongue.

"May the blessings continue to be with you always," the woman translates. "Aloha."

"Mahalo," Kate responds.

Kate turns to rummage through her colorful, quilted Vera Bradley weekender bag for her wallet. A split second later, she looks up to hand the woman payment for the lei, and sees that she is gone. Kate does a quick check around the area, but she's still nowhere to be found. She then walks the length of the corridor, but to no avail. Baffled, Kate walks up to one of the local vendors.

"Excuse me, but did you see a woman wearing a white dress, selling leis?" asks Kate.

"No, not that I can recall," responds the soft drink vendor, a young man who sports a blue and white floral print Hawaiian shirt. "Try up in baggage claim."

Kate walks over to the baggage carousel area, and as she waits for her luggage, continues to search for the woman. A half hour later with no sign of the mysterious lei vendor, Kate retrieves her two pieces of American Flyer luggage with a red fleur-de-lis pattern. Chalking up the strange encounter as both a lucky break and a good omen, Kate smiles with delight as she takes in the surroundings on her way to the rental car counter.

While the Lihue airport is busy, it's nothing like the stress-inducing crush of massive structures, crowds of people, bumper-to-bumper cars, copious exhaust fumes, and noisy honking horns that characterize JFK airport. Instead, the gentle, warm breezes, perfumed air, and lush surroundings of the Kauai airport emanate a calming, joyful spiritual energy or "mana" that would calm the most distressed traveler. Little does Kate realize that mana is just what she needs, and it's about to put her on a course that will change her life forever.

2

Kate's Hertz car rental is a cute silver PT Cruiser. The retro style compact auto has plenty of room for one, and it's the smart, economical choice for her basic island transportation needs—guaranteed to deliver at least twenty-four miles of gas per gallon.

Kate programs the car's GPS device for The Westin in Princeville, a five-star ocean resort tucked away at the end of a pretty residential street on Wyllie Road. From the online photos, the resort, which boasts a spectacular ocean panorama, is located right at the cliff's edge, some two hundred feet above the Pacific.

Kate drives approximately forty-three minutes along Highway 56. The lush views along the winding freeway's twists and turns are simply magnificent. Kate knows she's getting close to her destination when the GPS directs her through a roundabout into a residential area, which finally dead-ends at the resort.

Greeted by a lava rock sign that reads, "The Westin Princeville Ocean Resort Villas, A Vacation Ownership Resort," Kate drives the PT Cruiser around the circular driveway and parks it in the center of the hotel's front entryway. The Westin's Hawaiian plantation style structure has the feel of a stately mansion versus a hotel lodging. Large columns of lava rock support a Craftsman style roof, which extends like an awning from the front door to shade the driveway underneath.

This is awesome! Kate thinks to herself. *A perfect place for unwinding and writing, not to mention a sublime ending to a long plane ride.*

"Aloha, miss. Welcome to The Westin!" says a young porter dressed in khaki shorts and a handsome Hawaiian floral shirt. He takes Kate's keys as she exits the PT Cruiser and pops open the trunk to retrieve her suitcases.

Upon entering the lobby, Kate takes a moment to soak in the elegant, calming view. The wide-open room has a vaulted wood beamed ceiling and a sand-colored stone floor. Architectural accents of carved dark Kona wood are everywhere, including the furniture, which boasts plush upholstery in shades of burgundy and white. A captivating view of the resort grounds and the blue Pacific is visible through a wall of windows in the distance.

Kate sighs as she feels calming energy flood her mind. She's extremely grateful for the pampering surroundings that are to be her home for the coming week.

At check-in, she is given a key card to Room 452, a one-bedroom premium villa with an ocean view. Arriving at her suite ahead of the porter, Kate notices that the ample room is even more than she expected. It has the look and feeling of a well-appointed home. The design of the L-shaped kitchen with its granite countertops and stainless steel appliances and the décor of the plush living and dining space are impeccable. The ocean-view lanai, visible from the suite's entrance, is also sumptuous and spacious.

As Kate walks around the suite, she notices all the little homey touches that will make her stay both comfortable and memorable, from the large screen TVs, to the playful dishware and abundant utensils, to the master bedroom's luxurious jetted tub—a place she knows she will frequent at the close of each day.

"Can I get you anything else, miss?" asks the bellman after he delivers Kate's suitcases to the master bedroom.

"No, thank you. Mahalo," says Kate as she hands the bellman a tip.

Now that she's in Kauai, the first item on Kate's "to-do" list is to call her parents to let them know she's arrived safely. It's already midnight in New York, which makes it just about her parents' bedtime. Kate clicks the "Mom and Dad" tab on her cell phone's speed dial.

"Hello," answers Catherine.

"Aloha, Mom! It's me!"

"Honey!" Catherine says excitedly. "You're in Kauai?"

"Yup, at the hotel. The resort is just fabulous!" squeals Kate with delight.

"Tell me, tell me."

"My room's just gorgeous. It's so beautifully decorated, and has the most magnificent ocean view!"

"I'm so happy for you, dear. Take lots of pictures. Maybe we can even FaceTime while you're there and you can show Dad and me around?"

"That's a great idea. Tomorrow I'll be at Olivia's all day, so the timing will be a little off. But the day after that should work."

"Hold on, honey, Dad's waking up. He fell asleep a little earlier. But you know him, he doesn't want to miss a beat."

"Hi, sweetheart—glad you made it safely," says Glen.

"Dad, it's awesome! You would love it. I wish you and Mom were here with me. We'd have a drink on the lanai, and then go to dinner. We'll FaceTime in the next day or two and I'll show you around."

"It's a date!"

"I'll let you two go to sleep. I'll call you tomorrow, OK?"

"Good night, and God bless," says Catherine. "Love you, dear—to the moon and beyond."

"To the moon and beyond," echoes Kate before ending the call.

Scanning the list of her voice mail messages, Kate notices there's one from Cindy and another from her sister. Checking her text messages, she laughs at the selfies sent by Cindy, Henry, and Jasmine. In the photos, they're holding tropical cocktails and making silly faces.

Another text from Derek reads "Aloha," after which are two emoticons—a palm tree and a happy face. Kate replies to his text, "Aloha, bro! In paradise now. XO to all," and she ends the text with a pink hibiscus icon.

While Kate feels a little let down that there is no message waiting from Jason, after over five years of dating, she knows his MO by now.

He's probably giving her time to get settled in and will text her tomorrow. She decides not to read too much into his silence, and if one thing's for sure, she's certainly not going to text him. Let him make all the moves now.

Kate unpacks her suitcases and places her foldable clothing neatly in the master bedroom's attractive wood dresser. Next, she hangs up the four dresses, three skirts, and several pairs of pants she's packed. She's extremely pleased that she had the foresight to bring a variety of weights, colors, and fabrics. This way she'll have plenty of options.

With the rumblings of her stomach now audible, Kate decides she's ready for an early dinner. Should she order up room service to enjoy on the lanai? What about a visit to the resort's seaside restaurant, Nanea, which overlooks the pretty grounds and where people may be mixing and mingling?

Her mind now made up that it's welcoming faces and human interaction that she needs, Kate washes her face, freshens her makeup, and quickly changes into a casual jersey dress.

"*Nanea* means peaceful, beautiful, tranquil, or to pass your time with ease," says the perky waitress, as if reading from a dictionary.

She must've said this a hundred times before, thinks Kate, sitting at a prime table situated at the restaurant's poolside lanai.

"That's a perfect name for this place then," Kate smiles as she finishes the last bite of a delicious farm fresh salad made with locally grown beets, spinach, red onion, cherry tomato, and goat cheese, tossed in a light citrus vinaigrette.

"How did you like the salad?"

Kate flashes her a thumbs-up in approval as she takes a sip of her iced tea.

"Now *that* looks amazing!" Kate marvels as the waitress serves an impressive looking entrée of coconut shrimp with a side of spicy peanut sauce, jasmine rice, and grilled island pineapple.

"Enjoy. Let me know if I can get you anything else," says the waitress as she leaves to check on another table.

Kate picks up one of the plump, crispy shrimp and dips it into the delicious peanut sauce. "Mmmmm," she moans in ecstasy after biting into the tender, crunchy morsel.

Between bites of food and sips of tea, Kate decides to power up her constant companion, Mr. Laptop, and leisurely review her digital notes in final preparation for her interview with Olivia Larkin. Every so often she checks her email and phone in hope against hope she might hear from Jason.

What she does find is an email reminder from Connie Martin, confirming Kate's interview with Olivia the next morning, as well as the yoga and spa date for the following day, and a party invite for a barbecue at Olivia's home on Friday night. The rest of the time in Kauai will be Kate's to do as she pleases.

Cool, thinks Kate, her thoughts now focused on this week's exciting assignment. The moment, however, is short-lived as her mind wanders back to Jason.

It's OK. I did the right thing. Now, the hard part—the waiting, she thinks as she sits alone and watches the moon's glow light up the Pacific in one of the most alluring and romantic places on Earth.

3

A brief rain turns the gray skies vibrant blue on Kate's first full day in paradise. The morning air, slightly humid but still cool, makes it a perfect time to go for a beach run.

Kate descends the stone stairs located next to the resort's front entrance, which lead her to the sandy beach at the bottom of the cliff. In her jogging shorts, Nikes, and a form-fitting tank top, she runs a path along the water's edge. Thirty minutes into her jaunt, Kate hears a muffled "ping" from inside her waist pack.

I hope it's Jason, thinks Kate as she stops and excitedly pulls the phone out of her pack.

"Aloha! Hope you had a smooth trip and good luck on your interview today," the text reads. "Thinking of you. Luv, Jason. XO."

Kate's ecstatic. There's no question that the tropical heaven that is Kauai is awesome, but Jason's little "XO," makes a world of difference, even in paradise. Suddenly, the ocean looks bluer, the grass greener, and the sweet perfume in the air smells even more delicious.

It's gonna be a great day, thinks Kate as she continues the remainder of her run.

Anxious to shower and eat breakfast, Kate makes her way back up the beach stairway towards the resort with a spring in her step that wasn't there before.

The exercise, combined with the fact that her body clock isn't sure which way to turn, has stepped up Kate's appetite. Once back upstairs, she quickly orders room service to get her day started right. A half hour later, a wholesome breakfast tray arrives loaded with a veggie egg white omelet, whole wheat toast, a few sublimely sweet pineapple slices, and a rich Kona coffee. She takes the spread out to her room's lanai. As she eats, she mentally reviews the combination of outfits she might wear to meet Olivia.

In Manhattan, Kate's customary interview attire would consist of a tailored jacket paired with a crisp pair of pants, a simple dress, or a pretty skirt and blouse combination. In Kauai, where tropical weather dictates business norms, Kate is thrilled to be a bit more casual.

To keep it professional with a look that's pulled together, Kate selects a pretty burnt coral knee-length linen skirt and a simple white jersey tank top with a lace neckline. She complements the outfit with a striking leather belt and strappy beige sandals. The decorative neckline of the tank top makes wearing a necklace unnecessary, so instead Kate opts for a pair of antique gold chandelier earrings.

Perfect! she thinks, looking at herself in the mirror.

How is it possible I feel this good? ponders Kate as she heads towards the resort's front lobby to retrieve her car from the valet. *I don't feel any stress anywhere in my body. Did I really need a break from my routine that badly?*

The one thing Kate knows for sure is that the feelings being aroused in her in Kauai are in direct contrast to how she feels going about her daily routine in Manhattan. Sure, she loves her friends and her job, even with its unending flow of deadlines and constant stream of networking events. Her work, after all, provides her with a very nice lifestyle, and she's doing what she loves—being a journalist.

So what's the problem with that? Kate thinks.

On the other hand, her day job makes it very difficult to find time enough to pursue her other passion: writing creative fiction. Since she spends most of her "usual" workday sitting in front of her laptop screen, repeating the same scenario when she gets home at night is the last thing

Kate wants to do. The brainpower creative writing requires just doesn't seem to be accessible after her customary eight to ten hour workday.

In a perfect world, in addition to finding a way to balance writing for the magazine with prioritizing her own creative pursuits, she would also opt for the quiet harmony of nature's country green versus the city's concrete and grey.

Maybe someday, Kate thought. *For now I've got to focus on the present.*

Once in the PT Cruiser, Kate programs the GPS with Olivia's Princeville address, which is off Kuhio Highway, not far from Anini Beach. The valet has already set the radio to soft instrumentals, a delightful blend of harmonious chords that immediately complements the tropical surroundings.

"Keep straight," announces the electronic female voice on the GPS, as Kate pulls away from the curb.

"Mahalo," Kate says out loud with a chuckle.

Kate enjoys the music that plays on the car's radio as she drives the curves of Kuhio Highway. She makes a mental note of the Hawaiian slack-key guitar instrumental title, "Kekaha Chimes," which the radio announcer says is by a local musician named Paul Togioka.

Kate slows her vehicle when she spots the driveway to Olivia's gated estate. The gold numbers of the address are easy to read against the black Hawaiian lava rock. Kate powers down her driver's window as she pulls up to the intercom and presses the call button.

"Aloha," answers a welcoming female voice.

"Aloha, this is Kate Grace from *New York View Magazine*. I'm here to interview Olivia Larkin."

"Hi Kate! This is Olivia. I'll buzz you in, just follow the driveway up, and I'll meet you outside on the lanai."

"OK, got it! Mahalo," answers Kate, a little surprised that it's Olivia on the other end.

Olivia is a very well known, sought-after, award-winning TV personality and media mogul, not to mention a philanthropist, humanitarian, and all-around amazing human being. In Kate's experience, most of her high-profile interview subjects were so busy that they made it a point of having an entourage of helpers to assist them with such mundane details as answering a phone or a front gate buzzer.

As Kate navigates through the gated entryway and down the meandering paved road, she feels as if she's driving through a tropical rain forest. There are palm trees and ferns in various shapes and sizes, kahili ginger, bird of paradise plants, and other flowering beauties mixed into the tall, abundant green.

Nearing the end of the private road, Kate sees an impressive two-story white plantation style home with a huge wraparound porch peeking out from behind the native foliage. A magnificent towering royal poinciana, which sits in the front yard to the left of the home, takes Kate's breath away. With its huge umbrella-shaped crown and mass of scarlet colored blooms, the tree is unlike any other she has seen before.

As Kate takes in this glorious setting, she begins to feel the energy in her body changing once again. The air feels light and fresh, and her senses are razor sharp.

It's definitely not the cup and a half of Kona coffee I had for breakfast, that's for sure! Kate thinks to herself. *So, what is it, then?*

Regardless of where the feeling of heightened awareness is coming from, Kate knows she is on the precipice of something big, but can't quite put her finger on what exactly it is. Her adrenaline spiking, she parks the PT Cruiser and begins to walk towards the front door.

"Aloha! Kate!" Olivia calls to her from the front lanai.

A beautiful and charismatic presence, the forty-two-year-old icon, dressed in white linen pants and a form-fitting lime green scoop neck top, looks age defying. Her shoulder length black hair, with its expertly cut jagged ends that flip this way and that, showcases a pair of attractive white hoop earrings that pop against her flawless, smooth black skin.

Olivia's warm greeting makes Kate feel instantly at ease—more like she is reconnecting with an old friend versus someone she's just met.

"Aloha, Olivia."

"Come in, please."

The foyer is a large area with vaulted ceilings and beautiful, rich, dark wood floors. The white paneled walls are decorated with colorful tropical landscapes and island people in the style of the famous French Post-impressionist painter, Paul Gauguin.

"The folks at *New York View Magazine* really appreciate your taking the time to do this interview."

"Oh, sure. My pleasure," says Olivia. "My publicist Connie told me she's set up a few adventures for us, so we're definitely going to have some fun. Follow me."

Kate enters the bright, welcoming home and immediately notices that the lush tropical foliage from the outside has been carried through to the walls of the home's large circular entryway which are decorated with an exquisite, hand-painted mural depicting a serene island setting. The sounds of trickling water that emanate from the stunning floor to ceiling fountains that grace either side of the foyer further add to the breathtaking ambience. As Kate follows Olivia down the central hallway into the heart of the home, she glances up and notices the soaring rich koa wood cathedral ceiling and takes note of more colorful island art that decorates the light walls. A minute later, the two arrive at the beautiful great room at the center of the lavish home.

"Wow!" cries Kate, unable to conceal her excitement as she gazes out the impressive all-glass retractable wall and soaks in the million-dollar view of lush grounds and the sandy beach beyond.

"It is pretty cool," agrees Olivia.

"It's breathtaking. I feel like I'm on another planet."

"As opposed to?" chuckles Olivia.

"As opposed to New York, which *is* another planet."

Olivia laughs out loud.

"I'm just in awe, I guess—at everything. I can't believe how different it is here."

"You got that right!" Olivia smiles. "Have you ever been to Hawaii before?"

"Yes, not Kauai though. It feels so primal here."

"I know what you mean. It's pretty amazing, which is precisely why I call this place *home*. Don't get me wrong; I love New York. I enjoy my place there, and I love working and playing there, too, but my soul lives here. This is where I breathe. It's where I think, and it's where I'm truly me."

"I can see why," says Kate as she peruses the room.

Overstuffed white sofas that sit in the center of the room are adorned with accent pillows in floral shades of coral, blue, red, yellow, and green, which pick up the calming hues in the magnificent artwork on the walls. Hand-painted tables, chairs, and hutches create a mix of casual and eclectic elegance.

Taking a deep breath, Kate inhales the sweet floral scents from the perfumed white ginger and other exotic floral arrangements that are displayed throughout the sumptuous living space. Gazing to the left of the living room, she spies an expansive kitchen with white wood cabinets, stainless steel appliances, and accent colors of blue and beige, which create a warm, beachy feel. A row of high back wicker chairs make their home in front of the massive kitchen island with a butcher-block countertop.

"Great kitchen! It's so bright and airy," Kate exclaims as she drinks in the beautiful natural lighting and tropical views through the white shuttered kitchen windows.

"Yes, it is," says Olivia. "It has a great energy, too, doesn't it?"

Kate nods in agreement.

"It's so quiet too. All you can hear are the sounds of nature," Kate notices as she listens to the bird chatter through the open windows and doors.

"It's a place where I get to think, relax, and regroup. I get some of my best ideas and inspiration here. Come, let's sit outside," motions Olivia as she and Kate walk through the great room's retractable wall out to the large covered lanai.

To the right of the lanai is another living area complete with an outdoor kitchen. Ten comfortable wicker chairs upholstered in a red and white floral pattern surround a large, rectangular wood table. To the left is a sitting area with comfortable sofas and chairs in a complementary floral pattern.

"Please, have a seat," Olivia says, sitting on one of the sofas. Kate sits opposite her.

A pleasant looking Polynesian woman in her mid-fifties now enters the lanai. She wears a floral sundress and her dark hair is tied back in a ponytail.

"Aloha," says the woman.

"Kate, meet Halia. Halia, Kate."

"Aloha. Pleased to meet you, Halia," chirps Kate.

"May I get you a coffee or a passion fruit iced tea?"

"An iced tea would be lovely, thank you," Kate answers.

"Make that two iced teas, Halia," Olivia interjects. "Mahalo."

Kate digs into her bag and pulls out her laptop as Halia exits the lanai. "If you don't mind, I'd like to take notes on my laptop while we speak."

"Go right ahead."

"The article will definitely mention all of your endeavors, from being an award-winning talk show host, to your magazine, TV and film productions, and all the philanthropic work you do," begins Kate as she adjusts the table for easy typing access.

"However, the main focus of the piece will be about living here, why you chose Kauai, and as you just mentioned, why you consider this place to be home above all other places you've lived and worked. So, first, if I may, what was it about the island that made you want to purchase a home here?"

"Ah! Getting to the good stuff right away, I see. This is going to be an enjoyable interview. Now mind if I get comfortable?" chuckles Olivia as she kicks off her shoes and tucks her legs beside her on the couch.

"Not at all."

"Well, to begin, the first time I visited the Hawaiian Islands was about fifteen years ago. I was on vacation, and I liked that trip so much that I kept on coming back, going from one island to the next."

"Growing up, I spent most of my time in urban areas. So I found the lush tropical foliage of the islands . . ." Olivia pauses to get it just right, "The perfumed air, the magnificent beaches, the warmth of the people, well, Hawaii just seemed to call to me."

"What was it about Kauai, specifically?"

"How do I explain it? I had a certain knowing almost immediately about the place. From the start, I've always felt a special affinity, like I belong here."

Kate nods in agreement. Instinctively she knows exactly what Olivia is talking about.

"And it's the little things," remembers Olivia. "For example, after the show's second season when we did a week on location in Kauai, I stayed on for a brief vacation. I noticed it would rain for a bit in the mornings or maybe late in the afternoons, but then the sun would always come out shortly afterward. Showers here feel gentle and comforting, like some sort of cocoon. I've never felt like that about the rain anywhere else."

"As you've probably already also noticed, it's not crowded or built-up here, which makes it feel timeless," continues Olivia. "I can walk the white sands of Anini Beach and gaze out at the ocean for hours. I'm aware of my thoughts, and I can feel nature's energy. It empowers me."

"You feel nature's energy?"

"Yes!"

"How? In what?"

"I feel it in the flowers, the trees, the Earth, the human body—all of nature and everything in our world is made up of energy. It permeates everything and connects us all. You've heard of quantum physics?"

Kate nods.

"Science has proven that the world is changeable. It's made of atoms, which are composed of subatomic particles or energy. Even our thoughts are energetically charged. So, when you allow yourself to be still in nature, you will begin to tap into the almost electric sensations that flow between us. You can then begin to develop a sensitivity to other people's auras, and determine whether they are emitting a positive or a negative energy."

Kate continues to listen, mesmerized. Olivia speaks what she knows to be true, but she has never heard this idea so eloquently expressed before.

"Here's another example," Olivia adds with excitement. "No matter how many times I drive across that historic one-lane steel truss bridge that leads into Hanalei and see those jagged mountain tops and nothing for miles but tropical green to my left and the blue Pacific to my right, I feel like I've been transported to a more peaceful, gentler time. When I take in this harmonious, divine energy, I feel so complete, and so full in my heart and in my spirit," says Olivia as she wipes a tear from her eye.

"Just talking about it gets me so emotional—in a good way. And I'm not PMSing, if that's what you're thinking. Or am I?"

Both ladies laugh out loud.

"I think it's wonderful that you feel that way. I can see that you really love it here."

"I do! I love the community, the people, how they live, what they inspire," Olivia replies. "There's a Hawaiian word for family, 'ohana.' This place, these people—they're my ohana."

Halia enters with a full tray of delectable looking goodies and sets it down on the coffee table. While she pours each of them a glass of passion fruit iced tea, Kate can't help but eye a basket of assorted pastries and baked goods.

"I see you've spied my favorites. You've got to try a muffin or scone with one of our local jams. Just killer," says Olivia.

"Are they homemade?"

"They are, but I didn't make them!" laughs Olivia. "They were made fresh this morning at The Plumeria Café in Hanalei. It's a breakfast and lunch place in the heart of Hanalei that I co-own with a friend. We sell all types of bakery items, local coffees, teas, jellies, curds, and jams."

Kate starts to fix herself a plate.

"The pineapple ginger jam is yummy, but my favorite is the Meyer lemon curd. Actually, either is to die for. A little bit of that on a blueberry muffin or a whole wheat cinnamon scone is simply divine," Olivia says as she rubs her hands.

"Can I get you ladies anything else?" asks Halia.

"This will do for now, mahalo."

"I didn't realize you were part owner of a café," Kate says. "I'd really love to see it if we have time."

"Absolutely! We can have breakfast there tomorrow. I'll have Connie move our yoga session to 11:00 a.m., and we'll do our spa treatment and lunch after that at The Westin."

Kate beams and gives Olivia an enthusiastic thumbs-up.

"So, why don't I pick you up early, say around 7:30 a.m. and we'll drive over to the café together. Afterward, I'll show you around the town a bit so we don't do yoga on a full stomach. It's such a quaint place, you'll love it."

"I'd like that a lot, thank you," Kate responds. "On another note completely, I'm sure your publicist told you that the magazine hired a local photographer to take some pictures here today. Is it OK if he snaps a few shots of you at the café, too?"

"Of course!"

"How long have you had this house?" asks Kate after washing down the last bit of scone with iced tea.

"Oh, about ten years. The minute I stepped foot in this house, I had that same feeling as when I first visited Kauai. It felt like home to me and I knew I had to buy it. Sure, I had to do a bit of fixing up and re-modeling to make it my own, but it was one of the best moves I've ever made."

"It's very special," Kate nods.

"Since this is your first trip to the island, I hope you're not just going to work while you're here. Did you set aside some time to explore a little?"

"That I did!" exclaims Kate broadly. "I told my editor I definitely wanted to take a few extra vacation days."

"Great! Because once you explore the island, you'll understand what I'm about to tell you."

Kate ears perk up.

"I get chills even remembering," says Olivia as she rubs her arms.

"First . . ." Olivia struggles a bit to find the right words. "Someone who has come to be a wonderful friend once told me that 'aloha' is more than just a greeting of hello or goodbye. You've heard the terms, the 'aloha spirit' or the 'way of aloha'?"

Kate nods.

"Do you know what aloha really means?"

"Well, besides being a greeting, it encompasses love and affection."

"Good start. To the Hawaiians, aloha is actually a very sacred and spiritually powerful word. It incorporates caring not only for yourself, but also for your neighbors, the community as a whole, the Earth, sky and ocean—all of nature. Living aloha or in the spirit of aloha means to live generously, to respect one another, and to honor, love, and protect all that surrounds us. In ancient times, aloha meant 'the God in us.' It's a code of ethics to live by, but it's also more than that. It's something that's part of our soul and in us all, and all we need to do to access it is to be open to recognizing it."

"I read once that the ancient Hawaiians viewed nature as being part of them, not separate."

"That's also part of the meaning of aloha," says Olivia. "It embodies nature. Mother Earth gives to us, and we must commit ourselves to caring for and protecting her. Plants produce the oxygen we breathe, and soil is nourishment to grow the food we eat. The ocean provides marine life in which we also can partake, but if we decimate our lands and seas, we're not only *not* following aloha, we're also destroying ourselves."

"So, aloha, besides being a greeting, is a way of life, a belief that we're all connected—at one with nature and with each other," summarizes Kate. "Sort of a 'do unto others' philosophy?"

"Precisely. The Hawaiians also believe that when your heart is filled with aloha, you have the capacity to influence those around you by living it, and the more you love and the more compassion you express, the more it grows in others, and in yourself. We all create this powerful 'mana,' which is a spiritual, magical force, with our thoughts and actions, so we better get it right."

"How beautiful," exclaims Kate. "You know, I've been here less than twenty-four hours, and I think I can already feel that energy, that 'mana' as you call it. Actually, I know I can recognize it."

"Woo-hoo!" claps Olivia. "The girl's one of us."

Kate chuckles as she finishes typing some notes into her computer.

"Olivia, tell me about your life growing up," Kate says. "Let's start at the beginning when you were a child."

Kate, having already done her research for the interview, knows Olivia's story well. However, hearing Olivia recount the poignant details of her life—a rags-to-riches story of an underdog who, with hard work and dedication, achieved astounding success—proved to be more moving than Kate could've ever imagined.

Olivia grew up poor, with her father and mother working a series of odd jobs to keep things together. When she was seven, her parents divorced, after which her father slowly but surely disappeared from her life—first by making periodic appearances, and then stopping altogether after he remarried and started a second family.

To cope with financial strain after the divorce, Olivia and her mother moved in with Olivia's maternal grandparents. Real tragedy struck when she was twelve. Her mother died of cancer and left Olivia in the sole care of her grandparents from there on out.

"Nana" and "Pops" were both hardworking people, "salt of the Earth," to quote Olivia, and their only grandchild meant the world to them.

They taught Olivia the joys of learning and excelling at school, and encouraged her in activities such as speech and debate.

While she was loved and doted on at home, at school, due to the fact that she was slightly pudgy and had a problem with acne, she was often ridiculed. It was a vicious cycle; the teasing and ostracism she received from the world outside her home led her to seek solace in food and the comfort of reading. This made her somewhat of a hermit, a "bookworm" as Nana affectionately called her. Whether she realized it or not, being the butt of her schoolmates' jokes gave her great empathy for others in future years, and the fact that she excelled in academics never went to waste.

It wasn't until her late teens and early twenties that she began to blossom into the beauty that she is today. The breadth of experience she obtained in her own transformation—regular exercise, a healthy diet, proper grooming, body/mind/spirit balance, as well as following her professional and personal passions—plus putting time into spiritual and emotional development by "paying it forward" and focusing on the positive, all became part of her raison d'être that today encompasses every facet of her life.

With a degree in journalism from NYU, Olivia worked her way up the television ranks as a field reporter, then anchor. Later, she hosted a local talk show which eventually led her to host her own nationally syndicated top-rated TV series, *The Olivia Larkin Show.*

On the personal side, she married in her early thirties, but both her and her spouse's hectic work schedules meant that they were often separated for long periods of time. After six years, they amicably decided to divorce.

"My personal story has a very happy ending, I'm glad to say," grins Olivia. "I now make my home with my soul mate Grant Anderson."

"Grant is a real estate developer, correct?"

"Yes, and he's also a business entrepreneur. He's a living doll, and I thank my lucky stars we found one another."

Front doorbell chimes are heard in the distance, and a few moments later Halia enters the lanai with a young Asian man.

"*New York View's* photographer Mr. Ken Yoshida is here," announces Halia.

"Aloha," smiles Ken. "Sorry if I interrupted you. Would it be okay if I took some candids while you finish your interview, then later maybe we can do some set-ups?"

"By all means," says Olivia. "Had my hair and makeup done earlier this morning, so I'm camera ready."

Ken begins to snap photos of Kate interviewing Olivia. Later, after the interview, special setups are coordinated at various locations inside and outside of Olivia's home. As usual with these types of photo shoots, Kate watches and makes suggestions for poses to Ken, knowing the type of shots that will please her boss Edward.

"I think we've got some great options for the cover today," enthuses Kate as she, Olivia, and Ken snack on the delicious lunch buffet set out by Halia.

The smorgasbord features a curry chicken salad on pita bread, Hawaiian sweet potato and taro chips, a tropical fresh fruit salad, crudités with hummus, decadent chocolate chunk macadamia-nut brownies, more passion fruit iced tea, and cappuccinos.

"I have my computer in the van out front—do you want to look at some of the digital images now?" asks Ken.

"That would be awesome!" says Kate.

"I'd love that," Olivia adds.

Olivia and Kate continue to enjoy the buffet as Ken sets down his lunch plate and makes a beeline towards his van.

"I feel like I'm doing a lot of eating today," Kate laughs. "Between breakfast at the hotel, then the scones and muffins, and now this lunch spread. Good thing I went for a run this morning!"

"You have nothing to worry about, my dear, trust me," says Olivia as Ken excitedly returns and powers up his computer on the large wooden lanai table.

"Ah, they look gorgeous!" cries Kate when she views the slideshow.

"Mmhmm!" Olivia agrees, pleased with what she sees. "I guess I've still got it going on, don't ya think?"

"You can say that again!" exclaims Ken.

"The colors and the lighting are fantastic, too," Kate gushes. "Edward will be so pleased. Mahalo, Olivia, for all your time today, and the wonderful hospitality, and to you Ken, for these beautiful photos!"

"I really enjoyed the interview," Kate says to Olivia as the two women walk to Kate's PT Cruiser.

"It was such a pleasure to meet you, too. I'm really looking forward to our spa day tomorrow. I'm warning you ahead of time, today you got to ask all the questions—tomorrow, it's my turn," says Olivia with a large Cheshire cat grin.

"What?"

"You heard me, what's good for the goose . . ." chuckles Olivia.

"OK, well then, I guess I'll have to answer, but my life definitely isn't as exciting as yours."

"I'll be the judge of that, thank you very much," smiles Olivia.

Olivia's down-to-earth attitude and genuine kindness has made an impression on Kate.

A class act, she thinks.

Out loud she says, "It's a deal."

"See you bright and early tomorrow at 7:30 a.m.!"

"Sounds like a plan," smiles Kate.

4

Back in her room at the resort just after 5:00 p.m., Kate feels the need for a refreshing swim. Slipping on a pretty beach cover-up over her sexy aquamarine Tory Burch one-piece, she makes her way down to the resort's luxurious infinity pool that sits on the edge of a cliff overlooking the ocean.

Kate kicks off her rhinestone-studded silver flip-flops and places them under the poolside chaise lounge she has claimed with her cloth sun hat and quilted bag. She removes her cover-up next and places it neatly on the chaise.

The sun still burns brightly, so Kate decides not to remove her sunglasses. She walks over to the pool's edge and skims the cool water with the toes of her right foot.

Sublime, thinks Kate. *The perfect temperature.*

She slowly descends the pool's tiled staircase and rotates her arms and hands in a flowing butterfly motion through the refreshing waters before settling her shoulders just beneath the surface.

"Ahhhh," sighs Kate, as she revels in the delicious feeling of the cool water caressing her sun-warmed skin.

Kate suddenly realizes that she hasn't thought about Jason all day long.

Not an easy feat! she thinks in awe of the accomplishment. *Imagine. Not even once, until now.* Of course now that Jason is front and center in her mind, Kate instinctively knows she is probably going to obsess about him for the rest of the evening.

Instead, she decides to make a bargain with herself: *For the next twenty minutes or so, I'll just try to think about something else. For example, the amazing ocean view . . .*

Kate looks at the endless horizon with its gorgeous palette of pinks, oranges, purples, and dark shades of royal blue filling the sky.

It's been such a good day, she thinks as she relaxes into the enveloping cocoon of water.

Kate runs over the scenes and conversations from the day's events in her mind. She is very pleased with how well the interview went. Relaxing in the pool, she even begins to start to write the article in her mind. It was such an enjoyable experience, and she knows the words will easily flow as soon as she sits down at her laptop to compose the piece.

Tomorrow's spa day, and the party later in the week will be the icing on the cake, she thinks.

Luxuriating in total peace and harmony, Kate emerges from the pool forty minutes later. She unfolds the large towel sitting on top of her chaise to spread beneath her, and closes her eyes to drift off into a blissful alpha state.

"Excuse me, miss," says a young waiter, interrupting her respite. "Would you like anything from the bar?"

"Iced tea, please, and do you happen to have an appetizer menu I can look at?"

"Here," the waiter says as he pulls a small menu from underneath his arm and hands it to Kate.

"Mahalo."

Kate peruses the one-page menu quickly for something light to hold her over until morning.

"The goat cheese wrapped in smoked salmon on panko encrusted zucchini rounds sound fantastic, how is it?"

"One of my favorites. Shall I place an order for you?"

"Mahalo," nods Kate as the waiter smiles and then heads for the pool bar.

I could really get used to this lifestyle, thinks Kate as she watches the sun begin to slowly set into the colorful horizon.

Later that evening, after a leisurely shower to remove the chlorine from her skin, Kate checks her emails and text messages while she sits on the large king-size bed in her master suite.

"Aloha!" reads the first text message followed by a row of red heart emoticons. "Love, Mom and Dad."

Kate texts her parents back, "Interview with Olivia was awesome!" followed by a happy face icon blowing a kiss.

Kate laughs out loud when she views Cindy's funny selfie—a shot of her with her hair teased to the limit, looking like she stuck her finger in an electrical socket. With her face contorted, eyes bulging, and mouth open wide in a horrified scream, Cindy's text reads, "Woman on the verge of a nervous breakdown. Trip to paradise needed NOW!"

"Now I know you are certifiable," replies Kate. "But you know I love you anyway."

There's also a text from Edward congratulating Kate on the interview and mentioning that Olivia's publicist had contacted him to let him know that her client had a great time.

Ditto, thinks Kate.

Last, but definitely not least, there's a text from Jason.

"Hope all is going well. So sorry babe, but it's really busy on this end. There's no way I can make it to Kauai. I'm traveling now, so with the flights and the time difference, I'll try and call you tomorrow. XO, Jason."

Hit by a sudden wave of depression, Kate does her best to come to terms with what she probably already knew would be the case.

Oh well, you didn't really think he'd be able to join you in Kauai, now did you? Kate asks herself.

And, truth be told, she didn't.

Note to self, don't get depressed, think only positive thoughts.

"Speak to you soon," Kate whips off a text to Jason.

Normally, she would end with a red lipstick kiss. However, this time she pointedly leaves it off.

Enough with emails and texts for tonight! So what to do at 9:30 p.m. to keep my mind off of the constant Jason chatter disrupting my calm? thinks Kate as she plops her head back on the row of fluffy pillows lining the head of her bed.

After a few seconds of scanning the room trying to find something to distract her, Kate picks up the TV remote and decides to channel surf the myriad of cable stations as a means to numb her persistent thoughts. As it turns out, it's actually the perfect medicine, for within twenty minutes she is fast asleep.

5

The morning's showers give rise to an earthy scent that permeates the outside of The Westin's front entrance as Kate sits waiting patiently for Olivia to arrive. The sun's rays, which have begun to penetrate the blotchy, cloudy sky, hold the promise of another beautiful, sunny day.

Dressed for this morning's yoga class in formfitting black yoga pants, a pretty pink and white sleeveless top, and pink Nikes, Kate fiddles with her oversized tote packed with her accouterments for the day's events—her digital Nikon Coolpix 100 camera, a swimsuit, change of underclothes, a sundress, sandals, various toiletries, and makeup.

Just as Kate is about to check her text messages again–especially for any from Jason–a white Mercedes-Benz wagon pulls up to the curb. The electronic passenger window rolls down to reveal Olivia's bright and cheerful smile.

"Aloha, Kate!"

"Aloha!"

"Don't you look all cute and pulled together in pink."

"Well, gotta dress the part for yoga class," laughs Kate as she picks up her tote. "I love to run, and I'm an avid gym rat, but I must admit it's been a while since I've done any yoga," she continues as she opens the car door and slides into the passenger seat.

"Well, you'll love this one. Shannon, the instructor, is a dynamite teacher. It's power yoga, so it's a little intense and they turn the temperature up a bit, but you'll feel fantastic afterward."

"No pain, no gain they say. Besides how bad could it be?"

"That's the spirit!" says Olivia.

Olivia and Kate drive down Wyllie Road and pass the Princeville Shopping Center, an attractive collection of restaurants and shops, as they take Kuhio Highway towards Hanalei. Looking outside her window at the passing views, Kate spies a field of splendid, leafy plants.

"Wow, what are they growing over there? The colors are gorgeous. It looks like a patchwork quilt," Kate says as she pulls her camera out of her tote to snap photos of the sea of vegetation in glorious shades of red, green, and purple.

"Those are taro fields. It's a root vegetable and a major crop in Hawaii. I love its beautiful purple hue, and I also love that it's really high in fiber. Taro has been a staple of the native Hawaiian diet for centuries."

"Don't they use it to make that starchy dish, poi?" asks Kate.

"Yes, and it's also used to make taro chips, like the ones we had for lunch yesterday. Taro powder is used in everything from baked goods to noodles and ice cream, and even soft-serve frozen yogurt."

"Would you mind if we pull over so I can get some shots?" asks Kate.

"Not at all," Olivia replies as she pulls over.

"May I take a photo of you with the taro fields behind you?" asks Kate. "Don't worry. I promise not to tweet it or post on Facebook."

"Actually, I was planning on asking you to email me the photos you take today so I can tweet them and post them on Facebook," laughs Olivia.

"OK, as long as I get final editorial approval," chuckles Kate.

"Hey, isn't that supposed to be my line?" Olivia laughs even louder.

"Please stand a little to your right–I want to frame you so the fields are in view behind you."

"OK?"

"Perfect."

"Now let me take one of you," says Olivia, taking Kate's camera.

After Olivia snaps a few shots, they get back into the car to continue their journey into Hanalei.

"Look at that!" exclaims Kate, pointing at the historic one-lane steel truss bridge standing in the midst of acres of nothing but green fields. "I feel like we're going back in time."

"You are! That's the famous Hanalei Bridge. It's an exact replica of the one that was originally built in 1912. In fact, around 2003 the bridge was rededicated after a hard battle was won to keep the original design rather than replace it with a more modern structure."

"I'm so glad they stayed true to the original design! It's . . ."

"Magical?"

"Yes—in fact, that's precisely the word I'd use to describe the feeling I have about this place," Kate says as she gapes in awe at the inspiring green vistas set against the jagged purple mountaintops on the edge of the Pacific. At the entry point to the bridge, where Highway 56 becomes the 560, Olivia pulls her car to the right, making way for five vehicles waiting to pass over the single lane.

"If you like the look and feel of this area, just wait until you see Hanalei Town. It's really charming and has a great mana."

"If you allow yourself to feel it, you can really tune into the spirituality of this place. That feeling, or 'mana' if you will, is one of the reasons why the people that live here fought so hard to preserve the integrity of that old bridge we just crossed over. It would have been a crime to destroy the natural beauty and heritage of this amazing place."

"My sentiments exactly," agrees Kate as they enter Hanalei.

The shades and rays of light reflected from the mountains and filtered through the mist from the ocean create a warm, pleasing glow over the picturesque and transcendent Hanalei Town. On either side of the two-lane road sit groupings of single story shops and restaurants, many constructed in the familiar plantation style design. Some of the storefronts are painted white, while others are green or blue, or simply sport their natural woods' hues.

Olivia pulls the car into The Hanalei Center, an attractive grouping of shops, behind which sits a row of jagged mountain peaks.

"Wow! Look at those mountains! I almost feel like a dinosaur is going to come out from behind one of them or something," Kate exclaims excitedly.

"Well, they just might. They filmed parts of *Jurassic Park* right here on Kauai. May I introduce you to Mount Hihimanu, Na Molokama, and Māmalahoa?" chuckles Olivia as she playfully points in the direction of the majestic masters.

"I've just got to get some pictures," Kate says as she jumps out of the car and immediately starts to snap photos.

"Go ahead, I'll be right behind you."

Kate captures one great angle after another of the regal beauties rising from behind the center shops.

"Nature's perfect lighting is working like a charm," yells Kate from behind the lens. "I'm getting awesome shots."

Finally satisfied with her bounty of images, Kate walks back towards Olivia, who is shaking her head and laughing a bit.

"What?" inquires Kate, suddenly self-conscious.

"You're like a kid in a candy shop! It's nothing bad. Just amusing. Heck, I was like that when I first saw this town. Come on, let me show you the café."

Kate and Olivia walk up a small stairway to a wood lanai landing belonging to the one story plantation style shop. A sign written in pretty calligraphy and interlaced with images of white plumeria blooms hangs over the red-painted wood door and reads, "The Plumeria Café."

Both the inside of the café, as well as outside on the lanai, are bustling with early morning risers that sit at little wooden tables sipping their coffees.

Inside, at the back of the café, stands a large glass counter which displays all types of luscious baked goods in tantalizing arrangements, behind which a bevy of baristas rush about filling customers' orders. Hawaiian instrumental music plays softly over the loudspeaker.

Malie Kapule, a pretty, slender thirty-one-year-old woman of mixed Hawaiian, Dutch, and English descent, is busy supervising the staff.

Her long, silky dark hair is pulled back in a ponytail. She wears jeans, sandals, and a short-sleeved white top with a thigh-length baker's apron in light beige. In the center of the apron are the words, "Aloha, and welcome to The Plumeria Café," in lettering that matches the same floral graphic style of the café's door sign.

The aroma of freshly roasted Kona coffee fills the café and mingles in a sweet potpourri with other intoxicating scents—from cinnamon baked apples to fresh rosemary bread being pulled out of the oven, to subtle hints of toasty lemon and blueberry scones—all of which encourage a very good reason to break the morning fast.

The café itself is a homey environment. The décor is an eclectic mix of wooden tables, chairs, cushy sofas, and book and magazine racks brimming with good reads. The local artwork—everything from paintings to photographs, greeting cards, tabletop picture books, and hand-painted wood pieces—is available for purchase and proudly displayed on the walls and in quaint, artistic hutches.

"Aloha," says Malie as she moves from behind the large glass countertop to greet Olivia with an embrace.

"Malie, this is Kate Grace with *New York View Magazine.*"

"Aloha, and welcome to The Plumeria Café," Malie smiles, extending her hand to Kate.

"We're here on unofficial business," says Olivia. "Kate interviewed me at home yesterday, and today we're just taking in a few of my usual activities to capture some of the local flavor and color."

"Wonderful. Why don't you two get comfortable and take a seat on the lanai. Let me bring over some breakfast," Malie suggests as she pulls a notepad and pen from her front apron pocket. "What'll it be?"

"Something light," says Olivia. "We'll be taking a yoga class later this morning. So, for me, a nonfat latte, a small fruit cup, and one of those mini lemon blueberry scones."

"That sounds perfect. I'll have the same," Kate chimes in.

"Comin' right up," says Malie, turning toward the kitchen.

Olivia and Kate sit at a quiet table on the lanai. A delightful, cool breeze blows past the pair every now and then, taking the edge off of the sticky morning air.

"I just have a few more orders of business, and then it's play for the rest of the day," promises Kate.

"I can handle that . . . so shoot."

"Ken, the photographer from yesterday, told me that he'll be coming by the café this morning to take a few shots for the story."

"Right, no problem."

"He'll also snap a few photos before yoga class. Then later, when we're at The Westin for lunch, he'll do one or two set-ups."

"Works for me."

"Great! Then the article will be *fini*!"

"Perfect. All photos get cleared through Connie, though, correct?" asks Olivia.

"Absolutely."

"Good. I wouldn't want any unattractive or risqué yoga images of me doing down dog, cow pose, or God forbid, happy baby, out there for mass consumption."

Kate and Olivia laugh out loud.

"Breakfast will be out shortly, enjoy," Malie says as she delivers Olivia and Kate's lattes.

"Mahalo," Olivia replies.

"So, now, being the interviewer that I am," says Olivia, "it's my turn to ask you questions."

"Oh, no. Like I said yesterday, my life isn't as exciting as yours," Kate laughs demurely.

"I'll be the judge of that."

"OK, shoot," Kate acquiesces.

"How long have you been working for *New York View Magazine*?"

"Since I graduated from Hofstra University, about eight years ago."

"Really? What was your major?"

"Journalism with a minor in communications."

"I was a journalism major with a minor in communications in college too," says Olivia. "Grade average?"

"3.9."

"I thought so, Ms. Smarty Pants," Olivia chuckles. "Tell me about your family."

"I grew up in the suburbs of New York. I have a sister and brother who are both in their forties and married with kids. I'm the youngest, and not married. My parents, Catherine and Glen, have been happily married for fifty years, and they're still very much in love."

"Sounds like a beautiful family," says Olivia.

"It is. I'm lucky," Kate replies. "We love each other, and more than that, we actually like each other's company."

Olivia smiles.

"Got someone *extra special* in your life?"

Kate takes a moment to answer. She's not really sure anymore, and the reality of it hits her like a ton of bricks.

"I think so," says Kate. "I hope so."

"What do you mean?" asks Olivia gently.

"Jason, my boyfriend and I, well, we've been dating steadily for about five years now, and just before I left for Kauai, we had a . . . *a talk*."

"Oh, one of those," Olivia nods knowingly. "So, how did it go?"

"Not so great. We're using this week apart to think. Or I should say, he's using it to think. I hope. I told him I need to know if we're still on the same page. I always thought we were, but now I'm not so sure. I want to know we want the same things, and that he wants them with me."

"Things such as . . . ?"

"Marriage, family."

"Did he ever tell you he wanted those things with you?"

"He did. He knew that marriage was a nonnegotiable for me right from the start. When we first became a couple, we agreed that that was where we were both headed," continues Kate. "But I think I've spoiled him a little, waiting longer than I had originally intended for him to deliver on the commitment, and in light of some recent conversations we've had, I'm not sure if marriage is that important to him anymore, or even if it ever was."

"Marriage, especially these days, is never as important to a man as it is to a woman," Olivia says frankly. "You were totally right to say what you did; you have to see where he's at. It's all about communication. I think, though, after five years, he should know you well enough, and also be clear about what he wants as well—at least enough to make a decision to move forward, or not."

"That's exactly what I said to him, almost word for word."

A young waiter serves Olivia and Kate their fruit cups and scones. They thank the waiter, and then Kate begins to eat slowly, obviously deep in thought.

"Kate, I'm sorry if I upset you."

"No, I'm OK. I'm putting it all in God's hands. I'm meditating, praying, and trying to be strong in knowing what's right for me and for my life. It's not easy, but it's important. I should have done this a long time ago. I do feel that Jason really cares about me; he just needs to sort things through."

"This scone is delicious by the way," Kate adds, changing the subject. "What about you, how long have you been with Grant?"

"For about four years now," smiles Olivia. "We knew right off the bat we were right for each other. It's a good thing too; we're both very independent and lead busy lives."

"Would you like to marry him?" Kate asks.

"Maybe because we've both been married and divorced, there isn't the same urgency that you may feel as a younger woman who's never been married before. But, yeah, I would like to marry him, and I'm sure someday we will."

"Any time soon, you think?"

"We've talked about it, but we're not in a rush. To be honest, I have a feeling that eventually we'll just do it. But for now, we're just happily going along taking it day by day."

"Will he be at the party Friday night?"

"He will. He flies in Thursday night, so you'll get to meet him."

"Great, I'd like that. Can I ask you one more question about marriage?"

"Sure, one more, but then I get to ask the questions, remember?"

"OK, one more. When you got married the first time, did you think he was 'the one'?"

"Well, let me answer it this way. When my ex-husband and I started dating, we really hadn't even given any thought to the future. However, once some of my friends and business associates started getting married, I began to think about it. I thought it was the right thing at the time, but I also wasn't as conscious as I am today. Our marriage was good for a while, but then we grew apart. In actuality, we were so young when we met, and we both went through so many changes. After a few years, while we were friends, it wasn't the type of love connection that would make it for fifty years like your parents' has lasted."

"Then again, as you know, my grandparents raised me," continues Olivia. "Now, they had a marriage like your parents'. So I know the type of example that sets, and why, coming from that environment, it's important to share your life with someone that way."

"Are your grandparents . . . ?" begins Kate.

"No, they've both passed. I hold them dear in my heart, though, and they're still as alive to me as ever. I talk to them every day."

"You do?"

"Sure! I believe they're living around me in spirit as sure as I can see you sitting across this table."

Kate smiles at the thought.

"So I say 'hello' or 'aloha' to them whenever I think of them, and sometimes I tell them about my day. I feel their presence often, and they visit me in my dreams."

"I believe in spirit, that we live on, maybe even that we come back," Kate nods. "You mentioned something about not being 'as conscious' in your twenties as you are now. Three of my grandparents passed away when I was a lot younger. My mom's mother passed when I was in my teens, and I know I wasn't as conscious as I am now. Even so, after my grandmother's passing, I always felt that she was around me. I guess I've been really fortunate that I haven't had to deal with the death of a loved one since then."

"Of course it's a difficult experience, but then again, it's a part of life that all of us have to experience at some point. That's why I believe in that saying 'live, love, laugh.' We have to take those words of wisdom to the max, and follow our passions and our truths."

"You sound like my mom," chuckles Kate. "She is always telling me to follow my passion."

"Well then, I think if I met your mom, I would like her a lot."

"I think you would," Kate smiles.

"Now, it's my turn to ask the questions, remember?"

"OK, I promise," says Kate with a sheepish grin. "No more questions."

6

"OMG! I stretched muscles I didn't even know I had," moans Kate.

"Me too, girl," chimes Olivia. "I can't wait to hit the saunas. Since we'll be doing photographs later, Connie made me a hair appointment. After that we'll have lunch, OK?"

"Works for me!"

Once back at The Westin, Kate takes a shower and dresses for lunch, arriving at Nanea Restaurant's outdoor terrace just in time to meet Olivia.

"I ate here my first night in town," Kate says. "The menu is fab."

Kate orders a large green salad of spinach and romaine mixed with cranberries, macadamia nuts, and avocado topped with a sizeable piece of wild salmon, and Olivia chooses a classic Caesar salad with grilled chicken. The pair chat like old friends over lunch, sharing their ideas and opinions about everything from fashion and music to world events.

"Kate, I'm so glad the magazine assigned you to do my interview."

"Me too."

"I've got to tell you straight up, I feel like I've met you before—as if I know you from somewhere. We've never met on a junket or at an event have we?"

"Funny you should ask that," says Kate. "I've seen you on TV, I've read about you, and I've interviewed hundreds of people in the media, but I can't say like I've felt I've known them previously. But I feel like I've met you before, too."

"So it's not just me?"

"No."

"OK then, maybe it was in another life," Olivia chuckles. "And whatever it is, I'm glad we met. I feel a real affinity for you, and I hope after you go back to New York and the article's been published, you won't be a stranger. Maybe we could have lunch sometime, or double date with our men?"

"Really?" Kate blurts out.

"Really," smiles Olivia.

"That would be great!" Kate fumbles with excited energy. She's elated that Olivia would make this suggestion, and completely thrilled that she feels a mutual kinship. "I would just love that."

Kate finds herself wanting to phone Cindy, her mother, and Jason to share the good news about her new friendship. When her thoughts turn to Jason, however, Kate feels an immediate stab of pain right in her heart as she's reminded of how uncertain things are between them.

"Oh, Mom, I've been having a blast!" Kate excitedly exclaims, leaning back on the cushioned chaise lounge on her bedroom lanai. "Olivia's really cool, very solid and down-to-earth. It feels like we've been friends forever, and she said she wants to keep in touch even after the interview is published!"

"That's wonderful, hon," replies Catherine. "I certainly know she's definitely found a good friend in you. Will you start to write the article while you're in Kauai?"

"I'll look over my notes, but I think I just want to soak up the environment here, have time to digest everything before I start to write. I'll play it by ear though."

"That sounds like a good plan."

"Hey, Mom? Want to see the view from my bedroom?"

Kate turns her phone around to let her mother get a glimpse of the gorgeous resort grounds on FaceTime.

"See the Pacific?"

"I certainly do! I feel like I'm there. Well, I guess I am, electronically."

Kate laughs.

"Oh, Kate, take lots of photos. I want to see them and hear about every detail when you get back. I'm so glad you're having such a good time."

"Is Dad still awake?"

Catherine turns around to check. "No, hon, looks like he fell asleep while we were gabbing."

Kate glances at the time at the top of her cell phone screen and realizes it's midnight in New York.

"Oh, Mom, it's really late where you are. Let me say goodnight and let you go to bed. We can talk tomorrow."

"OK, sweetie. It's been wonderful talking to you. I love you *soooo* much you know. To the moon and beyond," says Catherine, blowing Kate a series of kisses that seem to fly right through the cell phone screen to her daughter's cheeks.

"Love you too, Mom, to the moon and beyond," Kate blows kisses to her mother in return. Both women then touch their phone screens, virtually connecting their hands. The soulful look in Catherine's eyes is so heartfelt that Kate can feel the loving energy permeate the screen and sink into her being.

Kate hits the red disconnect button on her FaceTime screen and her mother's image disappears. She then checks her text messages. There's nothing from Jason, but then again, he said he would be traveling and would touch base when he could.

Maybe tomorrow, thinks Kate. While she briefly considers sending him a little message and maybe a few photos from the day's events, she ultimately decides against it.

It'll be better if he reaches out to me right now.

Kate sets the electronics aside and leans back on the chaise. Her mind immediately searches for tender memories of Jason and she remembers their first meeting.

She had met him by chance one night after work. Jasmine had asked her to go out for sushi. When she asked the waiter about a particular dish on the menu, Jason, hearing her inquiry from the next table, chimed in. That one question soon led to an evening's conversation with Jason and his business associate, followed by the men treating Kate and Jasmine to a lovely dinner.

Kate was immediately attracted to Jason; it was hard not to be. He was gorgeous and, as she soon found out, intelligent, successful, and a gentleman. Like her, Jason grew up in a well-to-do area on Long Island's North Shore. He descended from a long line of successful, Ivy League educated bankers and real estate developers, and Jason himself had graduated with honors and a degree in economics from Yale. Yes, she had to admit to herself that she was smitten from that very first night. The fact that Jason enjoyed being in control, was sometimes a little arrogant and selfish, and lived a little too much for the thrill of making the big financial "score," was something she had not realized during the early days of their courtship. By the time she finally came to that realization, and saw how that behavior might negatively impact their relationship, her heart was already committed for the long haul.

As for Jason, he always told her how he was immediately attracted to her natural beauty and her sweet, feminine demeanor—but he was also thrilled to find out that she could be sexy, playful, and loving, too. He often expressed his appreciation of the fact that she, like him, came from a good family, and he frequently praised her other major attributes: the fact that Kate is considerate, honest, loyal, smart, and well, "just plain lovely."

In Kate's mind, however, some of the things that Jason loves about her also appear to occasionally irk him. She can feel him retreat at odd times—especially when she's going out of her way to be sweet, understanding, flexible, and willing to compromise.

The lights that now illuminate the grounds of The Westin are so atmospheric and romantic that Kate, sitting all alone in this gorgeous paradise, begins to get even more nostalgic. Her mind wanders to her first official date with Jason, categorized in her memory under, "too romantic to be believed." It was a stunningly beautiful summer day. The weather was picture-perfect as they drove in Jason's convertible BMW from Manhattan out to the Hamptons on Long Island's South Fork for a seaside picnic.

For their déjeuner, Jason had picked up an amazing gourmet basket lunch complete with baguettini sandwiches, fresh fruit, a selection of gourmet meats and cheeses, and decadent chocolate covered strawberries for dessert. He also packed a vintage bottle of Château Margaux, which was a gift from a client. He'd told her that he'd been keeping it to share with someone special.

Kate is all smiles as she remembers that amazing day—their picnic underneath a large weeping willow, their playful jaunt in the ocean, but most of all, the taste of his delicious lips, and his strong, hard, muscular arms wrapped around her.

Now, her thoughts turn to remembrances of subsequent dates and events—family parties, cooking in the kitchen together, lazy Saturday afternoons, fun European vacations . . . And then on to more intimate moments—the warmth of his body when he holds her tight, his arousing kisses on her neck, the lightness of his tongue as he teases sensuous pathways along her arms and neck, up towards her mouth.

Kate relives these memories as if they are happening now—bits and pieces from glorious times. She can actually feel her body growing tense with desire. She feels a need to wrap her arms around Jason, to rub her body against his, to hear him call her name in a way that tells her how much she is wanted.

With those images in her mind, Kate bolts upright to break the spell of her reverie. Shocked, for a second she is unable to comprehend where she is. The distant sounds of chatting, happy vacationers as they take evening dips in the pool slowly float up to Kate. A cool tropical breeze slowly starts to envelope and soothe her, bringing her back to reality.

At 7:00 p.m. the neighborhood streets are now dark, and being cautious as a single woman alone—even in paradise—Kate opts to drive to Princeville Center rather than walk. She set her sights on dining at CJ's Steak & Seafood and, once inside, the hostess escorts her to a wood table on the restaurant's enclosed lanai where Kate dines on freshly made crab cakes with garlic aioli and a large green salad.

After dinner, Kate peruses the Center's store windows, as some of the shops are still open for business. The wonderful scent of perfumed candles, lotions, and soaps lure her into Island Soaps & Candle Works. A host of attractively packaged bath and body products displayed on pretty wood shelves and hutches entice Kate to pick out several items to bring back as gifts for her sister, Cindy, and Jasmine. In a jewelry display case, pretty, locally handmade shell necklaces also catch Kate's eye, and she selects two of the unique designs as gifts: one for her mother and the other for herself.

Happy with her purchases, but still not ready to leave the Center just yet, Kate makes her way towards a man selling CDs from a large booth in front of the Foodland Market. Intrigued by several customers wearing bulky headsets to sample the music, Kate decides to give it a try.

"What CD do you suggest?" Kate asks a congenial looking man of about fifty wearing a baseball cap. "I'd like to hear something from a local artist."

"OK, got it," says the man, looking over the massive collection of music. "Here's one I'd recommend. Paul Togioka. He's a local known for his beautiful slack-key guitar instrumentals. Here's his latest CD, *Here, There, and Everywhere*."

"Oh, I heard that artist's name on the radio the other day," remembers Kate as she places the headset over her ears. As soon as she hears the sublime tones, she knows she has to add it to her collection.

It's almost 10:00 p.m. by the time Kate gets back to her room. Exhausted from the day's events, she washes and undresses, and places her new music purchase in the CD player of the master bedroom's entertainment console.

With the bedroom lights now dimmed to almost nonexistence, Kate crawls underneath the silky sheets of the king-size bed and is lulled peacefully to sleep by the soothing sounds of the slack-key guitar strings.

7

The next morning, sitting on her lanai and enjoying a cup of morning Kona brew, Kate Googles, "places to go and things to do in Kauai." Pages and pages of activities and events pop up on her computer screen, and while they're all enticing, all Kate can seem to think of is returning to explore Hanalei.

I've got to go back . . . take more time to peruse the shops, soak up the atmosphere, and maybe walk by the shore to the Hanalei Pier . . . Think of all the great photo ops.

Her plans for the day are now set; Kate dresses in a comfortable, knee-length blue and white Calvin Klein jersey sundress and flip-flops. She wears her Tory Burch bathing suit underneath her clothes in case she feels the urge to swim later, and smiles at her reflection in the full-length mirror.

"That'll do," she says out loud as she adjusts her Solumbra hat.

She packs two totes; one overflows with a large towel, toiletries, and a change of underclothes. The other, a smaller quilted bag with a floral tropical print that she bought in New York exclusively for the trip, is packed with sunscreen, her wallet, a tube of Bobbi Brown lipstick, a compact of mineral powder, a small brush, a large bottle of water from the resort's marketplace, and her camera.

Kate loops the long handles of the totes, one set around each of her shoulders, and carries her laptop just in case she feels inspired to do some of her own creative writing. Before she leaves, she also grabs the slack-key guitar disc from the CD player, as this music is perfect for her journey into Hanalei.

Armed with her arsenal for the day, Kate heads out to the resort's valet station to retrieve her car. Before pulling away from the curb, she pops the slack-key guitar disc into the CD player on the car's console and is immediately transported by the harmonious sounds.

The man who sold her the album mentioned that slack-key guitar, or *kī hōʻalu* in Hawaiian, is a genre of music meant to accompany the rhythms of Hawaiian dancing. Its harmonic structure and unique sound require a certain fingerstyle technique, as well as the loosening (or "slacking") of several strings on the guitar.

As she crosses over Hanalei's magical steel truss bridge and takes in the magnificent vistas, a chill runs up Kate's spine, and she instinctively knows she is in for a wonderful adventure. Once in Hanalei Town, Kate parks next to the cluster of shops that sit adjacent to The Plumeria Café. After her walk, she decides she'll drop by the café to say aloha to Malie and maybe grab a latte and another one of those delicious scones.

Kate pulls the tote with her beach towel and camera from the trunk and slings it around her shoulder before walking down Aku Road in the direction of the water's edge. Some of the homes along the residential street are typical beach cottages—nothing fancy, and in need of some paint—but others are picture-perfect, charming, and quaint.

She follows Aku Road to the end where it borders the water and meets Weke Road. As she takes a right onto Weke, she notes the street has its own unique feel, perhaps because of its close proximity to the bay. While boasting an eclectic mix of housing styles, it is home to more midsized residences and stately gated mansions.

As she makes her way in the direction of the pier, Kate notices that the palm tree-lined slice of heaven is ever so quiet. There is nobody in sight, and all she can hear are the sounds of nature—birds chirping in the trees, swooshes of the cool morning breezes as they finger through the tropical foliage, and the pebbles that crunch underneath her feet as she walks along the road's edge.

Each home is unique and enchanting. One plantation style cottage has a lava rock wall and paved driveway that's lined with palm trees and bursts of red ti plants and ginger, which serve as a welcome aloha on both sides of the gated entrance. Views of the bay and mountain vistas just beyond the property peek through the tropical green.

While some structures appear to be family compounds, others are more modest cottages, and the street is also dotted with a number of large, vacant lots with unobstructed water views. Growing up in the suburbs of New York, Kate is no stranger to living in homes possessing ample acreage and sporting lush, green landscapes; still, she has never experienced anything quite like this.

Living and working in Manhattan, Kate is now accustomed to the hustle and bustle, the crowds, and the endless "white noise" of the city. Here, she notices that the town has a similar type of quiet she can compare to where her parents live on Long Island. And yet the feel and the atmosphere are vastly different. This tropical climate, the sensation of the warm sun on her skin, the shades of light that fill the sky, the balmy breezes—they all make for an otherworldly experience that brings harmony to Kate's soul.

As she walks, she is aware of every feeling in her body. Strolling along, a sense of delicious relaxation sweeps through her and allows the usual cramping and stiffness that plague her neck and shoulders from hours spent at the computer to dissipate. For a moment, Kate thinks about the story she must write and deliver to the magazine, but she knows her process. For now, she will put that task aside and only entertain thoughts about the article that slowly dance in and out of her consciousness, preparing her for when she does sit down to write. She is in no rush, and is content to jot notes on her iPhone when she feels inspired. She deserves today. Today is her time to just be.

It feels magnificent, she thinks. The freedom of not being on a schedule, of having to do this or that, or go here or there. Today, structure falls away, and as Kate allows herself to go with the flow, she begins to get glimpses of her true spirit.

"So, this is what time off feels like," she sighs out loud.

As Kate continues her walk towards the pier, she quietly starts to sing "Somewhere over the Rainbow," in the version of the song made famous by the Hawaiian music legend, Israel "Iz" Kamakawiwo'ole, which she has now heard numerous times on the radio. She sings softly to herself as she walks in a trance of sublime happiness, at one with nature, and with her cares and worries truly far behind her. On the road in front of her, the green foliage to her left opens up to a large clearing. The closer she gets, she can see a myriad of cars and trucks scattered about an open grassy area.

Must be the attraction of the pier, she thinks. As soon as Kate turns into the parking area, she sees it. *Wow!* The magical Hanalei Pier sits directly in front of her. She has seen this image a hundred times before in magazines and photographs, but in person, its magnificence cannot be compared. The pier juts out into the water some 340 feet, and at the end of it is a roof structure that shelters residents and visitors alike as they laugh, talk, and snap photos.

Although it's a clear, sunny day, a fine mist hangs low in the sky and seems satisfied to sit just below some of the waterfall-lined mountain peaks, creating a mystical, dreamlike view of this timeless place. Excited by the multitude of amazing sights with the type of awe-inspiring lighting that only nature can conceive, Kate reaches inside her tote and pulls out her camera. She takes a photo of a lone canoe on the sand that lies underneath a palm tree. In the shot, the mist is low on the horizon and the subtle, diffuse lighting it creates gives the image an appearance of a painting rather than a photo. Sailboats that happily sway moored in the bay also become digitally immortalized.

When Kate is satisfied that she has captured all the images possible from where she currently stands, she walks towards the pier's canopied end.

Awesome! she thinks as she snaps shots that richly capture the water's various blue hues and the hillside's hearty greens. When a tropical beat starts to chime inside her tote, Kate grabs her cell and answers.

"Aloha."

"Aloha," comes a sexy male voice on the other end.

"Hello?" Kate responds quizzically. She doesn't recognize the phone number, and the voice, though familiar, doesn't quite register.

"It's me, Jason."

"Oh, Jason! Sorry, I'm a bit distracted, and whatever number you're calling from isn't in my contacts. It's good to hear your voice."

"Yours, too."

"Where are you?" asks Kate.

"Back in Manhattan for a day. Then it's 'Hasta la vista, baby,' and off to Miami I go, and after that Park City and San Francisco."

"Wow, you really are traveling a lot," Kate says, as she walks back to shore.

"I know, but things are going great. We locked up the Miami deal last night, so I need to go to sign the paperwork and schmooze a little. The other cities were just booked—one of my partners got a lead on some buildings that will make great condo conversions."

"Congratulations," Kate replies, a trace of sadness in her voice.

"Miss you, you know."

"Really?" says Kate.

If he misses me, couldn't some of his new appointments have waited a few more days? she thinks.

"I do miss you!" insists Jason on the defensive. "I've been thinking a lot about you. I can't wait to hold you in my arms and . . ."

"Say the words I long to hear?" Kate finishes his sentence.

There is silence for a minute.

"Ah, OK, I see where you're going with this," says Jason.

Kate pauses, not wanting to speak until she has more of a read from him. Unfortunately, there is nothing but awkward silence. To let off some nervous energy, she starts to kick some pebbles.

"So, you'll be flying back to New York on Monday night, right?" Jason asks.

"Yup."

"OK, shall we say we'll get together for dinner next Tuesday night then?"

"OK," agrees Kate, a little reserved now, feeling hurt by Jason's non-committal attitude.

"Well, sweetie, I have to run. Got to meet with a client. Because of the time difference and traveling and all, I'll call you Friday or Saturday around this time?"

"OK," sighs Kate. Jason appears oblivious to her tone.

"Bye," Jason says, the line going immediately to dial tone.

"Wait! What?"

Kate is incredulous that Jason didn't even give her the chance to say goodbye. She sticks her tongue out at the phone and shakes it. Then, in a fit of fury, she kicks a nearby rock, hard.

"Ow! Damn it!" yells Kate grabbing her hurt toes with one hand, while hopping around on the other foot in a crazy circle.

"You OK?" she hears a male voice call out.

Kate looks up and sees a really cute, muscular guy staring at her. She stops her dance.

"Yeah," says Kate sheepishly, "I'm OK."

"I like that little dance you were doing," he laughs, as he pulls some items out of the back of his Land Rover. "Try and be more careful, OK? Otherwise the next time you might find yourself having to take a trip to the hospital."

"Mahalo, but I'm just fine," Kate replies, rather embarrassed now.

"OK, then. Aloha, and have a good day now," the hunk waves and walks off, turning his head back once to look at her again before he disappears from view.

"I must have looked like quite a nutcase," she mutters under her breath.

Kate spreads out the towel she brought with her from the hotel onto the sand beneath a shady tree, and plops both herself and her tote down. As she watches the beachgoers, she runs the conversation with Jason over in her mind.

We'll get together for dinner next Tuesday night . . . Does that mean he'll be ready to talk seriously about moving forward in our relationship?

Before Kate allows herself to despair, she remembers the power of positive thinking and shifts her perspective.

Maybe. And as long as I believe he's open, then perhaps things aren't that bad.

Kate makes a few quick calls—first to Cindy, then to her family.

"Just remember, when you meet up with Jason, hold firm," instructs Cindy. "You know he is quite the wordsmith when he has to be, and you want to be sure you know where he's coming from and if he means business."

Her sister Carla and her mother also reinforce what Kate already knows; they are her cheerleading squad when it comes to sticking up for her principles and her dreams. All three women, especially her mom, have been her support in so many situations throughout the years. She's lucky, and she knows it. She has never needed a lot of friends—like the hundreds of casual "friends" people collect on Facebook. Her small, solid sisterhood who she loves dearly, and counts on through thick and thin, who knows her innermost thoughts, passions, and desires—they are her rock, and she is the same for them.

After several hours of resting and reading at the pier, Kate's rumbling stomach gets her to think of all the scrumptious delights at The Plumeria Café, prompting her to pack up her things and walk back towards town. As she strolls leisurely down Weke Road, a charming little white plantation style cottage seems to stand out. It's one that she hadn't noticed earlier in the day. On either side of the pastel blue wooden front door are stained glass windows depicting pretty scenes of tropical birds and flowers. Two large picture windows with plantation shutters the same color blue as the front door grace both sides of the home. On the spacious lanai behind a pretty white Hawaiian style railing sit two wicker chairs.

A winding row of pavers leads through the velvety green front landscaping up to the cottage's main entrance. Vibrant hibiscus in yellows, reds, and whites and other tropical foliage intermixed with strategically placed lava rocks and boulders line the front of the house. Two plumeria trees laden with white blossoms stand on either side of the front stairway landing.

Kate stands in the middle of the road, looking at the house, mesmerized. Feeling the warm sun bake her bare shoulders, she is aware of the stillness of the surroundings. Then, she sees it. A swoosh of color in the window. Moving closer to the edge of the street in front of the cottage, she sees the shadow again. Is it a shadow? A person? There's no one looking out the window. Suddenly a breeze, seemingly from out of nowhere, filters through her hair and across her skin like a gentle caress.

"Kate!" she hears her name being called softly by a high-pitched, ethereal voice. Kate turns around to see who might have called out to her. There is no one else anywhere in sight.

"Aloha!" she hears this time as clear as day. Prickly tingles run up and down her spine and arms. Kate tries to keep her composure as she processes what is happening. The voice is not one that she's ever heard before. Kate remains for a time standing in the same spot, waiting to see if there is any further movement, or if she hears anything more. There is nothing.

OK. I'll just file that under strange, thinks Kate. Despite whatever just happened, she is not frightened. Instead, she feels thrilled and intrigued.

What is it about this house? Why am I feeling this way? Instinctively, she pulls her camera from her tote and takes several photos of the charming home. Then, for a reason she can't explain, she feels herself not wanting to leave the house, even though she knows she must.

"Aloha, till we meet again!" she says out loud without thinking. She smiles and waves to her new friend, and then continues down the street, lost in thought and humming to herself contentedly.

BACK AT HER CAR, Kate places her bag in the trunk, removes her wallet, and grabs hold of her laptop before heading over to The Plumeria Café.

Now that the lunch hour rush had passed, it's the perfect setting for a leisurely bite.

"I'll have a large mango iced tea and the grilled veggie panini with the house salad. Please put the citrus vinaigrette on the side," Kate addresses the attendant at the counter. "Oh, and one of those pineapple coconut muffins to go. Mahalo."

Kate pays the cashier and takes her iced tea out to the lanai. A large wooden hutch, which displays gift items like prepackaged bags of Kona coffee and coffee mugs, candles, greeting cards, and local paintings and photographs, grabs her eye just before she reaches the door to the outdoor seating area. Kate thumbs through a large wicker basket with a sign that reads, "All prints, $25.00." The watercolors, five by seven inches in size, depict colorful scenes of the Hanalei bridge and pier, boats docked in the bay, the mountains and palm tree lined sky, and Hanalei Town. When Kate gets to the last image, she gasps.

It looks like an exact replica of the pretty white cottage on Weke Road. Kate scans the image looking for the artist's name. To the bottom right is the signature, *Leilani.* Kate knows immediately that she has to buy the print. At the register, Kate sees Malie placing freshly baked items into the display case.

"Aloha, Malie!"

"Well, aloha!" says Malie smiling broadly. "How nice to see you again."

"I have a day off and wanted to explore more of Hanalei," Kate says.

"Well, I'm so glad you came back to the café!"

"I was hungry, and I thought I'd sit out on the lanai, have lunch, and maybe do some writing."

"I thought you said you had a day off?"

"My own personal creative writing. The kind that I don't get to do because I'm always busy writing other stories," Kate responds.

"What can I get you?"

"I just ordered a panini, but I'd really like to buy this watercolor," says Kate placing the print on the counter.

"Oh, yes, sure."

"Do you take American Express?"

Malie goes to take Kate's card, but decides against it.

"No. This is your first trip to Kauai, and this print is special, so please, let it be my gift to you."

"No! Really?" Kate asks.

"Really."

"Mahalo."

"How long will you be in Kauai?" asks Malie.

"Just for this week. I leave Monday."

"Olivia mentioned you'll be coming to her place for dinner Friday night. My husband Aukai and I will be there as well."

"That's wonderful. I'm really looking forward to the party."

"Me too."

Malie hands Kate the print, which she has placed in a reusable cloth bag imprinted with the café's logo.

"Great bag!" Kate exclaims.

"We love our home, so we do what we can to keep it sustainable around here," smiles Malie. "Enjoy your lunch, and your writing. I look forward to seeing you again Friday night."

"Looking forward to it. Mahalo, for everything."

At 10:00 p.m. Kate sits in her nightgown on the living room sofa in her hotel room. She sips chai tea and thumbs through a stack of tabletop books filled with information on the history of Kauai.

"Hello?" Kate answers her cell on its second ring.

"Aloha Kate, this is Olivia."

"Hey, how's it going?"

"It was a long day of meetings, but now I'm just relaxing on my lanai. *Heaven*," Olivia trills. The funny singsong way Olivia says "heaven" makes Kate laugh.

"I was thinking if you don't already have plans for tomorrow, would you like to go to lunch?" adds Olivia. "There's an amazing restaurant called Gaylord's that's located on the historic Kilohana Plantation in Lihue. It's a bit of a drive, but a pretty one. Are you game?"

"That sounds fantastic. Count me in!"

"OK, then. I'll pick you up at ten thirty tomorrow morning."

"I'll be waiting curbside," Kate says without missing a beat.

That night Kate sleeps peacefully and deeply. In her dream she sighs with contentment as she walks down pretty Weke Road. As Kate passes in front of the white cottage with the pastel blue door and matching shutters, she stops and faces the home head on. As she does, a woman's voice gently calls out, *"Aloha, Kate . . . Aloha."*

Kate is startled awake from her dream. Something about it is so real . . . *that voice.* She's heard it before—it sounds like the voice she heard when she stood in front of the cottage on Weke Road just the other day. Kate looks at the clock on the nightstand. It's 3:00 a.m.

The hour of the spirits, thinks Kate, knowing that three o'clock is known as the time when spiritual energy is at its peak. While it is known to many as the "witching" hour, it is also a time that is considered by many more as a holy hour. As Kate thinks about how the dream made her feel so comfortable and at peace, she slowly drifts back to sleep.

8

"Kate, while you're here, you've really got to visit the Princeville Botanical Gardens," says Olivia as she drives with Kate on Highway 56 towards Lihue.

"I read about the gardens in a book I found in my room last night," Kate remarks as she sips her latte.

"It's really an amazing display of tropical landscapes. They've got all types of exotic flowers and fruit trees . . . AND they make chocolate on the premises and even give out samples."

"Well, that settles it, if there's chocolate, I'm in," chimes Kate. They both laugh.

"That's Anini Beach over there," Olivia says, pointing to a calm body of water. "It's a little slice of heaven. I've never seen it very crowded, and you can go snorkeling, there are tables to picnic on, and also plenty of trees if you just want to sit under one and read, or in your case, write."

"I'll have to remember that."

"WOW!" exclaims Kate when they drive onto the Kilohana Plantation grounds, and she sees the expansive 16,000 square foot stately Tudor-style manor built in 1935. "This place is gorgeous!"

"It was owned by Gaylord Parke Wilcox, one of the island's well-known sugar barons," says Olivia.

"There's that tree again. You have one in your yard. What kind is it?"

"A poinciana," Olivia replies as she and Kate admire the tall tree blooming with a massive umbrella of stunning red flowers.

"The grounds here are extensive, 104 acres," she continues. "There are fruit tree orchards, and they grow pineapple here and sugar cane, too.

They even have taro fields and a tropical rainforest on the property. We can take a tour after lunch if you'd like."

"Cool," says Kate. "Mahalo for taking me here."

Inside Gaylord's, an outdoor restaurant located in the manor's original courtyard, Olivia and Kate are shown to a table with distant views of Mount Waialeale.

"I think you'll love the food," Olivia says. "They have a 67-acre sustainable farm right here where most of the produce comes from. Are you hungry?"

"Bring it on!"

For lunch, they split an appetizer order of shrimp and scallop spring rolls served in butter lettuce cups with a rice vinegar papaya dipping sauce. For her main course, Kate selects the fresh catch of the day, grilled ono, with a field green salad made with cherry tomatoes and served with basil dressing. Olivia opts for the grilled ahi over roasted herbed veggies and mixed greens.

"This is definitely going to be my food intake for the rest of the day," says Kate, taking one last bite of the restaurant's signature classic banana coconut cream pie made with Koloa rum, whipped cream, and topped with toasted coconut, candied walnuts, and butterscotch sauce. "I'm glad I ran this morning."

"I hear ya," Olivia agrees. "You have to indulge every once in a while, though. It's good for the soul."

"Well, if you put it that way, just one more itsy bite," says Kate as she maneuvers her spoon around a candied walnut, which she pops into her mouth.

"When I was growing up, for dinner we always had salad, followed by the main course, and some kind of dessert. I honestly don't know how I didn't turn out to be huge," Kate laughs.

"Moderation is how," smiles Olivia. "Do you cook?"

"Yes, I love to!"

"You do?"

"Oh, yeah. While I usually grab most of my lunches on the run and eat at my computer, for dinner, even if it's just me, I really like to go to the market, shop for what appeals to me, and then try out different recipes. I also often make up my own dishes. I keep it pretty healthy though—organic meats, sustainable fish, and lots of veggies or vegetarian dishes. I find cooking to be a relaxing, different type of creative release from being at my computer all day long."

"Well, I wish I could say the same. I'm afraid my culinary skills are limited at best," comments Olivia. "But, I must say, I've got great utensils."

They both burst out laughing.

"In fact, tomorrow night, since it's just a small gathering, Grant's going to be the grill master, cooking up some of Halia's yummy marinated seafood, steak, and veggies."

"If you like, I could whip up a salad or side dish or two, and maybe a dessert."

"Really?" Olivia asks, incredulous.

"Sure, it would be fun! I can go shopping tomorrow afternoon and come over early, if that works for you."

"Yes, I'd love it. You're on!"

After lunch, Olivia and Kate peruse the gift shop on the second floor of the stately home, and then take a forty-minute train ride through the expansive plantation grounds. By the time Olivia drops Kate back at the resort, it's 4:30 p.m. She decides to call her parents early enough so that her dad won't be asleep. Kate places a FaceTime call.

After exchanging pleasantries and listening to Kate's excited description of her day with Olivia, Catherine changes the subject and inadvertently hits a sore spot with Kate. "Have you heard from Jason?"

"He called yesterday. He's traveling a lot and said he'd call again once he settles. He told me he closed the Miami deal, and he sounded really good."

"So, he can't make it to Kauai?"

"No, but I'll be seeing him on Tuesday night for dinner."

"Well Tuesday's not so far away. Has he given any indication as to next steps?" asks Catherine gingerly.

"No, but I'm taking dinner Tuesday as a good sign."

"I hope so, but be strong, hon," Catherine says. "If he knows what's good for him, he'll run, not walk, to the altar."

"Thanks, Mom."

"Kate, you're an amazing woman, so never underestimate that. Any man would be proud to call you his wife and close the deal before another guy maneuvers his way in. That's what your dad did with me."

"But Dad did maneuver his way in," laughs Kate.

"Precisely! And then he made sure he closed the deal!"

They both laugh.

"You're lucky, Mom. Dad wanted you, you wanted him, and he took action."

"That's how it is when it's right, sweetheart. It's a different time now, though. Back in my day, men and women had to marry; it's not necessarily the case anymore. That's why if one person values getting married, and the other doesn't, the person that does has to hold onto that truth about him or herself, and sometimes that person may have to face a tough choice."

Kate looks like she's about to be sick.

"Don't worry, dear, I think you'll know what's what when you see Jason on Tuesday. You've spent quite a bit of time together, and it's only fair you confirm whether or not you're both on the same page. If not, you'll have to gracefully part ways so you can find your true partner."

"Oh, Mom, if we're not, I think I'll just want to crawl under—"

"Don't even go there!" Catherine interjects firmly. "Remember, *you* are the prize. You're beautiful, smart, loving, loyal, and you'll make a great wife and mother. If Jason doesn't want marriage now, and moreover can't commit to being in your future in a meaningful way, then he may not be ready for a long, long time, *if ever*. If I remember correctly, he enjoyed playing the field before he met you and had somewhat of a reputation as a ladies' man, am I correct?"

"Yes," Kate sadly admits.

"Well, it may be that he feels he hasn't sewn enough wild oats yet, and that's what's holding him back."

"I don't think that's it, Mom."

"Kate, I don't want to upset you, but trust me. Some men may be fun to go out with and date, but they may not be marriage material. You want a friend and lover, someone who you can trust and be open with. You don't want to play games; you want to be real with each other. After five years of dating, Jason should be able to tell you if he's ready to move forward with you."

There is silence for a moment as Kate digests her mother's words.

"Kate, honey, I hope I haven't hurt you with my bluntness."

"No, Mom. You're right. It's time that Jason and I have a serious talk. I get scared sometimes when I think of a possible future without him, but I need to stay strong now. Thank you for reminding me."

"I love you," says Catherine. "Dad and I only want the best for you."

"I know."

"That's right, Katie poo, we only want the best for you," chimes in Glen sticking his face next to his wife's on the screen. "I can't believe you two are still gabbing."

"Hey, Dad we're just talkin' girl stuff."

"Precisely why I left after our initial hellos and went to my man cave."

They all laugh.

"Well, Mom and I just wrapped it up for tonight, so I'll call you guys tomorrow, OK?"

"Of course, dear," smiles Catherine.

"Love you, hon," adds Glen before he moves off screen.

"Love you to the moon and beyond, dear," Catherine says as she blows a kiss to Kate.

"To the moon and beyond, I love you, Mom," Kate replies, returning the kiss.

9

Kate shops the grocery aisles at Foodland on a mission to figure out the perfect recipes to complement the grill menu at Olivia's barbecue that evening. She wants to keep it simple, tasty, and healthy.

When Kate sees the locally grown Roma tomatoes, Maui onions, garlic cloves, and fresh basil in the produce aisle, she decides on the first recipe, a bruschetta appetizer. Then she contemplates recipes for the two side salads she'd like to make that would go great with either the grilled fish or meat. For the first, Kate chooses a mix of fresh spring lettuces and baby spinach, red onion, goat cheese, cherry tomatoes, and candied pecans. She picks up a few lemons and limes, white vinegar, olive oil, and honey to make a citrus vinaigrette dressing. For the second salad, she decides on orzo with sundried tomatoes, artichokes, and shrimp in a simple dressing of olive oil, Italian seasonings, and freshly squeezed lemon juice. For dessert, Kate elects to make lemon cupcakes with vanilla bean frosting topped with sweet shredded coconut.

As Kate checks off the last of the ingredients from her shopping list, she decides to pick up a cupcake tin just in case Olivia's "great utensils" don't include bakeware. Kate smiles remembering Olivia's funny delivery of her shortcomings.

"Et voilà!" Kate declares as she claps her hands, pleased at what she's accomplished thus far.

After her grocery run, Kate heads over to Olivia's.

"Hey, girl, how ya doing today?" Olivia calls out as she walks over to help Kate unload the groceries from the PT Cruiser.

"Just fab! Looking forward to playing with your great kitchen utensils."

"What did you buy? Is there anything left in the store?"

"Don't worry," laughs Kate. "I promise not to take over your kitchen entirely. I'm just going to make a few simple dishes, fresh salads mostly. The only thing that will take some bake time will be the lemon coconut cupcakes."

"Yummmy!" Olivia exclaims at the mention of the delectable sounding dessert.

In Olivia's kitchen, Kate starts to unpack the bags of groceries on the massive center island. "I'll make the cupcakes, bruschetta, and what I can of the salads now. Then, just before the guests arrive, I'll finish adding in the salad ingredients so that they are nice and fresh when we serve them."

"You got it, mi casa es su casa. Just let me show you around the kitchen so you know where things are. Actually, I won't lie to you, it might be educational for me too," laughs Olivia as she proceeds to open all of her drawers and cabinets, periodically stopping to marvel at her own wares.

"You weren't kidding when you said you had 'good utensils,'" comments Kate, which prompts both of them to burst out laughing.

Next to the large picture windows that look out to the ocean and lush grounds stands a gorgeous hand-painted hutch, which displays all types of glass and kitchenware.

"In here you'll find silverware and some great kitchen tools," says Olivia as she opens the hutch's large center drawer.

"And down here," she adds, opening the two large cabinets below, "on this side are all types of mixing bowls, and on the right, the electric mixer."

"OK, I think I have the lay of the land," Kate says.

"Let me know what I can do to help."

"The dishes are so simple. Maybe just sit at the center island and keep me company?"

"Now that I can do," chuckles Olivia. "Can I get you something to drink, a passion fruit iced tea perhaps? I was just about to pour myself a glass when you drove up."

"That would be great, mahalo."

Kate sets out the ingredients to make the bruschetta, cupcakes, and orzo salad.

"I'm impressed already. You're quite organized," says Olivia, pouring the iced tea into two tall glasses.

"It makes it more fun and the process runs smoother this way," Kate replies.

"Whatever you say. You're the master chef!"

"I'd hardly refer to myself a *master*, but experienced home chef, for sure."

"Have you ever catered?" asks Olivia.

"Not really, although friends and family have had me cook for their dinners and parties, and I occasionally whip up some goodies for the office. But it's all for the joy of it, never professionally."

Kate picks up the container of Roma tomatoes and fresh basil and moves over to the sink to wash and ready them for the bruschetta. Afterward, she retrieves a large glass bowl with a blue lid and a large wooden cutting board from the hutch, which she brings over to the kitchen's center island. Then Kate pulls out a sharp knife and peels and dices the ingredients. Tossing everything in a bowl, she mixes them together with a few squirts of lemon before sealing the glass container with its blue lid.

"I'll just let these marinate in the fridge and add the other seasonings later."

As Kate begins to sort through the ingredients to make the cupcakes she notices a series of photos on the kitchen windowsill. One image is of Olivia with her boyfriend Grant. Kate recognizes him from the dozens of photos she's seen of them together in the press. In another, there's a pretty young girl, about seven or eight, with a woman in her twenties. Their arms are wrapped tightly around one another and they smile broadly for the camera—clearly it's Olivia and her mother.

In another photo, Olivia is now a young teen, and she's standing in between an older man and woman—Kate guesses her nana and pops—arms intertwined, everyone grinning from ear to ear. The last photo is a shot of Olivia as an adult with her elderly grandparents standing in front of a Hawaiian beach with beautiful leis around their necks.

"What lovely photos of your family, Olivia. Your mom, nana, and pops, right?"

Olivia gets up from the center island and walks over to Kate by the sink.

"Oh, yeah," Olivia affirms nostalgically. "Happy times."

"You can really see the family resemblance between your mom, grandmother, and you," says Kate, zeroing in on the photos.

"Yeah, you sure can. I wish I had a chance to get to know my mother better. I was so young when she died."

"Twelve, right?"

"Good memory," Olivia nods. "There were so many things I didn't get to experience with her."

Olivia picks up the more recent picture of her grandparents and her.

"This picture was taken right here, just a few years ago, outside the lanai in front of the water."

"It's beautiful. Everyone looks so happy."

"We were. My nana and pops just loved this place. For the last few years of their lives, they lived right in that guest cottage out there where Halia and her husband live now. How old are your parents, by the way?"

"My dad's seventy-five, mom is sixty-eight," Kate replies as she begins to measure the ingredients for the cupcakes.

"You're lucky to still have them," says Olivia.

"I know. Growing up, it's amazing how much we take our parents for granted and assume they'll always be there. I think it was in my twenties that I began to look at them differently . . . right after I graduated college. They actually became more than just my parents; they became my friends."

"It was that way for me, too, with my grandparents. Because I lost my mom early, they became my parents. As I got older, instead of just being providers and disciplinarians, they became like friends. I feel them around me all the time."

"You mentioned that at lunch the other day."

"I think that's one of the reasons I feel such an affinity to this island and to Hawaii in general."

"What do you mean?"

"Well, for one, I can relax and be myself here. No one seems to be too impressed by me being a TV personality. Secondly, I can . . . how do I put this . . . feel myself. Being close to nature, the peacefulness of it all, I can think and create with ease. Being here rejuvenates me. I know I mentioned this to you the other day, but the thing that impacts me the most, and resonates with my soul, is living aloha and for ohana."

"For family," confirms Kate. "That's what it's all about, isn't it?"

"Yes, and it goes beyond this plane of Earth."

"How so?"

"Hawaiians believe that ohana not only nourishes your body and soul, they also believe that we are bound together in this world and the next. Even after your ohana pass from this world, family ties remain unbroken, and it's the living's duty to always remember and honor them. When I'm in New York, or other parts of the world, I take my ohana in my heart, but for some reason, I really feel and connect with them here. I think it's the land, the atmosphere, the culture, and other things I might not even be conscious of. All I know is this place is my heart, my true home, my soul place."

"Ooh, the writer in me likes that line, '*This is my heart, my true home, my soul place.*' I love it. Do you mind if I use it in the story?"

"Sure, why not?" Olivia responds with a smile.

10

An hour before the guests arrive, with the house ready for entertaining, the salads and cupcakes made, and the meat and fish ready and waiting to be grilled, Kate freshens up in Olivia's guest room. After she washes her face and reapplies her makeup, she changes out of the t-shirt and jeans she's been wearing and puts on a pretty tropical print halter and attractive white capri pants, then heads for the great room.

A cool breeze pours in from the retracted glass wall and soft instrumental music filters through the home audio system, setting the stage for the evening's soiree. At the kitchen's center island, Halia pours some Chardonnay into two chilled wine glasses.

"What type of wine glass marker would you like?" asks Halia. "A pineapple, palm tree, or hibiscus?"

"A red hibiscus will do just fine," says Kate. "Do you need any help with anything?"

"No, thank you. Here you go," Halia says as she hands Kate a glass.

"Mahalo."

Olivia, looking gorgeous in a long, flowing tropical patterned sundress, enters from the lanai. Olivia wolf whistles when she sees Kate. "Don't you look stunning!"

"You look amazing, too."

Halia hands Olivia a chilled glass of wine.

"Mahalo, Halia," says Olivia. "Why don't you pour yourself a glass of wine and relax? You've been working hard all afternoon."

"Maybe just a little bit, then I have to get ready to leave for my daughter's. My husband Naoki and I are dining at her place tonight," Halia explains to Kate.

"Kate, come. I have someone on the lanai I'd like you to meet."

"Sure," Kate replies, following Olivia outside.

Olivia's boyfriend, Grant Anderson, rises to greet Kate.

"Aloha," he extends his hand to Kate.

"Aloha, nice to meet you," Kate says as they shake hands.

Grant is very handsome, dressed in a pair of khaki Dockers pants, sandals, and a Tommy Bahama shirt in beige, blue, and white. He is even more classy and distinguished in person than in the photo sitting on Olivia's kitchen windowsill. His perfect white smile is genuinely welcoming and sparkles against his ebony skin.

"Olivia mentioned that you two have been having a grand ole time this week," says Grant, putting his arm around Olivia's waist.

"We have. Not only was she gracious enough to do the interview, but she also showed me around Hanalei and Kauai's East Coast from Anahola to Lihue."

"I think in my next life I'll probably be a tour guide," chuckles Olivia. "I get such pleasure from it."

"You'd make a great one, hon," says Grant. "You're a pretty good party hostess, too."

"Just call me the hostess with the most-ess," jokes Olivia as she kisses Grant's cheek.

"Come on, let's sit down and take in the beginnings of what looks to be a super amazing sunset," Grant suggests.

"I'll toast to that," chimes Olivia as they all clink glasses.

"Kate, just so you know, tonight I've invited a few close friends," adds Olivia. "My show's producer Morgan Armstrong and her husband Tom. They're in town for meetings and for a little R & R. Our friends Sukey and her husband Kamal are also coming—they're both local artists who run a gallery in Princeville. You'll also meet Elaine and Trevor Harrison.

Elaine's my realtor friend who sold me this house, and her husband is an architect who builds green buildings. Last but not least, my Plumeria Café partner Malie and her husband Aukai are coming. Aukai owns a surf shop in Hanalei."

"And Malie's brother Kai might also be coming," adds Grant. "He's an ER doc in Kapaa."

"Sounds like an interesting crowd," says Kate.

"They are," agrees Grant. "All fantastic, really nice people doing good for the planet in their own way."

"Here, here," chimes Olivia. "Let's definitely toast to that!"

Before Halia leaves for the evening, she sets out several pretty long necked silver tablespoons next to the orzo salad displayed in a pretty glass bowl. The long wooden lanai table, which serves as the appetizer bar, also displays an impressive assembly of crudités with a selection of red pepper and pesto hummus, taro chips and an onion dip, as well as fresh fruit, assorted cheeses, and Kate's bruschetta. A gorgeous spray of tropical flowers expertly arranged in a large vase serves to give the table a celebratory feel.

"Everything looks so beautiful," comments Kate as she helps Halia with the table display.

Just as Kate is about to continue her conversation with Halia, Elaine and Trevor appear on the lanai.

"Aloha, Halia. And who do we have here?" asks Elaine Harrison, giving Kate a friendly once over. I'm Elaine and this my husband, Trevor.

Kate replies, "I'm Kate Grace from *New York View Magazine*. I'm doing a profile on Olivia. She's told me a lot about you—I hear you're a fabulous realtor," Kate embellishes, sensing that Elaine will enjoy the flattery.

"Moi? Oh that Olivia—she's too kind. Pleasure to meet you, Kate," says Elaine.

"Aloha, my dear, I'm so pleased to make your acquaintance as well," Trevor adds, taking Kate's hand and giving it a gentlemanly kiss.

Trevor, like Elaine, originally hails from London. He has a marvelous lilt to his voice and bears a slight resemblance to a younger version of the famous British actor Michael Caine.

Olivia, hearing the commotion out on the lanai, makes her way excitedly through the great room onto the lanai.

"Elaine!" cries Olivia.

"Olivia!" Elaine yelps, pulling Olivia into a huge hug. "You look simply smashing, daahling."

"Did I hear someone say he needs a drink?" asks Grant, looking directly at Trevor.

"You didn't, at least not aloud anyways. Lucky for me you know me well enough to read my mind," answers Trevor, eyebrows raised.

"Come, my man," says Grant as he drapes his arm around Trevor's shoulder. "Let's get thee to the bar."

"Aye! Now we're talkin!"

Once everyone has drinks, Kate strikes up a lively conversation with Elaine and Trevor, who are world travelers, sophisticated, and very funny. As the rest of the guests begin to arrive, Kate is supremely entertained by the Harrisons, as they take jabs at each new arrival and also each other.

Hosts Grant and Olivia check on their guests to make sure everyone has what they need. Grant makes the rounds taking drink orders, while Olivia makes sure she spends one-on-one time greeting everyone. Finally she makes her way to her producer Morgan. Morgan is an energetic Asian woman, who sits beside her husband Tom, an attractive black man who is a studio production executive and, like Morgan, in his mid-forties. They look every bit the power couple.

Across from the Armstrongs sit Olivia's artist friends, Sukey and Kamal. Kate finds out that Sukey, a beautiful Japanese woman with an eclectic style and personality to match, is a jewelry maker, and her husband, a handsome Eurasian man with a commanding presence and charming smile, is a painter, photographer, and a procurer and seller of fine art.

Trevor, taking over as bartender for the moment, stands mixing a drink and trading one-liners with Aukai, a muscular, athletic type and Kauai local with a laid-back and welcoming demeanor.

"'My wife and I were happy for twenty years. Then we met.' Rodney Dangerfield," says Aukai as he recounts a familiar one-liner.

Trevor laughs out loud.

"OK, I've got another one for you," Trevor returns. "'I never mind my wife having the last word; in fact, I'm delighted when she gets to it.' That's Walter Matthau."

"I want you to know that I heard that one *daahling*!" calls Elaine playfully. "You wouldn't be insinuating *that I . . . ?*"

Trevor makes a pouty face, then blows Elaine a kiss.

"That's right, you better blow me kisses. Or else . . . !" jabs Elaine.

"Or else what my luv? You'll spank me? Oh, please, please . . ."

Everyone laughs out loud now.

"I've got one for you," says Kai Stevens, Malie's hunk of a brother, as he walks onto the lanai. "'By all means marry. If you get a good wife, you'll become happy. If you get a bad one, you'll become a philosopher.' Socrates said that." Kai's spot-on delivery elicits more laughter from the group.

"Good one, but how about, 'My wife told me to go out and get something that makes her look sexy, so I got drunk,'" laughs Trevor.

"Hey!" shouts Elaine.

"Only kidding, daahling. You know I think you're the sexiest woman alive!"

"Oh, now he's just trying to butter up the designated driver," quips Elaine, rolling her eyes.

"That's right folks, when you drink, drive responsibly," says Kai.

"Yes, Doctor!" Trevor salutes Kai.

"Hey, that's no laughing matter!" chides Kai playfully as Olivia embraces him.

"Hello, handsome," Olivia says. "Don't worry, Doc, we'll make sure anyone who needs a designated driver will get one."

"You're looking gorgeous as ever," Kai smiles as he hands Olivia the bottle of wine he's brought.

"Mahalo," Olivia replies.

"Kai, can we tempt you with an adult beverage?" asks Elaine.

"After the day I had, I think I could be tempted with just about anything right now."

"Uh-oh ladies, better watch out!" calls Trevor.

"Now, now, Kai and Trevor, you two better behave. I'm warning you," says Elaine. "I also want to make one thing very clear. *NO* picking on me tonight."

"Ah, but Elaine, you're so much fun to pick on," winks Kai, smiling devilishly.

"Kidding aside, what can I get for you, my fine fellow?" asks Trevor.

"Cabernet, if you've got it," Kai replies, walking to the bar.

"Coming right up."

"He's a real charmer," Elaine whispers to Kate.

Kate watches as Kai sips his wine. As she stares at him, she notices he looks familiar.

Where has she seen him before?

It's hard not to notice Kai, who is thirtysomething. He stands about 6'4" with short dark hair, chiseled good looks, and a killer body to match.

A young Harrison Ford type, thinks Kate. And then she makes the connection: *Oh my God, it's the hunk from the beach the other day that saw me dancing around like an idiot when I stubbed my toe!*

Just as Kate is about to slink away or die of embarrassment, Kai turns around where she can get an even better view of him.

"He's Malie's brother?" whispers Kate to Elaine. "They don't really look alike, do they?"

"Malie looks like her mom, who was Hawaiian. Kai resembles his dad, who's half Dutch and half English."

"You said her mom *was* Hawaiian?"

"Yes, she passed away two years ago. A tragic boating accident."

Elaine stops talking when Kai begins to walk over from the bar to where she and Kate sit.

"Kai, this is Kate Grace. She's a journalist in from New York," says Elaine.

"Nice to meet you," Kai says as he extends his hand to Kate.

"Nice to meet you, too," Kate replies, wondering if Kai recognizes her.

Kai reaches around Kate's much smaller hand, and as his thumb interlocks with hers, his long fingers naturally wrap around her wrist, completely encompassing it in the handshake. The surge of warm energy that emanates from his hands to Kate's sears into her skin and catches her off guard for a second. Kate also notices that his handshake, while firm, is also quite gentle, and his skin is like velvet to the touch. His green eyes, which lock with hers, seem to bore deep into her soul.

Kate is the first to pull away. She tries hard to catch her breath and be nonchalant in the process.

"You look so familiar, don't I know you from somewhere?" asks Kai smiling, somewhat amused.

If he doesn't remember the other day, she's not going to volunteer the information. She was wearing a large hat and dark sunglasses so . . .

"I'm, well . . . I'm from the East Coast, and it's my first time here."

Kai smiles broadly at her, clearly amused.

"What's that look about? Do you have something against the East Coast?" asks Kate, her heart racing.

"Not at all. It's just that you seem familiar . . ." Kai lingers on the last word, but Kate won't give anything up.

"You look like you could use a refill," notes Kai, finally changing the subject. "Can I get you some more wine?"

"Sure, I'm drinking the Chardonnay," Kate says, not knowing quite what to make of their interaction. She watches Kai as he walks to the bar to freshen her drink.

OMG! she thinks. *He is so, so . . .* 'Hot' is the only word that comes into her mind. Kate bites her lip with a smile. She is blown away by this strange, unexpected chemical reaction she is having to Kai.

"Here you go," says Kai a few moments later, handing Kate back her glass.

"Mahalo."

"OK folks, I have an announcement," calls Olivia, projecting her voice so everyone can hear her over the chatter. The crowd quiets down allowing Olivia to speak in her normal tone.

"Thank you all so much for coming. It's soooo good to see everybody! As you probably know, appetizers are out here on the table to the right of the bar. Inside, on the dining room table, is a buffet for dinner. I'd like to give a big shout-out and say mahalo to my friend Kate here for making the bruschetta, delicious salads, and the lemon coconut cupcakes we'll be having for dessert."

Kate bows her head as people clap.

"Mahalo Elaine, Trevor, and Kai, for the selection of wines."

More clapping.

"And to Malie and Aukai for the brownies, Sukey and Kamal, the fresh baked breads, and Morgan and Tom, for the cognac we'll have après dinner. Oops, almost forgot—last but not least, to Grant for being the grill master and bartender extraordinaire."

"Hey, I thought I was the bartender!" says Trevor, feigning hurt feelings.

"No, you just tend to drink everything at the bar," yells out Kai in jest.

The guests howl with laughter.

"Hey, I can't help it if I never met a drink I didn't like," Trevor retorts.

"That's enough now, Trev, I'm starving!" says Elaine.

"OK, folks, *mangiamo*!" yells Olivia. "Or as they say in Hawaiian, e `ai kākou! Let's eat!"

11

Looking at her reflection in the bathroom mirror of her hotel suite, Kate rubs moisturizer onto her freshly washed face.

Dinner at Olivia's house was just amazing, she thinks.

Finished with her nightly beauty ritual, she switches off the bathroom light and makes her way through the darkened bedroom towards the open slider and out to the lanai. The moon's glow and the resort's outdoor lamps are sufficient light for Kate to maneuver in. Despite it being 1:00 a.m., Kate's much too alert to go to bed. A beautiful, balmy breeze flows in from the ocean and sensually caresses Kate's body.

"Aaah," she sighs with contentment before lying down on the plush chaise to enjoy the dark night sky, which is studded with sparkling white gems. The resort is quiet now, and the only sounds Kate can hear are those the balmy breeze makes as it fingers its way through the trees.

What a magical place, she thinks.

Scenes from the evening's party play over and over in Kate's mind like little snippets of film. She thinks about preparing the food in Olivia's kitchen earlier that day, their talk about their families, meeting Grant and all the wonderful dinner guests . . . and, most memorably, shaking hands with Kai. *"He's a real charmer,"* she remembers what Elaine said about him.

Yes, he was that, as well as handsome and funny. In her mind's eye, Kate reviews the lines of Kai's gorgeous body, and replays the feeling of his warm hands and the velvety touch of his long, strong fingers around her wrist, the warm glow in his green eyes, and a look that seemed to bore into her soul. When he asked her if they had ever met before, she knew the answer, even though she kept it to herself. However, now that she has actually gotten to know Kai a little better, she feels as if she's known him not just from the chance meeting at Hanalei Pier, but for a long time prior to that—even though she had never met him before this trip.

How is that possible?

As Kate thinks of Kai, she begins to breathe more rapidly. She becomes aware of a longing deep inside her. Surprised by the depths of her thoughts, she bolts upright and attempts to shake off the sensation. She takes a cleansing breath to release the pent-up energy from her reverie. Relaxing now, she walks back into the bedroom and picks up her cell phone to check if there are any new text messages.

"Missing you, Aloha, Jason XO," reads the only new text.

Kate smiles broadly as she places the phone back down on the table. Now, fully back in reality, and feeling rather spent, she crawls beneath the silky sheets and marvels at their welcome engulfing softness as she drifts into a deep sleep.

In her dream, Kate walks down the beautiful, tropical tree-lined Weke Road, home to that pretty white cottage, which is so similar to the watercolor print Malie gifted her with from The Plumeria Café. The sun feels warm against her skin, and the birds chirp happily.

As she walks down the street by herself, she suddenly becomes aware that her mother walks beside her. No words are necessary between the two women as they happily continue on towards the cottage. Kate feels her mother's warmth and love, and she knows her mother feels the affection Kate has for her in return. When the women reach the stone walkway that leads up to the cottage's blue door, they stop and look towards the house.

A lady peers out at them from the large picture window just to the right of the front door. A few seconds later, the door opens. The lady, a pretty Hawaiian woman in her late sixties, wears a simple sundress with a flower tucked behind her left ear. She stands in the doorway and looks at them with a welcoming smile. She beckons to Catherine and Kate with outstretched arms.

"*Kate!*" She hears her name being called as real as the day is long.

In a flash, Kate wakes up from her dream. She looks around the room to get her bearings, then turns to view the clock on her nightstand. It's 3:00 a.m. As Kate lies awake in her bed, she can still hear that voice calling her name. It felt so real. *How is that possible?* Pondering the details of the dream and wondering what it means, she once again falls into a deep slumber.

12

The next morning Kate wakes up unusually late at 10:00 a.m., but clearly she needed the sleep. Refreshed and rejuvenated, she's ready to enjoy a leisurely breakfast on her lanai. Although the sky looks rather dark, and the air smells of rain, Kate likes the feel of the cool breeze pouring through the windows and doors, and reckons that even if it does rain, she'll be protected under the lanai roof.

After a bowl of oatmeal with fresh fruit and coffee, Kate powers up her laptop to check her emails. Nothing urgent. She sends a few quick hellos to her family and Cindy, and also writes a special thank-you to Olivia for the lovely dinner party, and for arranging a private tour of the Princeville Botanical Gardens for later that day. Thanks to Olivia's connections, the family-run garden, normally closed on weekends, is making an exception for Kate to view the lush topography of this sacred paradise.

Kate then goes online to check out the forecast, and just as she suspects from the clouds, periodic spells of rain are predicted. She gets dressed for the day in shorts, a t-shirt, and flip-flops, and makes sure to throw a lightweight, waterproof, hooded jacket in her tote before she heads down to the resort's marketplace to see if they have umbrellas for purchase.

"You're in luck," says the cashier. "It's our last one until our next shipment arrives later this week."

The Princeville Botanical Gardens is a quick, easy drive from The Westin but as Kate views the darkening skies above, she wonders if her tour might get cancelled. Little droplets of rain begin to appear on her

PT Cruiser's windshield as soon as Kate pulls into the garden's parking lot, and seconds later, it starts to pour. To keep her camera safe before she exits the car, she buries it underneath the safety of her jacket.

As Kate approaches the entrance, she sees a woman in her early fifties wearing a large brimmed hat, khaki shorts, and a navy raincoat waving to her from the reception desk. Kate waves back, and even though she makes a beeline for cover under the reception canopy, her exposed legs and feet get drenched from the downpour.

"Aloha! Welcome to the Princeville Botanical Gardens. I'm Caren. You must be Kate?"

"Aloha, yes."

"I'll be your guide today."

"I appreciate it," says Kate. "So the tour is still on?"

"Oh, sure, this is nothing—the rain will stop shortly," Caren replies confidently. "Even if it lets up, it may start again when we're in the gardens, so we'll just take cover if we need to until the rain subsides. This happens all the time."

"Well, great, then. I'm really looking forward to it!"

About twenty minutes later, just as Caren promised, the rain tapers off and Kate enthusiastically follows her guide's lead through the flowering pathways.

"This area was previously cattle land," says Caren. "Over time it became an unruly jungle of plants that pushed out the native flora. When the Robertson family purchased this property, they started reintroducing native plants and sustainably treating the soil so that everything would thrive. Then, what actually began in 2001 as just a hobby, became this garden, and they're still adding to it all the time."

Kate witnesses firsthand the labors of love in every detail. The amazing garden is full of native "canoe" plants, plumerias, poinciana trees, fruit trees, ti plants, potent medicinals, rare and endangered exotic species, and florals in every color, shape, and size from around the world—the likes of which Kate has never seen before.

Midway through her tour, Caren takes Kate to the area where chocolate tastings are held. A host of dark, sweet, and milk chocolates are sampled and compared, and Kate loves the fact that there are a number of candy samples made from the garden's cacao harvest. After the tasting, Kate and Caren venture out into the forest again, only to be met with another torrential downpour. They take cover under the umbrella of a grouping of trees until the rain subsides some ten minutes later.

"Oh, wow!" Kate exclaims excitedly as she pulls out her camera and begins shooting pictures of the vibrant red and pink hibiscus surrounding her. "I can actually see the individual drops of rain on the leaves, and the way the light peeks through the foliage is making for some awesome shots."

"Snap away," encourages Caren.

It's as if Kate has lost all sense of time and space in the magnificent garden. Intoxicated by the colors, textures, smells, and sounds, Kate is more present and in the moment than she's ever felt before. In a blink, hours pass, and she has hundreds of photos to prove it.

"So, what do you think?" inquires Caren. "Would you like a spot of tea?"

"Yes!" Kate doesn't hesitate to respond. "And . . . maybe just a tad more chocolate?" she adds playfully.

Kate knows she has captured some amazing shots, and her mind is already processing which ones she might frame as holiday gifts. She's a bit anxious to get back to the hotel to download the images to her computer and get a more intimate look at her day's bounty. However, at least for the moment, tea and chocolate is at the forefront of her mind.

On Sunday, in celebration of her last full day on the Garden Isle, Kate remembers what Olivia told her about the North Shore's Anini Beach.

"A great place for a picnic, to write . . ."

So, in preparation for her excursion to Anini Beach in Kalihiwai, Kate stops at Foodland Market and orders a freshly made turkey sandwich with avocado and tomato on whole wheat, and picks up a package of raw veggies with hummus, a large bottle of Hawaiian Springs water, and a plump nectarine.

As Kate travels Highway 56 towards her destination, she feels confident she's going to have another great day relaxing, reading, and getting a head start on her article if the mood hits. Or better yet, maybe it's the perfect time to jot down some notes for that novel she knows she's destined to write.

Kate parks on Anini Beach's grass and sand parkway. Armed with her totes packed with the day's essentials, she walks towards the pristine shore. There aren't many people. A family of four snorkel just off the calm shoreline, there's a couple at the water's edge holding hands, and there are a few other beachgoers resting on blankets and swimming in the crystal waters. The sky is an exceptional blue with white cotton puff clouds so large and so close to the earth that they look as if she could jump up and touch them.

Kate picks out a picnic table with a perfect view that's shaded by a group of tropical trees. The water before her sparkles with little bursts of light from the sun's rays and is colored in several beautiful jewel shades of blue that blend seamlessly, one right into the other. The water closest to the shoreline is translucent teal blue. Further out, it turns deep aquamarine until in the distance, it transforms into a cool, deep azure.

Kate breathes deeply and releases a huge sigh as she becomes mesmerized by the view. There is so much awe-inspiring wonder about the island that she's had to take in and digest, and breathing deeply and then releasing it works to calm her spirit and create balance within. After sitting for a time in this meditative state, Kate reaches for her quilted tote on the wooden picnic table.

OK, Kate, what will it be? Reading for fun or just relaxing and enjoying the view? Maybe writing stream of consciousness style to see what comes out? Or perhaps I should get a head start on the article that's already starting to write itself in my head?

Kate pulls the bottle of spring water out of her bag, opens the lid, and takes a gulp before she pulls out her laptop.

"OK, writing! We'll see where that takes us," she says out loud as she powers up her computer.

For the last few days, Kate has had several ideas swimming around her head about how to begin the article on Olivia, and in this beautiful setting, inspiration hits, and so she begins to type. One hour quickly leads to two. By the time Kate looks up, she is well into completing her first draft.

OK, enough of that for now. I'll pick up where I left off on the plane, thinks Kate. *Now for some R & R.*

After lunching on her market purchases, Kate snaps a few shots of the picturesque beach, then packs the PT Cruiser with her valuables to free herself up for a long walk and relaxing swim. Whatever else she decides to do today, she is confident she will be able to find a myriad of ways to enjoy her stay in this little piece of heaven.

THE NEXT MORNING, her final day on the island, Kate wakes at dawn, brews a cup of coffee, and takes it out to her lanai in order to drink in the last of the glorious sunrise. Looking through her camera's viewfinder for just the right setup, she snaps a quick succession of photos of the multicolored sky as a reminder of this wonderful trip. Only when she is satisfied that she has captured just the right shot does she sit quietly on the chaise to sip her favorite Kona brew.

Before Kate boards her plane at Lihue airport, she sends off a flurry of texts to her family and friends, plus a special one to Olivia to once again thank her for her hospitality and to tell her that she's looking forward to keeping in touch. While Kate is anxious to see everyone in New York, she feels extremely melancholy about leaving Kauai. The trip had gone even better than she ever could have anticipated, and she is so grateful for her new friendship with Olivia.

What is it about this place that makes me feel so despondent about leaving? she wonders. *Maybe it's because for the first time in a long time, I've actually taken some time to relax? Or perhaps it's the friendly people, the hospitality, and the natural beauty of the place that has touched me?*

Kate has really connected with the environment, and with parts of herself as well, yet she feels there's so much more to explore. She has a sixth sense that she's on the brink of something.

But what?

Laying her head against the plane's glass window, Kate watches as the lush green of the island and stunning blue waters surrounding it grow farther and farther away, until they disappear altogether beneath the white cotton puff clouds. And when they do, Kate feels a stream of warm tears on her cheeks, and an unexpected longing in her soul.

Part Two

HER LOVE IS A BEACON

New York

13

"Your article's fantastic, Kate!" says Edward as he sips his morning coffee.

"I'm thrilled you like it," Kate replies.

"I'm impressed you got it to me your first day back."

"Well, inspiration hit while I was in Kauai, and then there was the long plane ride back to New York."

"You never let any grass grow under your feet, do you?" chuckles Edward.

"No, but maybe I should sometimes," replies Kate, a little nostalgically. "I found out I really liked kicking back and hanging loose."

"Well, you're a hard worker and never take time off," Edward remarks. "I'm sure I'm not the first to tell you that it does a person good. You still have a few weeks of vacation left, you know. So, as long as you give us advance warning, we'll figure a way to work around it."

"Thanks, Edward. I really appreciate that."

"The photographer will email us a complete zip file of photos by this afternoon, so after lunch, I'll buzz your office," says Edward. "We'll review them with the photo editor and pick out a few cover possibilities along with the images for the inside spread."

"Sounds like a plan. We'll have to get photo approvals from Olivia's publicist, though," Kate reminds Edward.

"Absolutely."

"For my next piece, I was thinking about talking to some high-profile chefs about what's in season and their farm-to-table recipes.

What inspires them and why. Maybe a mix of family traditions and modern inspirations?"

"I like it. Gather some ideas, and we'll regroup in a few days to talk more."

"Cool. Oh, I almost forgot," Kate adds as she pulls a small gift box from her shoulder bag and hands it to Edward.

"What's this now?"

Edward opens the box. It's a beautiful glass paperweight in shades of teal, white, and blue. Inside the round ornament is hand blown glass that resembles ocean waves.

"I know how much you love the sea, so I thought why not bring a little of it into the work place? It's from a gallery in Princeville that's run by two of Olivia's friends."

"It's a perfect gift for me. I love it!" says Edward, examining every detail. "But you shouldn't have. Thank you." He gives Kate a fatherly hug. "And actually, what I meant to say is, mahalo."

THE NEXT DAY KATE TAKES special care getting ready for her important dinner date with Jason. Tonight she'll find out where they are headed, and in light of their recent communication since the "big talk," she is both nervous and tentatively hopeful about their future.

If Jason didn't have a change of heart, or something positive to talk to me about, then why would he be taking me to dinner? she thinks.

But then again, I also have to be prepared for nothing to be different. Either way, I'll know what's what, and there will be some relief in that, right?

Intent on looking her absolute best, Kate checks out her form for the umpteenth time in her full-length mirror. Her deep green, form-fitting, lace, strapless dress is designer perfect. She looks fantastic in it, and it accentuates her beautiful green eyes. She has only worn the dress once before, to a friend's cocktail party a little over a month ago. As usual, Jason couldn't attend because at the last minute he was called out of town. The rave reviews she received that evening, not to mention the plethora of attention she got from a few of the male partygoers, makes her feel that this dress is the perfect choice for tonight.

To complement her attire, Kate puts on a sexy pair of black silk stockings and pumps. Her hair is styled in casual waves that hang provocatively about her face and shoulders. Strands of her hair, bleached by the Hawaiian sun, highlight her facial features in all the right places. Her makeup, done to perfection, and the long, dangling silver earrings she wears, complete the sexy look. The rest and rejuvenation she enjoyed on her trip only add to her allure.

"Not bad, even if I say so myself," says Kate aloud.

Dinner is at one of the most romantic spots in Manhattan's West Village, the upscale One if by Land, Two if by Sea. The restaurant, a 1767 landmark carriage house that once belonged to Aaron Burr, who served as vice president under Thomas Jefferson, has exquisite décor featuring cozy fireplaces, a private garden, and plenty of old-world charm. It's also well known as a setting where many people get engaged and hold special occasions like weddings, anniversaries, and other important celebrations. Knowing this only adds to Kate's excitement and anticipation for the evening's rendezvous.

Kate arrives at the restaurant at 7:00 p.m. to meet Jason in the restaurant's cozy piano bar. The room is dreamily lit with several large chandeliers that cast an alluring glow. A pianist adds even more atmosphere to the room as he plays romantic tunes from bygone eras at the baby grand in the corner. From the bar's entryway, Kate sees Jason sitting at a table in the back.

I feel like I'm on a movie set, thinks Kate. *But this is no cinematic trick, this is my life . . . and it's about to get interesting.*

She takes a deep breath and walks towards Jason.

"Wow! You look absolutely amazing," Jason says, standing to greet Kate with a kiss on the lips.

"Mahalo, I mean thank you," laughs Kate as Jason pulls out a chair for her to join him.

"Mahalo. Hmm, I see going to Kauai has made quite an impression on you."

"I kind of got into the habit of saying thank you that way while I was away."

"I'm sorry I couldn't make it, but I want to hear all about it. I'm having a scotch on the rocks, can I get you something to drink?"

"Chardonnay," Kate answers. Jason goes to the bar and returns a few moments later with the drinks.

"Scotch on the rocks?" questions Kate. "Normally you order a Cab or a Merlot."

"Well, I kind of got used to it with some of the new clients," Jason replies as he takes a sip of his drink.

Kate smiles sweetly at Jason. She suddenly realizes that she feels completely confident and totally at ease. Maybe it's knowing that her ohana is looking out for her, or perhaps it's the peace she found in taking real, relaxing time for herself, but whatever it is, she feels renewed and refreshed . . . and not so concerned about what may or may not unfold next.

Jason must sense this shift in her, and he studies her intently, as if trying to read her mind. He furrows his brow for a minute, seemingly confounded about something.

Finally he says, "I really can't believe how great you look."

Kate takes a good look at Jason before she answers. She instinctively feels as if he wanted to say something else, but for now she's content with taking in how much he's fawning over her.

"Wow, I must have really looked like I needed a vacation before I left, then," grins Kate.

"Well, you were a little . . . *tightly wound*."

"Excuse me?" Kate says, now not so laid-back.

"I'm sorry, that came out wrong. What I meant to say is that you, um, were a little stressed, working too much, and seemed to have a lot on your mind. It does a person good to take a break now and then," explains Jason, trying to recover.

"Yes, it does, and you should try it. When was the last time you took a break?"

Jason thinks for a moment. "Touché! You got me."

"We're not fencing here," Kate says, placing her hand on top of Jason's. "We both have been working hard for a while now. I realized when I was away how good it feels to take some time off."

"From each other you mean? Or just in general?"

"Just in every way. To think, rest, and rejuvenate, to get in touch with my inner self. For me, I found it was a great way to connect to my creativity. I found it really easy to write there. The article I did on Olivia just flew out of me. I even had time to jot down some ideas for that novel I'm always telling everyone I want to write."

"That's wonderful for you. So it was a good trip?" asks Jason, taking another sip of his drink and becoming increasingly distracted and almost nervous.

"Does it bother you, that I had a *good* trip?"

"No, I think it was great—*for you*," Jason replies. "I think I'd be bored out of my mind in a place like that, though."

"What? Why?"

Jason only shrugs.

"You'd actually be bored taking a few days off to enjoy a gorgeous tropical paradise, sunning by the ocean, and taking walks in nature? You realize that you'd still have all the amenities of a five-star hotel and access to your computer and cell? It's not like you'd be going to another planet."

"That's probably true," says Jason. "It's just that I find a lot of excitement and pleasure in my work right now. Besides, I really can't take the time off at the moment."

"Yes, you've mentioned that before, numerous times, and I understand your reasons why you couldn't join me, I do."

"Well, good. By the way, I'm actually expecting an important call from a client in the next half hour or so, and I'll have to take it, but it will only be for a minute or two. I'm just warning you ahead of time."

"OK."

Both Jason and Kate sip their drinks in silence. Before it becomes too uncomfortable, Jason suddenly gets a sly smile on his face and reaches out to stroke Kate's bare arm and shoulder.

"You look very sexy tonight, you know," he murmurs in a low voice.

Within seconds, Kate can feel her body begin to respond. Jason bends into Kate just enough so she can feel his warm breath on her skin in a way he knows excites her. He kisses her gently on her cheek first, then lightly runs his tongue along her neck and around her ear before gently kissing her lips. Kate lets out a little moan of pleasure as Jason slips his tongue into her mouth.

"Jason," says Kate as she breaks away to cool things down.

"You are so lovely," Jason breathes, taking hold of her hand and kissing it. "I missed you."

"I missed you, too."

"I want to make love to you so much," moans Jason softly into her ear. Kate feels herself start to tremble with delicious memories of their lovemaking.

"Hey, I've got an idea," says Jason. "How about we order takeout from here, and then go back to my place, where we can get reacquainted and then enjoy dinner in bed?" Before Kate can answer, Jason gets up to alert the manager.

Kate sits trying to sort through her feelings and organize the mishmash of thoughts running through her head. She is keenly aware of the fact that she is weakening to Jason's charms, and she also needs to hit the brakes before getting physical with him if she is going to get the answers she so desperately needs.

Jason's cell phone starts to ring and vibrate frantically jumping about the table. Kate scans the room, but Jason is nowhere in sight. If this is the important phone call he's waiting for, then he's going to miss it unless she answers it for him.

Should I do it? she wonders. As the phone continues to ring, Kate makes an executive decision.

"Hello," answers Kate. It's a FaceTime call. A gorgeous brunette appears on screen.

"I'm calling Jason Latham," says the woman, who is about Kate's age. "Is this his office?" she asks, sounding incredulous.

"No, this isn't his office. We're out right now."

"*Who* are *you,* may I ask?"

"I, uh . . . I'm Jason's girlfriend, Kate. He said he was waiting for an important client call and he got up from the table and forgot to take his phone, so I . . ."

"Oh, ah, well," the woman pauses, taking a very business-like tone. "Please tell Jason that Heather called, and that I have some news regarding the Clark deal. I need to talk to him immediately, as it's quite urgent."

"Do you want to hold? He just stepped away for a second . . ."

"No, just tell him to call me, thank you," Heather replies curtly as she abruptly ends the call.

Jason returns to the table seconds later.

"The manager's cool with us cancelling our table for tonight. I placed a take-out order for us . . ."

"Jason, sit down for a minute please," orders Kate with a sudden calmness of purpose. Jason sits and Kate begins to speak slowly and firmly.

"We had a conversation the evening of my parents' anniversary party. Have you thought about what we said?"

"Oh, baby, let's not do this now."

"Jason, it's important. I want to know what's on your mind."

"Yes, I've thought about it."

"And?"

"And, I thought about it, period," says Jason in a defiant tone.

They stare at one another for a bit. Kate's blood is starting to boil, but she's doing her best to handle herself. Jason fidgets and then gulps down the last droplets of scotch in his glass before he speaks.

"Look, I'm not ready to make any commitments right now." Kate swallows hard as she digests what Jason has just revealed.

He continues, now more pointedly. "I'm just not ready for marriage."

"Right now or just to me?"

"I just feel I'm too young to get married. Maybe in a couple of years or so, I don't know. There are a lot of things I want to do, and I can't be tied down."

"Oh, so you view marriage as being tied down to such a point that you can't do what you want?"

Silence.

"You don't view it as a partnership born out of mutual love?"

More silence.

"Do you even really love me Jason?"

"Of course I love you," he says, but not with the passion and conviction Kate hopes for.

"Jason, we've been dating for five years. There isn't anything we don't know about each other. It's not like we're in our early twenties just out of college. I'm not a burden, not someone that is going to tie you down. I love you, and I'm here to support you. I want to share a beautiful life together with you. After five years, if you don't know that, then I honestly don't know when you will."

"You know, Kate, we have a good thing, but I've got to be honest with you; I really don't appreciate the fact that you're trying to manipulate me into marriage," says Jason, a cruel note in his voice.

Instead of reacting in her normal fashion—which would be to back off and not confront him—the calm and inner peace Kate has been feeling since she's returned from her trip gives her clarity and a renewed conviction in her beliefs. The earlier FaceTime call from Heather is also making Kate's delivery easier.

"You know, Jason, I don't appreciate you accusing me of manipulating you. You knew from the moment we started dating what my true intentions were. I've never hidden anything from you. At that time, I'll remind you, we were both on the same page, and agreed we'd get engaged if we were still together in a year. Cut to five years later, and I shouldn't even be having this conversation with you."

"Look, I'm not getting into a negotiation with you," Jason replies, shocked at this new Kate before him and trying to turn the tables once again.

"I'm not asking you to," says Kate. "That's really your problem, Jason. To you, everything is a game. A fencing match. You're all about making this deal or that deal, angling to see how you can get control or a leg up. You know something? That is not what love is."

Kate stares Jason down.

"All this time, I thought that you truly loved me," she continues. "Otherwise I wouldn't be with you. Now I think that perhaps you're avoiding marriage as a way to keep enjoying the benefits of a committed relationship while you continue to play the field for as long as possible without any real responsibilities."

"What's that supposed to mean?"

"I don't know, why don't you ask your client . . . *Heather?*"

"What?"

"She called on FaceTime when you were looking for the manager. I thought it was your important client call, and I was going to place it on hold until you returned to the table."

"You picked up my phone?"

"Yes, innocently, out of care and concern for you and your work. Not to spy. I'm not that type."

"All woman can be that type," Jason counters.

"I beg your pardon?"

"She's just a client," says Jason firmly. "Yeah, she's trying to make it more personal, but it's not the other way around. I'm just trying to take the deal to a smooth conclusion."

"Yeah, I'll bet you are. She didn't know you have a girlfriend."

"You talked about that?"

"No. I didn't have to. I read between the lines of what she *didn't* say, and her attitude towards me."

"I can't help how she acted," Jason shrugs.

"No, but that's what I'm talking about. I need a man who isn't afraid to let the world know that he's in love, that he's off limits . . . that he's *married*!" says Kate, shocked at the words flowing from her mouth, but feeling empowered pronouncing her truth.

"I'm sorry, Kate, but like I said, I'm not going to get married right now."

Kate takes a sip of her wine for fortification.

"I hear you, loud and clear. Thank you at least for finally being honest with me."

Kate gets up and turns to leave.

"Wait," Jason says as he reaches out and grabs Kate's arm. "Don't you want to come back to my place? Maybe we can work it out . . ."

Kate's mouth drops open. "No. I'm not going back to your place. Haven't you heard anything I've said to you?"

Jason looks at her with puppy dog eyes.

"I need a man who feels the same way I do, who mutually embraces the idea of marriage as a joy, not as a burden. Who is willing to share his life with me as his wife, not just as his girlfriend."

"So, it's really all about you, then, isn't it?"

"Jason, I'm not going to let you manipulate me this time. You've led me to believe we were on the same page all this time, but in reality you were taking what you could get by saying the things I wanted to hear, or behaving in ways that kept me hoping. *So that really makes it all about you, doesn't it?* This is not a game to me, Jason, it's my life. After five precious years of giving you all my love, my time, and my devotion,

I'm not willing to continue without a genuine commitment. So, if and when you're able to make that commitment, only then will I consider moving forward—not a moment before. But I'll tell you this: I can't promise that I'll be available. For now, I have to get on with my life without you."

Kate leans over and kisses Jason on his check, fighting back the tears about to roll down her face. As she walks slowly out of the bar, she can't help but turn and look over her shoulder through the lingering crowd. She sees Jason sit deep in thought for a second, and then, without even looking in her direction, he walks up to the bar and orders another drink.

The reality that Jason has just let her walk out of his life makes her lose all sense of calm, and her tears begin to flow freely now. She gathers all the strength she can muster to make her way out of the restaurant without making a scene. When she finally steps onto the busy New York street, she feels desolate and completely alone, even though she stands among the throng of passersby.

14

"Like an idiot, I kissed him on the cheek before I left the bar," Kate tells Cindy.

Instead of going home after the fiasco with Jason, Kate ran straight over to her BFF's apartment for comfort and validation.

"You were being your genuine self. Never feel bad for that," Cindy says as she gives Kate a much-needed hug.

Kate starts to cry.

"I spoiled him," Kate chokes out. "So, it's my fault too. I believed him, but I should have been firm a long time ago."

"Don't worry, hon, if it's meant to be, he'll come around, and if he doesn't, it's his loss. Big time."

Kate sits next to Cindy on her living room sofa. Cindy, ready for bed, wears her hair pulled back into a ponytail and a large oversized nightshirt inscribed with the words, "*Voulez-vous coucher avec moi ce soir?*" She picks up the open pint of Häagen-Dazs chocolate chocolate chip ice cream that sits on the coffee table and dives in.

"Hey, why am I eating all of this by my lonesome?" asks Cindy.

Kate smiles.

"See, at least I got you to smile!" Cindy says as she takes another heaping spoonful of the chocolate delight.

"Are you sure you don't want some?"

Kate shakes her head.

"You haven't eaten since lunch. How about I heat up some leftover pasta and meatballs? Vinnie's having dinner with his brothers tonight, and won't be home till late, so . . . ?"

"Maybe in a little bit. I'm not really that hungry."

"I'm so proud of you, girlfriend," says Cindy as she shovels another large spoonful of ice cream into her mouth.

"You are?"

"Are you kidding me? Now you'll know what he's made of—and if he's your man. Just curious though, what finally made you give him an ultimatum?"

"I guess the talk we had a P. J. Clarke's a few weeks ago about my biological time clock, not to mention Jasmine's engagement, got it started. Lately I've just felt the overwhelming need to know if Jason was with me for the long haul—or not."

"Well, it's about time you stood up for yourself. Who knows, maybe he'll come to his senses . . . if he knows what's good for him."

"Deep down, I'd like to think that, but after tonight, I'm not so sure. He seemed pretty firm. *He let me walk out of that bar.* It's beginning to dawn on me that maybe he loves me, but just not enough." Kate starts to sob again.

"Oh, no, baby, don't cry," Cindy implores, starting to tear up as well. "Never mind, maybe you should cry and get it all out of your system."

"So, you think I did the right thing?" asks Kate through her tears.

"Absolutely! If he didn't think you were serious before, he knows you're dead serious now. As my mom would say, sometimes men need a little push."

"I hope so," says Kate. "But I'm not going to hold my breath. I'm just going to pray for strength, and to be guided in the right direction," continues Kate as she plucks the spoon out of Cindy's hand and dives into the rest of the ice cream.

Hours later, after Kate's passed out in Cindy's guest bedroom in a fitful, sugar-induced sleep, something jerks her awake. She breathes deeply and hard, and it takes her a few seconds to get her bearings. The room is dark, with only a sliver of moonlight peeping in through the blinds. She turns her head toward the nightstand. The digital clock reads

3:00 a.m., *again*. Kate gets a quick shiver down her spine when she realizes that the witching hour is once again upon her.

Awake but tired, Kate lays her head back down on the pillow with a loud sigh and rubs her eyes. She thinks back on the details of the dream that woke her. She's in a house that's blazing on fire, and she is climbing up a stairway that's crumbling beneath her feet. She knows she will get out alive, but she is not quite sure how, and that's when she wakes up.

Calm down, everything will be OK, Kate tells herself.

"Please help me be strong, guide me to find my way, and lead me to the life I envision . . ." prays Kate.

Soon enough, her eyelids become heavy and she drifts back to sleep.

The next morning Kate wakes up to the familiar scent of Kona coffee brewing. Unable to resist the intoxicating smell, she slips out from under the bed covers and adjusts the oversized t-shirt she wears that has managed to cinch uncomfortably around her waist. She checks her cell for any messages from Jason. *Nada. Not one.* Kate feels a pang in her heart and a wave of nausea fills her empty stomach.

"How'd ya sleep, doll face?" asks Cindy, already sitting at the kitchen table munching on a bagel and cream cheese, a cup of steaming Kona brew in her hand.

"OK, all things considered," Kate replies as she opens the stylish wood cupboard. She pulls out an oversized coffee mug with a funny looking person that reads, *"Life's a Bitch"* with the "it" in "Bitch" crossed out and replaced with "ea" to read *"Life's a Beach."* The saying on the cup makes Kate chuckle.

"What's so funny?"

"The mug," Kate holds it up for Cindy to read.

"Yeah, well, accentuate the positive I always say."

"I'm so glad I stayed over. It's so comforting here."

"Help yourself to some Kona heaven—I always say a good cup of coffee has a way of making things right," says Cindy with a big smile.

"I love you sooo much," Kate sighs, giving Cindy a big hug.

"And I you, girlfriend."

Kate pours herself a cup of coffee and adds in some almond milk.

"I'm assuming you checked your phone. Any word?" asks Cindy.

"No," Kate shakes her head. "In a strange way, it's actually a relief. Even though it hurts, this morning I'm feeling in my bones I did the right thing. I want to share my life with my true partner, no one else."

"Now you're talking!" Cindy exclaims, slapping her hand down on the table in enthusiastic agreement.

"Here," Cindy pushes a plate of bagels with cream cheese and smoked salmon towards Kate. "Vinnie bought them for us fresh this morning. Let's eat up so we can get ready for work."

"That was so sweet of him," says Kate, enjoying the warm feel of the coffee mug as the heat permeates her hands clasped tightly around it. She takes a sip.

"I had a weird dream last night."

"Oh yeah, another one of your premonition dreams?"

"No, I hope not," Kate replies. "I dreamt I was in a house that was on fire, and I was climbing up a crumbling stairway. It was freaky, but I also had a good sense that I was going to make it out. And then I woke up."

"Maybe it just means that things are heating up right now, but they'll be fine in the end," reasons Cindy.

"Maybe. I hope so."

"I know so," Cindy asserts as she reaches out and squeezes Kate's hand.

15

The initial shock of the breakup with Jason behind her, each new day Kate finds herself slipping into the same mind-numbing routine. She sets her alarm to get up earlier than necessary, knowing full well that it will take a good thirty minutes of positive affirmations in order to motivate herself to get out of bed. Then it's a quick shower, a slap of makeup on her face, and finally a quick rummage to find the most comfortable outfit to wear. Her clothes these days, which are sometimes just picked off her cluttered bedroom chair and worn for a second day in a row for convenience, rarely make a fashion statement. It literally takes all she has to make it to work. Still, she is steadfast about fulfilling her daily tasks, but she does so without much real joy.

It's a Catch-22 situation; the very things that normally bring Kate pleasure are put on hold—morning workouts, cooking and entertaining, and even going out with friends—as the idea of feigning interesting conversation is overwhelming to her. These days, about all she can muster after work is picking up takeout to eat alone in her apartment while watching mindless TV for hours on end before being lulled to sleep by its numbing chatter.

Even the weekends don't break Kate's hermit routine. Tonight is a Friday night, and Kate has already assumed the now familiar position, sitting on her bed watching TV and eating Chinese food. The glass of Chardonnay sitting on her night table is a welcome treat that takes the edge off her loneliness, along with listening to the stubborn, tenacious Nancy Grace, the famous former prosecutor turned HLN legal commentator, journalist, and television host. Nancy's program fascinates Kate, most likely because viewing others' tragedies takes her mind off her own. She can commiserate with the victims and berate the perpetrators along with Nancy. It feels good.

"That's right Nancy, you tell that bastard!" Kate yells at the TV during this evening's episode where a husband stands accused of murdering his wife, and the man's legal team is making lame excuses for his obvious guilt.

At about 8:00 p.m., the doorbell rings. Kate looks through the peephole. It's Cindy and Carla. Resigned, she lets them in.

"Well, *hellooo* stranger," says Cindy.

"Hi, Cindy. Hi, Carla," Kate responds lethargically.

"Yes, she can talk, and she does know our names," teases Cindy.

Kate cracks a meager smile, then proceeds to straighten out her disheveled clothes in an attempt to look more presentable. Her messy hair is pulled back in a ponytail, and her clothes are oversized and mismatched. Takeout containers are strewn about the apartment along with just about everything else.

"Love what you've done to the place," continues Cindy, "and that's quite a look you've got going there. I may want to feature it in the magazine."

"Sorry, I wasn't expecting guests," Kate says.

"Yes, we can see that," Cindy rolls her eyes.

"Carla, why are you in the city?" asks Kate.

"Because you've had us all worried."

"I'm OK. I'm just having dinner and watching Nancy Grace."

"Yeah, what's your new BFF got that I don't?" quips Cindy. "I'm getting a little insulted that you prefer her to me lately."

Cindy feigns a pout, then gives Kate a big hug.

"I don't prefer her over you, it's just . . ."

"It's been weeks since you broke up with Jason," Carla says. "Mom and Dad are getting worried, too. They tried calling you last night and then again this morning. They left messages, so why didn't you call them back?"

Kate picks up her cell phone sitting on the coffee table. She sees on the screen that she has six messages.

"Oh, I'm sorry, I just didn't realize they called."

"It's your nephew's birthday tomorrow," Carla adds.

Kate gasps, covering her mouth with her hands.

"Don't you remember you told Mom and Dad you'd stay over at their house tonight so you could get up bright and early tomorrow to help us cook for Lucas's party?"

"I can't believe I forgot!" Kate exclaims, and then starts to cry.

"Kate, it's OK, it's OK," Carla soothes her.

Feeling the dam now breaking loose, Kate lowers herself onto the sofa.

"Ah honey," says Cindy, rubbing Kate's back. "You've been going through a hard time, we know."

Carla joins Kate and Cindy on the sofa. She opens her purse and pulls out a pocket packet of Kleenex, and hands Kate a tissue.

"Here, Sissy."

Kate blows her nose.

"Let's just get you packed with what you need for the weekend," Carla says. "I'll drive you to Mom and Dad's place, and we can stay up late watching Lifetime movies. I'll stay over too. OK? Mom will love it."

"What about Frank and Lucas?" asks Kate through her sniffles.

"They're happily watching sports on TV tonight, and they'll do boy stuff in the morning while we cook for the party. It'll be fun. Sound like a plan?"

Kate nods her head in agreement, finally managing a smile.

And a few hours later Kate, Carla, and Catherine snuggle up on the family room sofa to watch a marathon of Lifetime Movie Network flicks—women against the world, women in distress, and "he done her wrong" movies—just what the doctor ordered.

At around 9:00 a.m. the next morning, there's a knock at Kate's bedroom door.

"Breakfast in about ten minutes, hon," Glen calls.

"OK, Dad," says Kate, awake but groggy.

Resting in bed, Kate revels in how good it feels to be at her parents' place. Even though this home isn't the house she grew up in, Kate has always had a tremendous affinity for it—from the first time she ever visited. Her parents had sold the family home in Oyster Bay after Kate's father had retired. At the time, her parents wanted to try living in a new area, and they fell in love with the North Fork, home to many beautiful vineyards, farms, and quaint, picturesque towns, just a twenty minute ride or so from the famous Hamptons.

This home's location in Cutchogue—a quieter community than the bustling Hamptons—was ideal. Situated in a development of custom homes, each of which sit on an acre or two of lush green landscaping, Kate's parents scored a prime plot with incredible unobstructed water views of the Peconic Bay. They worked with an architect to design a home that would suit their needs and tastes in this new phase of their life as empty nesters.

Kate loves the fact that she can hear the crickets and frogs singing when she goes to bed at night, and an occasional rooster crowing *cock-a-doodle-doo* in the morning. She also adores how light pours into the kitchen all the way to the center of the home from the wall of French doors that line the entire back of the house. She constantly marvels over the beautiful view of the pristine bay as well.

On mornings like this, Kate feels safe in the all-encompassing warmth and unconditional love of her parents, which makes it nearly impossible to hold on to too much unrest or inner pain. Kate thinks about her parents now so much more than she did when she was growing up. Living her own life in the city, and watching her parents grow older, she's become keenly aware of how precious life is.

Catherine is Kate's hero. Growing up, she was not only her children's caretaker, she was also their teacher, champion, and protector. They always knew she loved them fiercely and wanted the best for them. She demanded that they be kind and respectful, and to do the same unto others. She also instilled in them from the time they were little the concept that they were on Earth to be their best selves, to work to achieve their dreams, and to use their unique gifts in an honorable way. She taught them to think positively, have faith in God, and to visualize their goals and work—physically, spiritually, and emotionally—to manifest them.

To Kate, there is something also quite mystical about her mother. She seems to know things without being told, and she has a keen intuition. She also has deep insight into other people, especially her own children, without them having to say a word. In this way, Kate is very much like her mother; she taps into others' energy, has precognitive dreams, and a sixth sense about things.

Kate is painfully aware that her mother has become fragile in the past few years. She now walks with a little shuffle, and takes extra time to do a task. After a mild stroke a few years back, she's also become more and more forgetful. In Kate's mind's eye, however, her mother will always be young, vibrant, courageous, energetic, magical, and invincible.

Kate's father was a college professor—a profession that was perfect for an intellectual, sophisticated man who loves history, music, and the arts. Early in his career Glen wrote a number of textbooks and had a multitude of published articles in his chosen field of health education. One summer, as Kate waited for her father in a classroom at the college where he taught, she overhead his students talking. Unbeknownst to them, their professor's daughter was sitting right in the room.

"Dr. Grace is such a cool teacher," said one student to another. "He's so laid-back, and he's got a great sense of humor. I really like his interactive labs, too."

"It took me three semesters to get a space in his class," said a third student. "So worth the wait, though. He really makes the material fun—I'm actually thinking about switching over to pre-med thanks to him." Kate could barely hide her deep blush of pride thanks to the students' heartfelt praise of her dad.

Glen was also a terrific planner and provider. His top priority was to be sure his family was well taken care of. He was always the strong, silent type, and her mother the more emotional one. As her father ages, however, Kate notices he's become more and more expressive with his feelings. She loves this new vulnerability and softness.

Lying in bed thinking about her parents, the wonderful aromas that emanate from kitchen make their way to Kate's nose, making it impossible for her to stay in bed. So she slips out from under the sheets into her slippers and heads towards the family hub.

As Kate enters the great room, she sees her sister and mother sipping their coffees around the breakfast table as Kate's dad stands by the cooktop, stirring batter in a large wooden bowl.

"Hey, sleepyhead," says Glen.

"Dad's treating us to his homemade pancakes," says Carla.

"We also brewed some of that delicious Kona coffee you brought back," adds Catherine.

"Smells great," Kate replies as she pulls a mug from the kitchen cabinet and pours herself a cup. "Thanks for making us breakfast, Dad. I would have done that."

"You ladies have a big day ahead of you," Glen smiles. "So I wanted to make sure you have a good start."

"Thanks, Poppy," says Kate as she gives her father a hug.

In a few hours' time, the Graces' serene kitchen is turned upside down as Carla, Catherine, and Kate prepare the various dishes for Lucas's birthday party.

"So what are Dad, Frank, and Lucas up to after golf?" asks Kate as she places trays of chicken scaloppini in the fridge.

“They’re going to a movie, then they’ll be back at the house just before everyone arrives,” Carla replies as she whips up some fresh pesto in the Cuisinart.

“OK, Mom,” says Kate. “All we have to do is just pop the chicken scaloppini in the oven to warm it before we serve. Carla’s done with the pesto and the vegetables are marinating in the fridge to be grilled later. What’s next?”

“Well, let me see, Derek’s bringing some appetizers, and he’s also picking up Lucas’s cake,” Catherine notes.

“Kate, wait until you see the cake,” says Carla. “It’s just adorable. It has a baseball theme, and it’s decorated with little figures playing baseball. He’s going to love it.”

“I’ll bet,” Kate says.

“He absolutely will adore it,” agrees Catherine. “Let’s get all the salad chopped and prepared. We’ll dress it later before we serve.”

“OK, sounds like a plan,” Kate nods as she starts taking vegetables out of the fridge.

“It’s wonderful cooking with my girls in the kitchen!” smiles Catherine. “I love a good party!”

“You’re a party animal, Mom!” jokes Carla.

“We love cooking with you, too, Mommydoo,” Kate adds cheerfully, giving her mother a squeeze.

After they finish up in the kitchen, the women begin to decorate the house for the party. Kate helps her mother with a large floral arrangement for the table. She watches her mother artistically place the cut flowers into an impressive vase.

Mom is something else, she thinks. Over the years, Kate’s watched her mother transform from a dynamic mom and top-producing real estate agent into such a sweet, ever-so-cute, cuddly grandma.

At one point during the afternoon, Kate hangs decorations and happily hums as she moves about. Without Kate noticing, Catherine nudges Carla, and they share a secret smile at seeing that Kate appears to be back to her old self.

"Mom, I think I'll run home, take a shower, and get changed. I'll be back in about an hour and a half or so," announces Carla as she takes the last sip of her iced tea and kisses her mother and sister goodbye.

"OK, dear," Catherine says, "see you in a bit."

"Later, Sis," adds Kate.

"Come on hon, let's take our drinks onto the deck and just relax for a while," Catherine proposes after Carla leaves.

"OK." Kate picks up her glass and follows her mother through the glass slider. The women set their iced teas down on a table positioned between two chaise lounges and lie back to rest and enjoy the water view.

"Ah, it feels good to be off my feet," sighs Catherine happily.

"I agree. I hope we can relax a bit. When do you think we should start getting ready?"

"Oh, in about thirty to forty minutes or so," Catherine replies, looking at her watch. "I'm so glad you're here, dear," she adds as she reaches over and squeezes Kate's hand.

"Me too, Mom," smiles Kate. "I wouldn't miss Lucas's party for anything."

"Sweetie, I know things haven't been that easy for you lately. But it's important you know that you're a beautiful, smart, caring, thoughtful, loving woman. I'm not just saying this because you're my daughter. You'll make an amazing wife and mother. Promise me you'll always remember that you are the prize."

"I do know, Mom."

"Do you?"

"What do you mean?"

"I know that right now you may not feel like getting out and dating again, and when you do, it may feel really awkward at first. But I think you'll find once you start moving in that direction, it'll get easier. When you meet the right man, you'll understand why I'm telling you this."

"I always thought Jason was right, and that we wanted the same things," says Kate. "I don't know, maybe I have a problem in the judgment department."

"No, it's understandable why you felt the way you did, and I'm sure it's shaken your self-confidence and makes you question yourself. But what's happened has happened, and you have to let it go and move on. I hope I don't sound too harsh, but do you understand, honey?"

Kate nods.

"They say that when God closes one door, he opens another. It's true; you just have to have faith."

"I know."

"You're too vital to be locking yourself in your apartment night after night."

"I don't seem to have a lot of energy for going out these days."

"Put yourself on a schedule to do things, go to the movies or out to dinner with friends, visit us whenever you want, start going back to the gym or take a yoga class. Pamper yourself—get a massage, go shopping, do the things that make you feel good and alive. You'll see that by taking little steps forward each day, you'll begin to feel better, you'll meet new people, and that will help you restore your joie de vivre."

"Do you think Jason will ever come back?" asks Kate wistfully.

"That's not what you should be asking yourself, or thinking for that matter, dear," Catherine says. "For whatever reason, he is obviously not ready or willing to make a commitment. Frankly, he might never be ready."

"I know, but sometimes I can't help but hope he'll change his mind."

"Kate, honey, you dated him for five years, and at this age, believe me, a man knows what he wants. Furthermore, he's made it clear that although he's happy to casually date you, he doesn't want any part of marriage. I'm not even sure how good a husband he would make."

"What makes you say that?"

"He's handsome, well-educated, and charming—I'll give him that. But he's also selfish. He always puts himself first, and he likes to be in control. Not to offend you, but in my opinion he's a bit of a manipulator. He grew up privileged, and his parents spoiled him. And his actions make me think that he's been leading you on for his own purposes. For that I'm very, very angry at him right now."

"I think I saw the potential in him, and I felt he loved me," says Kate.

"I'm sure he loved you, dear, in his own way, but is that enough?"

"No. I've come to realize it's not, at least not now. I want more, and with someone who wants the same things I do."

"Good, that's good. I'm glad to hear it. That's precisely why it's important to get back out there and take control of your destiny."

Kate sighs deeply.

"You know, your dad and I will not always be here, dear."

"Mom, don't talk like that!"

"Honey, it's a fact. Dad and I aren't spring chickens. I love you sooo very much, Kate, and my sincere wish for you is for you to find the right partner because I know you want it, and you deserve it."

Kate looks forlorn.

"Don't worry. You'll find your true love. Trust in that. Things happen for a reason. Know in your heart that you will be led to the right man, even if it doesn't make much sense at the moment. Pray to God and your guardian angels for guidance. I'll pray for that, too."

Kate's mother's sweet smile and support warms her heart, and for the first time in a long time, she feels that everything is going to be OK.

Later that evening, at 9:00 p.m., the birthday party is in its sixth hour.

Basking in the glow of a delicious meal followed by a decadently satisfying chocolate birthday cake, the adults enjoy a round of post-dinner cordials on the outside deck while the birthday boy plays video games with his older cousins downstairs in his grandparents' basement.

"The photos from your trip are just amazing, Kate," Derek remarks.

"Aren't they?" says Catherine as she turns to the next page of photos on Kate's iPad. "I especially love this pretty street in Hanalei . . . and this house," says Catherine as she points to Kate's photo of the white cottage on Weke Road.

"Hey, it looks like the house in the watercolor Kate bought you," Derek notes.

Kate walks over and stands behind her mother. She zooms into the photo for a closer look.

"That's why I got it," says Kate. "I saw the house on Weke Road and was compelled to take a photo. Then, when I saw the print, and the fact it looked so much like the house I loved, I had to get it because I knew Mom would, too."

"I do. I treasure that picture. Thank you, dear," Catherine says as she smiles up at Kate. Kate bends down to kiss her mother's forehead.

"Kate knows your taste," grins Carla.

"I miss our little beach house on Martha's Vineyard," says Glen. "Do you think we did a wise thing selling it?"

"I know you loved that cottage, dear, but we have the townhome in Florida now. We needed someplace warm to go during the cold winters."

"You can say that again! Last year was brutal. If I could, I'd pack up Julie and the kids, and we'd be living in a warmer climate like Florida, California, or heck, even Hawaii, in a heartbeat!" exclaims Derek.

"Hawaii, that would be nice," Carla says dreamily. "Maybe someday."

"What about you Kate, if you could live in a warmer climate, where would you live?" asks Derek.

Kate smiles broadly, her face suddenly extremely animated, "Kauai, hands down!"

"Well just make sure you get a place with a lot of space . . . you know, for all your family visitors," Carla grins.

16

Sunday morning and it's just Kate and her parents. She cherishes these moments alone with her folks and relishes the attention they bestow upon her.

After Mass at Cutchogue's Sacred Heart Church, Kate, Catherine, and Glen lunch at the quaint North Fork Country Club where Kate's parents have a golf membership. Founded in 1912 and situated on a beautiful green, the Club, which provides many active social events for its members, is also where Kate's parents dine at least once or twice a week.

"I'm surprised Dad let you out of his sight, Mom," says Kate as they shop the Tanger Outlets in Riverhead after lunch.

"Well, he made a golf date with his buddies as soon as he knew we had shopping on our minds," Catherine replies. "Besides, you know how much he dislikes browsing."

Kate chuckles as she peruses the sale rack.

"That Ann Taylor white summer dress is a steal," says Catherine, admiring one of Kate's finds.

After a few hours of visiting their favorite stores, Kate notices her mother looks tired.

"Had enough, Mom? Do you want to head home?"

"Do you mind, dear?"

Kate shakes her head.

"Imagine me saying I'd like to go home," Catherine sighs. "To think, it was only just a few short years ago that I would never have said that when it came to shopping. I'd still be searching the racks."

In the car on the way back to Cutchogue, Kate notices Catherine is struggling to keep her eyes open.

"Do you mind when we get home if we have some tea, and then maybe I'll take a little nap?"

"Of course not. Why don't you get a head start and close your eyes?"

"It's such a treat to spend the afternoon with you, I don't want to be a party pooper."

"You're not, Mom, don't worry about it."

"Well, I seem not to have the stamina I used to, that's for sure. I guess I'm getting older, and it sure isn't for sissies."

"You sounded like Grammy just now," laughs Kate.

"Well, here's another 'Grammy-ism': *'I hope your Dad doesn't bust a gasket when he sees what we bought,'*" laughs Catherine.

Back at the house Kate and Catherine sip their chai tea at the kitchen table.

"Mmmm, heaven . . . just what the doctor ordered," Kate says.

"I almost forgot!"

"Forgot what, Mom?"

"You'll see, I'll be right back," Catherine replies, leaving the kitchen.

Kate breaks off a piece of the lemon scone she's sharing with her mother and pops it into her mouth as she watches the sun's rays begin to fade on the calm Peconic waters outside. Kate looks forward to a quiet evening with her parents before she has to wake up bright and early the next morning to head into Manhattan on the Long Island Rail Road.

For dinner, the plan is to eat at a charming Italian bistro not far from the house. Later that evening, they'll change into their PJs and watch a good movie on Netflix. Kate loves this type of weekend evening with her folks. It's always so comforting and good for her soul. She notices that this weekend she has been thinking about Jason a little less—a real feat considering that until now her mind has been going to thoughts of her ex almost every minute of every day. Her heart feels lighter, too, surrounded by the love of her family.

Remember this feeling, Kate, she tells herself. *If you find yourself headed into a depression about Jason, or are experiencing overwhelming feelings of sadness, don't hole up in your apartment. Come and stay with family.*

Kate decides that if she has to, she'll work for a day or two away from the office. All she needs to get her job done is a phone, a computer, and an Internet connection. And she can certainly schedule meetings and appointments in the city in a way that would allow her to avoid heading into the office for days she would prefer to work from Long Island. She smiles at this newly realized safety net from her heartache and takes another sip of her tea.

"You won't believe what Dad and I found when we were cleaning out the basement," says Catherine as she places a large cardboard box marked "Kate" on the kitchen table.

"What's this?"

"A box of your cards, letters, and school things from when you were growing up," Catherine responds. "Your dad and I put together a box for each one of you children."

Kate opens the lid and starts examining the contents of the box.

"Wow, look at this card I made you and Dad for your anniversary!" exclaims Kate.

The front of the card, made with colored notepaper, has stick figures of Catherine, Glen, Derek, Carla, and Kate, all with big grins on their faces and the words, "Happy Anniversary" in a child's handwriting. Kate opens the card. The inside reads, "I love you to the moon and beyond!" followed by lines of X's and O's, and finally, "Love, Kate."

"How old was I when I made this?"

"Oh, about four or five, I think," answers Catherine.

"Oh, look at these!" Kate exclaims as she thumbs through some old family photos. One is a shot of a very young Kate, with her older siblings Carla and Derek.

"My three angels," says Catherine, beaming at the photo.

Kate pulls out several sets of stapled notebook pages covered in her own neat handwriting.

"What are these?" marvels Kate.

"Short stories you wrote in junior high and high school," Catherine replies.

"I completely forgot about these."

Kate looks at the papers. One of the stories is science fiction, about a future war and hope for a better world. The second work she wrote for a class assignment to create a "new myth" inspired by Greek and Roman mythology. The third piece is a much more extensive work of fiction entitled "Jessica," which has an elaborate cover featuring a beautiful woman with long flowing blonde hair. The story is about a close-knit family living through the trials of the Civil War. Kate received an A+ on all three assignments, as well as glowing reviews from her teachers.

"These aren't half bad," comments Kate after perusing the stack.

"They're excellent! I reread them. Your insight is uncanny and way beyond your years."

"I completely forgot I wrote fiction like this," says Kate. "It's funny, I've written for newspapers and magazines, ad copy and columns, you name it—and though I always said I wanted to write creative fiction, I've yet to write a novel."

"Well, if you really want to write fiction, you can do it. You've always had the talent."

"Actually, lately, I've been toying with the idea of starting a novel," Kate says. "When I was in Kauai, some ideas started turning in my head, but they're not really formulated."

"Well, keep at it, honey," encourages Catherine. "Figure out a plan and a schedule to write your stories, not just the ones for the magazine. It might take setting an hour or two in the morning or evening a few times a week. Just see what works best for you. Create an environment where you can be creative and not put pressure on yourself, but encourage ideas and words to flow. Then after a time, you'll see that even an hour or so a day a few times a week can generate something of note."

"That's a good idea, Mom. I'm so busy, but if it's ever going to happen, I need to carve out the time for my own creative endeavors."

Catherine, looking a little pale, suddenly yawns widely.

"Enough chatting, Mom. Why don't you get some shut-eye? I'll keep myself busy looking through the box. OK?"

"OK, dear," says Catherine as she kisses the top of Kate's head. "I love you to the moon and beyond."

"And me you, to the moon and beyond," Kate smiles watching her mother slowly walk towards her bedroom.

Kate feels the need for another cup of tea before reviewing the other boxed items, so she gets up from the table to put the kettle on. When the pot whistles, Kate pours the hot liquid into her cup. The image on her mug is a picture of the Breaker's West Resort in Palm Beach, Florida, an oceanfront Italian Renaissance style getaway near her parents' Florida townhome, their respite from January through May. Kate loves to visit her parents during April when the temperatures in Florida are magnificent, just before the hot, sticky summers.

Suddenly noticing the pretty evening lighting on the horizon through the wall of windows and doors in the back of the house, Kate walks through the kitchen into the adjacent living space, sipping her tea while keeping a firm grip around the warm mug. The great room is decorated with comfortable oversized furniture in soothing hues of antique white and pastels of blue, green, yellow, and pink.

She peruses the various framed family photos on the mantle, hutches, and walls—photos taken with her grandparents, of her siblings and her when they were kids, family weddings, anniversaries, and holidays. There's a fantastic shot of her parents in a golf cart on the green at Breaker's West, and others showcasing their travels abroad to places like Italy, France, Ireland, Norway, Sweden, St. Croix, and other choice spots from around the globe.

As Kate walks back around to the kitchen, she spots a familiar cartoon-type drawing hanging next to the kitchen entryway. The caricature is of her mother in her job as real estate office manager. In the drawing, there are little bubble images around Catherine with the sayings she is best known for, "*You'll thank me on the way to the bank,*" "*Nose to nose, toes to toes,*" "*What comes around . . . goes around,*" "*C'mon guys, call those FSBOS and EXPIREDS!*" A white bubble extends from Catherine's mouth as she sits at her desk surrounded by family photos and memorabilia, which reads, "*Glen, I'll be home in five minutes!*"

Kate smiles as she remembers those days. Catherine had to almost twist her husband's arm to go to work when Kate started elementary school. Being rather traditional, he didn't understand why Catherine wanted a career. However, once they finally reached an agreement, he would often find himself working as if he were part of her team of agents, assisting with open houses and helping her distribute and post residential listings.

The next image catches Kate off guard, even though she's probably seen it hundreds of times before. Taken some twenty or so years earlier of her parents on vacation, they sit in a restaurant and wear huge smiles on their faces and beautiful Hawaiian leis around their necks. They look so young, relaxed, and happy. Kate remembers how excited her mother was when she was awarded a trip for two to Oahu, Hawaii, having been named by her firm as one of the top producers.

I'll have to make a print of that photo, thinks Kate. *I'll put a copy of it next to my photos from Kauai.*

To Catherine, though, when push came to shove, her family was her life. As a wife, she loved her husband and supported him in all things. That's why when he retired, and he asked her to do the same, she did so without hesitation. Her parents cherish each other.

Kate's thoughts are drawn back to a winter a few years ago. It was a cold day, and she was visiting her parents. They went shopping, and it started to snow. When her father pulled the car into their driveway, the remote control to open the garage door wouldn't work.

"I'll let myself in the garage door and activate the wall remote," said Catherine before exiting the car. Glen watched his wife walk towards the house and then turned to Kate.

"Want to know something?" Glen had asked.

"What Dad?"

"I love your mother more deeply now than the day we got married."

It was comments like this that touched Kate's heart—it's why she believes in marriage. At the time her father made that offhand remark, her parents had been married forty-seven years.

Kate believes, as her parents do, that there is something beautiful about sticking together through thick and thin, and working out problems rather than trading in a partner for a newer model or for a "grass is greener" scenario. There is such tremendous joy to be had in sharing a life with one loving partner—the ups and downs, triumphs and aches, and the memories.

Her parents have stuck together like glue, and the constant that makes it so is unconditional love and respect for one another. Kate hopes and prays she will be blessed to have even a little of that someday.

"ALLA FAMIGLIA," TOAST GLEN, Catherine, and Kate just before dinner at the rustic Italian restaurant, Touch of Venice, situated on Cutchogue's Main Street. Once a fisherman's rest stop, the eatery has been transformed into a cozy, stylish room with wood and tile floors, tin ceilings, eclectic furnishings, and captivating art.

"So honey, when are we going to get a peek at the cover story you wrote on Olivia Larkin?" asks Glen.

"It'll be out in a few months. I can print you out a copy off my computer when we get home if you want," says Kate. "Edward's really pleased."

"I'll bet."

"I can't wait to read it!" enthuses Catherine.

"So what's on your agenda this week?" inquires Kate.

"The usual. A little golf, routine doctor's visits, card games at the Club," Glen responds.

"Your sister's having us for dinner on Wednesday, and then Derek and his wife are going to dine with us at the Club this coming Friday," chimes in Catherine.

"Sounds like you've got a full week then," says Kate.

"How about you dear?" Catherine asks.

"I've got a lot of meetings. I'm checking into some leads for new stories and meeting with freelancers. The usual."

"Got plans for next weekend?" asks Glen.

Kate ponders this.

"Well . . ."

"We don't want to keep you from your friends, but I hope you know you can come visit us anytime. We love having you," Catherine interjects.

"Here, here. I second that," says Glen, lifting his wine glass again. "Buon appetito!"

17

Early Monday morning Kate's father drops her off at the Long Island Rail Road station in nearby Mattituck to catch the 5:52 a.m. train into Jamaica, where Kate will change trains to head into New York's Penn Station. The trip is just two and a half hours, which leaves her plenty of time to take a leisurely walk to the office before her first appointment.

Kate sips her Starbucks grande latte and munches on a hard-boiled egg and some carrot sticks as she watches the foliage and buildings rush by outside her window on the comfortable commuter train.

As usual, it was a fab weekend, thinks Kate. *What would I have gone through had it not been Lucas's birthday?* she ponders. *Nope, too grim . . . I'm not going there.*

Without the distraction of her family, her thoughts now drift to Jason and what he's been up to.

Is he traveling? Home? No matter, his actions are speaking louder than words.

No phone calls, no texts, she confirms as she checks her phone again. Oddly enough, when she really thinks about it—heartache aside—she has no true desire to contact him. Coming off the buzz of being home, she wonders if later as she goes about her usual routines that feeling of wanting to crawl under the covers will suddenly hit.

One day at a time, she tells herself. *I feel good; let's work to keep that feeling.*

Kate texts Cindy, "Hey girlfriend, taking the train in this a.m. from Mattituck. What are you doing tonight? Want to do a potluck at my place or yours?"

Many times Kate and Cindy, with or without their significant others, would get together for an informal or impromptu dinner at each other's apartments. After feeling so bolstered by being around her family, Kate decides it's probably best to keep it up and make plans with good friends as much as possible.

Keep busy and do things that give me pleasure, thinks Kate. *Yup, just what the doctor ordered.*

Once Kate gets in to work, she goes to visit Cindy in her office.

"Thanks for rescuing me Friday night," she says, sitting on Cindy's office sofa.

"What are friends for? You'd do the same for me." Cindy gives Kate a big hug. "From the looks of the pics you texted me of Lucas's party, it looks like everyone had a great time. How are you doing, by the way? Are you really OK?"

"Yeah," nods Kate. "I finally think I'm through the worst of it. I'm not ready to get out there yet and start dating, but I do want to do the things that bring me joy."

"What have I been tellin' you?" claps Cindy.

"I know . . . I should have taken your advice sooner, but I was just in a dark place and had to process for a while."

"Well I'm glad you're back," says Cindy. "And yes, per your text, let's do dinner tonight at my place."

"Sure. What can I bring?"

"We'll grill some salmon, so how about a green salad?"

"OK, and maybe something delicious, decadent, and—*chocolate?*"

"Oh, you naughty little girl," Cindy admonishes with a devilish smile. "You know that totally works for me!"

Kate begins to revisit her morning workouts. She makes a commitment to herself to get back on track with eating healthy, getting proper sleep, keeping busy with activities she enjoys, and staying away from people, places, and things that are "downners." Slowly but surely she feels more and more of her old spirit coming back to life.

Seeing how good she looks and feels when she takes care of herself, she realizes without a doubt that her MO following the breakup with Jason—the bad habits of not eating well, drinking a little more than usual, and exercising with the remote instead of at the gym—was her way of medicating the pain away, and an unhealthy one at that.

"So, I can cut off about an inch or two and do highlights around your face?" asks the salon stylist during Kate's routine monthly appointment.

"Go for it!" exclaims Kate.

Kate finds her hair makeover so invigorating that she decides to review her makeup choices and wardrobe for even more of a pick-me-up. Combing over her closets and dresser drawers one Saturday, Kate pulls out and packs up anything that's been hanging in her closet for more than a year without being worn, and everything that doesn't look just absolutely fabulous on her. Five grocery bags of unwanted items that she plans to donate to Goodwill proves this is a long overdue exercise.

Next on her agenda, and perhaps inspired by all the HGTV DIY programming she's watched over the last several months, Kate decides to streamline and renovate her apartment.

Out with the old, in with the new, thinks Kate as she replaces several pieces of well-worn furniture with new finds, paints her apartment, and replaces dated accent items and artwork with new pieces. When she is finished, Kate feels unequivocally that the décor in her newly transformed home—which is bright, happy, calming, and comforting—fits her new energy and spirit perfectly.

"Wow, wow, and more wow!" is all Cindy can say as she tours Kate's renovated digs. "I liked your place before, but this is really extraordinary."

"I had a great time sprucing up the place. Most of the new accessories are bargain finds from garage sales and thrift stores, so the renovation didn't even cost me that much," gushes Kate.

"Move over Martha Stewart!" yells Cindy dramatically, which prompts Kate to laugh. "The colors, artwork, and accents . . . they're all so peaceful and relaxing. You know where this place makes me feel like I am?"

"Where?"

"In a tropical resort."

"Ah, yeah . . . I see what you mean."

"Hey, I like those prints on the wall," Cindy says, pointing at some beautifully framed prints of Hanalei's pier, the shoreline at Anini Beach, and other memories from Kate's recent trip.

"I took those photos in Kauai."

"OK, well, it all makes sense then. Kauai must have been your inspiration," smiles Cindy. "Now I know I'm really going to have to get Vinnie to get his butt in gear and take me there."

"Trust me," says Kate. "You'll have the time of your life."

THAT NIGHT AS KATE LIES IN BED in her comfortable, newly decorated surroundings, she listens on her iPod to a recording of the melodic sounds of waves as they crash upon the shore and drifts into a peaceful slumber that brings her to a familiar dream.

Kate and her mother walk down Hanalei's Weke Road without a care in the world. Catherine takes Kate's hand, and the women start to swing their arms just as they did when Kate was a child. Without the need for words, both Kate and Catherine feel their love for each other. It is as if their thoughts and feelings are the words themselves.

"I love you so much, to the moon and beyond, and I will always be with you."

The women stop in front of the familiar charming white cottage on Weke Road. The door opens, and as in previous dreams, they are greeted by the same pretty woman, who waves and bids them, *"Aloha!"*

Kate bolts awake from her dream. It's the middle of the night and darkness surrounds her. She turns her head to view the digital clock at her bedside and as usual, it reads 3:00 a.m.

Again? she thinks. *What is it about this dream, that house?*

Eventually her eyes close and she returns to a deep sleep.

18

"The layout and photos look spectacular!" says Kate as she stands in Edward's office and flips through the digital draft of her article on Olivia Larkin.

"The cover is really killer, too," beams Edward. "We'll get some advance copies over to Olivia's publicist with a note before it hits the stands."

"Good idea. I'd also like to send a few copies to Olivia with a personal thank-you."

"I'll make sure you get some. By the way, I like your idea about doing a food and wine pairing story with some of the top chefs and sommeliers from the North Fork. Let's feature an appetizer, main course, a side or two, and a dessert recipe—maybe a different local vineyard for each course. Work with our photographer and stylist on the staging once everything is booked. Just keep me posted."

"Will do. I've already got a list of my top choices prepared and ready to roll," says Kate.

"Then go get 'em tiger."

BY THE END OF THE WORKDAY, after placing numerous emails and phone calls out to perspective interviewees, Kate's locked in two chefs and three sommeliers. Just as Kate powers down her computer to leave for the evening, her cell rings.

"Hello, this is Kate."

"Kate, it's Carla."

"Hey, Carla, I was just about to—"

"Kate, I don't want to frighten you, but do you think you might be able to catch the next train to Mattituck?"

"What? Is everything OK?"

"Mom's in the hospital."

"What happened?" asks Kate, her voice a few octaves higher than normal.

"The doctors aren't sure. Something's not quite right. You know Mom's been tired more than usual lately, and that her vision's been giving her some problems. Well, her blood pressure was sky high this afternoon, so Dad brought her to the ER. They're doing a bunch of tests to figure out what's what. Remember Dr. Picard, that surgeon who put the shunt in her head a few years back?"

"Yeah, to drain the fluid off her brain after she had that stroke."

"Well, they called him in to give her an MRI."

"It's just after seven," says Kate, looking at the clock. "I'll grab a cab and pick up a few things at my apartment, then head out to Penn Station. I'll keep you posted about when I'll be arriving, so keep your phone close by."

"Will do. Sissy, I love you."

"Love you, too."

Kate, nervous and a little bit in shock, takes a second to regroup before she quickly gathers a few items from her desk, including the zip drive she just backed up.

Who knows how long I might be home? Might as well take whatever I'll be needing for a while, she thinks.

With only ten minutes to spare, Kate makes the 9:42 p.m. train leaving the city for Long Island. She calls her sister as soon as they pull out of the station.

"I get into Mattituck at 11:04 p.m.," says Kate.

"Lucas will be sound asleep by then, so Frank will pick you up. We'll be able to go over and see Mom first thing in the morning."

"Good," Kate says. "How's she doing?"

"Fine right now. She ate a good dinner, so that's a good sign. Dad's sleeping in the room with her. Hopefully we'll know something more tomorrow."

"I hope so. OK, Sis, see you soon. Love you," says Kate as she ends the call.

What is wrong with Mom? wonders Kate. *What will the tests show?*

Kate lays her head back on the cushioned train seat and stares out into the dark, black night. The shunt that was placed at the base of Catherine's brain a few years back after the stroke to treat her hydrocephalus was working well. Both her mom and dad were sticklers for keeping all their routine doctor appointments so there had been nothing out of the ordinary to report.

So what could it be?

Kate has a sick feeling in the pit of her stomach. She tries to shake it off. Normally, after some deep breathing and a few minutes thinking positive thoughts, she's able to turn her head around. However, this is different. The feeling sticks to her insides like a bad meal.

The next morning at the hospital, Kate holds her mother's hand and watches her sleep. Catherine looks so tiny and sweet lying in her bed, and all Kate wants to do is kiss and hold her and attend to her every need.

A clear breathing tube protrudes from Catherine's nostrils, wraps around both sides of her face, and leads to an oxygen tank nearby.

"Mommydoo," says Kate childishly when her mother starts to stir. She kisses Catherine several times on the cheek, "I love you. How are you feeling?"

"I'm in Happyville now that you're here," smiles Catherine.

"Are you comfortable?"

"Yes, dear. A little tired, but that could be the drugs they gave me. Where's Daddy?"

"Carla took him to breakfast down in the hospital cafeteria. They'll be back soon. Can I get you anything Mom? Water?"

"No dear, I'm OK. Don't you have to be at work?"

"I told them I'm here with you today. Besides, have computer, will travel, so I'll be able to take care of business from here, don't you worry."

Catherine smiles weakly.

"Would you mind very much dear if I went back to sleep? I'm a little tired."

"Of course, Mom, I'll be right here. I'm not going anywhere." Kate gently takes hold of her mother's hand again and watches her drift off.

Dr. Picard comes by Catherine's room once all the tests results are in, and when he does, he finds her asleep with Derek, Carla, Glen, and Kate, by her side. Dr. Picard motions for the family to join him in a private room down the hall. Once everyone finds a seat, he addresses the family.

"I want to be upfront with you. So please let me give you the full picture, and once I've finished, feel free to ask me any questions you may have."

The room is eerily silent, and Kate feels the acid turning in her stomach.

"I'm very sorry to tell you this, but Catherine has a large tumor at the base of her brain."

Kate and Carla gasp.

"Oh, no," chokes Glen, clenching his fist and bringing it to his lips as if to keep any further anguished sounds from escaping. Derek puts an arm around his father, his face distraught. The moment is so surreal that Kate feels as if she is having an out-of-body experience. Dr. Picard points to an x-ray of Catherine's skull on a large computer screen.

"Oh my God, I see it! That's the tumor, right there, isn't it?" interjects Kate, pointing to a huge mass visible even to the untrained eye.

"That's right," says Dr. Picard.

For the next minute or so, the family listens somberly, without questions, to Dr. Picard's every word.

"We're not sure if the tumor is cancerous or benign," begins Dr. Picard. "So, the first thing we'll do is an exploratory surgery and then a biopsy to see if it's cancerous or not. Once we know what the diagnosis is, we can figure out treatment, which would include another operation to remove as much of the tumor as we can, and then radiation, chemo, or a combination thereof. However, because of the tumor's size and position, even if we go in, we won't be able to remove it all, and there are risks involved which could include more limitations to her speech, walking, and other bodily functions. We just won't know more until we have more information. And unfortunately, regardless of what we do, and whether the tumor is cancerous or not, I still believe that Catherine has only six to nine months left. I'm very sorry."

"With all due respect, what's the point of putting her through two high-risk operations then?" asks Glen, wringing his hands.

The doctor looks at the grief-stricken family and swallows hard.

"It's my duty to let you know that surgery and treatments may help maximize the time she has left, but there are no guarantees. And it is possible that they could make things worse, and in her condition, could possibly even be fatal," says Dr. Picard.

Kate and Carla start to weep, and Derek, who has been trying hard not to cry, finally lets his tears flow freely.

"Oh, God," Glen groans as he buries his hands in his face.

"I understand how difficult this is for you," says Doctor Picard. "I will do all I can with whatever you decide."

"We appreciate that, Doctor," Glen replies. "We need to talk this over as a family, but I can tell you this right now, my wife is frail as it is. As you know, she had a really tough recovery when the shunt was put in. After the last surgery, she told me that she would never again let anyone drill into her skull."

"I'll leave you all to discuss this," says Dr. Picard as he hands Derek his business card. "You can stay here. I'll be on my cell and around all day today, so just call me if you have any questions."

"When your mother wakes up, I'm thinking we should tell her. What do you think?" asks Glen after the doctor leaves, looking around the room at his distraught children.

"I think we should," Derek says.

"Me too," adds Carla.

"So do I," says Kate, "but I know what Mom's going to want to do."

"She won't want the exploratory surgery," nods Glen. "It doesn't guarantee anything, and even if it did, they'd have to do another operation to remove what they could of the tumor, and there could be complications with that, too. And as the doctor said, it won't solve the situation. Either way, it's a six to nine month death sentence; she should have the best quality of life she can for as long as she has left. Don't you guys agree?"

"I agree that there's no way she'll go for surgery," Derek says.

"Especially since there would also be a long recovery period in the hospital, and for what? Iffy results at best are a pretty grim prognosis," reasons Kate. "In fact, she's known a few people that are younger than her and in better health with brain tumors who became vegetables after being operated on. I think she'll opt to celebrate life while she can."

Carla, too upset to speak, nods silently in agreement. Then Glen starts to sob, which causes everyone to break down. They hold one another and let their tears flow. Catherine has awakened and Glen tells her the truth.

"No operations, no hospitals," says Catherine bravely and with conviction as she holds Glen's hand. Her children surround her on both sides of her hospital bed. Everyone's eyes are red from crying, but Catherine hasn't even shed one tear. "I hope you understand and can respect that?"

"We do, Mom," Derek replies.

"Yes, dear," adds Glen as he squeezes his wife's hand. "After we talked to Dr. Picard, we discussed the prognosis, and we all knew you would feel this way."

"Good, then that's settled," smiles Catherine, breathing freely. "So, when can I get out of here?"

Catherine acting like being released from the hospital is akin to being let out of a lengthy prison term, causes the tension in the room to dissipate and makes everyone smile. Kate and Carla cover their mother's forehead, face, and the top of her head with kisses. Father and son follow suit. It is a heartbreaking show of love.

19

"Here's a folder of information on what to expect that you can go over with your father and siblings," says the head hospice nurse as she hands it to Kate.

"It has some phone numbers and services," continues a second hospice nurse. "We've also set up a schedule for our visiting nurse to come by your home regularly to check in on your mother."

"Thank you," Kate replies, with a pained smile.

Before going back to her mother's hospital room where her family is, she pauses for a moment just outside the nurses' office to gather her thoughts. She opens the folder and begins to peruse the materials in case she has any questions before she leaves for her parents' home.

"That sweet little woman in Room 444—how long do you think she has?" Kate overhears the hospice nurse ask her supervisor.

"With or without surgery, the prognosis is grim," says the head hospice nurse. "However, in my experience, I'd say it'll be much sooner. Two or three months at best."

Kate can't cry; this scene and the events of today are much too surreal for tears. Instead, she anxiously wrings her hands as she walks towards her mother's room with just one thought—to clear her schedule so she can spend as much time as possible with her family, and especially her mother.

WITH CATHERINE COMFORTABLY at home, the Grace children descend on their parents' house, leaving only when absolutely necessary. Kate makes arrangements with Edward to do as much of her job as possible via her computer and cell phone. She starts her days early, and she finishes them late, often working weekends to get the job done. Any "in person" meetings are organized back-to-back for quick trips into the city. The schedule that Kate had envisioned just weeks earlier suddenly is a reality, but not as a respite from her grief over Jason as she originally intended. She is painfully aware that every minute is precious.

Then again, in a strange, almost mystical way, this difficult time is also touchingly poignant. The family shares many meals together, just as they did before Kate and her siblings left the nest to build their own lives and families. Streams of aunts, uncles, cousins, and close friends also visit. Neighbors, when they learn of Catherine's illness, bring over trays of food, pastries, flowers, and other lovely gifts. During this time, while there is some talk of death, there is more discussion about life. It's become a long celebration and appreciation of what each person means to the other.

During Catherine's first five weeks after her release from the hospital, she appears to be her usual self. Perhaps she's a tad slower, but she truly loves every moment she spends with family and friends and has no desire to lay around in bed. As the weeks progress, it's an endless party, one dinner after another, where lots of happy memories are shared, laughter is abundant, and entertainment reigns supreme.

One morning Kate notices her mother is having a very hard time getting up from the kitchen chair after breakfast. The recently purchased walker doesn't do much to help steady Catherine on her feet. Dorothy, the pretty, perky, comforting fortysomething hospice nurse, checks Catherine's medications at around noon and then proceeds to do some physical therapy with her. After this Catherine is so tired that she asks to sit down to catch her breath. Moments later, she is sound asleep in the recliner.

"I think it's time for the hospital bed," Dorothy remarks to Glen, Carla, and Kate. "It will be covered by Medicare, and I can help arrange to get it here as soon as possible."

"My wife and I have already talked about the possibility of getting a hospital bed," says Glen. "She doesn't want to be in the bedroom cut off from everyone. Can we put it right here in the living room? That way she can continue to be a part of things."

"Not a problem. It's important to make her as comfortable and as happy as possible," answers Dorothy.

"I also think it will be a lot for your daughters and you to have to pick her up when she needs to go to the bathroom or to take a shower. Since your wife will be remaining at home, we recommend at this juncture that you get a 24-hour nurse to help. You're already going through quite a lot, and I'm sure you'll find the assistance invaluable."

When the new hospital bed arrives, it is strategically placed next to the living room sofa where Catherine can view all the family action in the kitchen and great room.

One afternoon, with Carla and Glen out grocery shopping, Catherine rests comfortably as Kate, sprawled out on the sofa next to her, navigates the movie selections on Netflix.

"Sweetheart, could we just talk for a bit?" Catherine asks.

"Sure, Mom, do you need anything?" Kate flips off the television and sits upright.

"No dear, just come closer."

Kate scoots over and takes Catherine's outstretched hand.

"I love you sooooo much, dear," begins Catherine, her radiant love shining through her eyes.

"I love you, too, Mom," Kate kisses her mother's hand several times.

"Your father and I have been so very blessed, finding each other, having you children, and all the many wonderful things we've experienced in between."

"And we've been blessed with you and Poppy."

"A mother always wants to see her children happy, to find their way in the world, use their talents, to find love, and get married and have their own families. I know how important that is for you dear, and I want you to know . . ."

Catherine struggles a bit through her emotion, then looks strongly and directly into her daughter's eyes. "Hear me and believe what I tell you. I know how important it is to you to find your soul mate and start your own family. After I'm gone—"

"Mom!" interrupts Kate.

"Wait, dear. I want you to know that I'll be with you always, to help guide you. If I can, I'll try to give you signs. I'm not sure how this will work yet, but look for me. I'm going to be with you, your dad, and your brother and sister always, even if I can't be here physically."

Kate starts to cry, but Catherine remains strong.

"Come here," Catherine holds her arms to Kate. As the women embrace, Kate's tears flow.

"I know, dear, I know," says Catherine rubbing Kate's back. "I don't want to leave, I wish I could get out of this mess, but here's the thing . . ."

Kate wipes some tears from her eyes.

"For me, being in heaven means not only being with God, but also being with my family."

Kate nods in agreement.

"So I asked God how there could be a heaven or how I could be happy there if my family is somewhere else. Do you know what the answer was?"

"What?"

"That I will *never* be far away from those I love. The answer was followed by a feeling of such joy and peace that I know that's how it will be. So remember, my love will surround you, and I will be by your side helping to guide you, *always.*"

One night, shortly after her conversation with Kate, Catherine sits at the family table and eats dinner with gusto. She even asks for a second helping of her favorite chocolate mousse cake. While the family is thrilled to see a glimpse of the "old" Catherine, the happy moment is short-lived. The next day, Catherine finds she no longer has the strength to get out of bed. While there is some discomfort in lying flat all the time, it's truly a blessing that the tumor is not painful or bothering her in any way.

The next afternoon, however, Dorothy sees that Catherine is having extreme difficulty swallowing properly. With sadness, Dorothy explains to the family what this means: Catherine's body is now shutting down. The end, in fact, is quite near, and the only solution is to give her small doses of morphine to keep her comfortable because she can no longer eat solid foods or swallow liquids because of the risk of choking.

The heavy reality takes its toll on the family. Well aware that they are all on borrowed time with their beloved mother and grandmother, they all make sure to hold her hand, kiss her face, and whisper into her ear what they need to say and tell her how much they love her.

Finally, one Saturday afternoon when there's a peaceful hum about the house, the inevitable happens. Kate is in the kitchen, placing an order to have the evening's dinner delivered while Carla sits holding her mother's hand in the living room. Derek, Glen, Frank, and the grandchildren are scattered around the kitchen and living room, playing board games while soft music emanates from the stereo. Derek's wife Julie makes tea.

"Something's happening!" announces Carla loudly with trepidation. Everyone drops what they're doing and bolts into the living room.

Suddenly Catherine's eyes spring wide open. Then a second or two later, she takes a large breath in before closing her eyes as she releases a deep exhale. The family watches, transfixed, as little swirls of light seem to dance around Catherine until they finally work their way up to the ceiling and eventually dissipate.

Carla and Kate wring their hands as they watch Dorothy check Catherine's vital signs. The silence is deafening as everyone tries to comprehend what is happening.

"I'm so sorry . . . she's gone," says Dorothy sadly.

Kate and Carla reach for each other, simultaneously bursting into tears. Glen puts his head in his hands and starts to quietly sob. Derek, also crying softly, goes to his father's side and the men embrace while Frank and Julie comfort the grandchildren. Kate watches as Dorothy puts a towel around her mother's head and jaw.

"We must do this," Dorothy explains, "otherwise her jaw will set in an open position."

The color is now draining from Catherine's face, and when Kate kisses her mother's cheek and forehead, she feels the coolness that is setting in.

Where is she? she thinks as she stares at her mother with a sense of awe. She knows her mother is no longer in her body. In an instant, Kate feels a warm energy around her, and a sudden feeling of peace enters her soul. She's knows that she's witnessed something divine.

From the moment of her mother's passing, Kate knows that the world will never again be the same. It takes on a new meaning; a new shape. From now on, Kate will forever look at life through new eyes and with a new understanding. Something has happened today, something beyond her dear mother's passing, but yet having everything to do with it . . .

For in Kate's heart and soul, she instinctively knows with every fiber of her being that although her mother is no longer in her earthly body, she is still here, and will live in and around her, as promised, *always.*

20

A month after Catherine's funeral, Kate walks down Fifth Avenue toward her office. Since her mother's passing, she feels strangely separate from the world. It feels so odd to her that life should go on as it has in the past, that the sun should come up in the morning and set in the evening, that every morning people hurry to catch trains and buses to get to their jobs on time, that things keep chugging along in so many mundane yet profound ways. Even the fact that hunger pains remind her of the need for food doesn't seem right.

Since her mother's death, Kate, who had always found her work to be engaging and rewarding, now finds it something she has to endure. Each day she finds herself living for 6:00 p.m. when she is free to be with her thoughts and allowed to continue to process her life without the pretense of conveying interest or engaging in idle conversation.

Kate plods through her day-to-day tasks, but she's not truly engaged with any of her usual pursuits. Everything is suddenly open for reevaluation—from her routines, to where she lives, to her work and her habits, even to her place in the world. Somehow, she feels the life she is leading is only part of what she is meant to experience, and now she needs to find a way to live authentically. However, right now, what she wants to do most is to just sit quietly and think, read, and tap into her spirituality. She craves to connect to the things she knows but cannot see with her physical eyes, to feel her mother around her in a new way.

Her father, on the other hand, is completely distraught. While he prays and goes to church, losing his wife of fifty years has created such an endless void inside him. He clearly doesn't know which way to turn. Glen keeps as busy as possible, and Kate realizes that he's willing to do almost anything to avoid sitting at home alone with his thoughts.

One day Glen announces that he intends to fly to Florida earlier than usual to stay at the winter home in West Palm Beach, returning to New York briefly for the Christmas holidays, then back to Florida with a possible return to New York in late April.

While Kate knows that it was always typical of her parents to spend the winters in Florida in order to avoid the frigid East Coast weather, and also because they have always had loads of friends in Florida, not to mention a network of trusted doctors, she can't help but wonder now . . . *How is he able to chart his life so quickly? Perhaps he is frightened of his own mortality, of realizing what he has lost? But she isn't truly gone, at least not spiritually speaking,* thinks Kate. *She is all around us.*

"I just hate roaming around in that big house all by myself," Kate has heard her father declare numerous times since Catherine's death. She knows it is just a matter of time before Glen puts the Cutchogue home on the market. She loves that house, and it makes Kate sad to think of it, but she understands why it must be difficult for her father to continue living there.

Kate appreciates the support she gets from her brother and sister and has always talked to them on a regular basis. They now connect daily, each of them providing support and love to one another in a way that only siblings can do when they have lost a beloved parent.

However, while her sister and brother have full lives with work and their spouses and children, Kate, now back at her apartment in Manhattan full-time, is the one who is left alone. And with her father going off to Florida, she's already missing him. Still, she is pleased that he is working to find his new path, and realizes so clearly now that each person really does have to find their way in their journey of life. Family and friends can certainly offer support and guidance, but it is up to the individual to listen to their souls and be guided by their own North Star.

Kate's friends provide her with tremendous comfort and support. But like her siblings, her friends Cindy, Jasmine, and her other friends also have busy lives, close partners, and family responsibilities. This huge emptiness Kate feels in her own personal life has actually been there for a long time. But now, with nothing else to focus on but her thoughts and her feelings, Kate's eyes are wide open to it.

What am I going to do about it? How am I going to find my peace and make my way? thinks Kate.

Kate rarely thinks of Jason now. With what she's been through, he seems like a distant memory. Now she has other things on her mind, and truth be told, she's only interested in surrounding herself with those who show their love and dedication to her. Now that she has her blinders off, she sees the selfishness behind Jason's indecision so clearly, and with each passing day, realizes more and more that she's happier without him.

ONE DAY, KATE COMES INTO WORK to find a beautiful spray of incredibly gorgeous tropical flowers on her desk. She sets down her purse and briefcase by her desk in order to open the little envelope held in the plastic cardholder protruding from the arrangement.

"Dearest Kate, We are so very sorry to learn of your mother's passing. We send you our prayers and sincerest sympathies. Much Love, Olivia & Grant XO"

Kate's heart is immediately warmed by Olivia's thoughtfulness. She rummages through her purse and retrieves her cell, immediately dialing up Olivia's mobile.

"Hello," a pleasant voice greets her. "This is Olivia."

"Olivia, it's Kate Grace."

"*Kaaaaate!*" cries Olivia as if she were greeting a long lost friend.

"The flower arrangement, it's just stunning!"

"I'm so sorry about your mother. I would've been in touch sooner, but Connie just heard from Edward, and of course she told me."

"Thank you," says Kate. "I know you get it, especially after our conversation at your home in Kauai. What you told me about spirit has really helped me through this rough time."

"Oh, Kate, I'm glad I could be of help, and I'm sending you big hugs right now."

"Thanks."

There's a slight pause before Olivia adds, "By the way, the cover story is just wonderful, Kate. I love it. Mahalo."

"You got the magazines?"

"Just yesterday, when we got back to Manhattan."

"I'm so glad you liked the story."

"Say, there's no pressure, and I'll understand if you may not be able to do so on such last minute notice, but if you're not doing anything for lunch today . . ."

"Yes, I'd love too! Just tell me when and where," Kate replies without hesitation.

"Fantastic! Let's meet a Smith & Wollensky for some good ol' comfort food. In addition to all sorts of grilled goodies, they also have a great mac and cheese dish that does a soul good. How does that sound?"

"Like heaven."

"12:30 p.m.?"

"You're on."

At Smith & Wollensky later that day, the hostess walks Kate to the back of the elegant steakhouse to where Olivia sits.

"Aloha," they greet and embrace one another.

"Can I have your waiter get you anything?" asks the hostess.

"An iced tea, please," replies Kate as she sits across from Olivia.

"I can't believe it's already been almost five months!" Kate exclaims.

"Let's not let it go on that long again," says Olivia.

"Promise?"

"Promise."

"How have you been?"

"Same old, same old," answers Olivia. "I had to do a lot of traveling the last month and a half, but all is good, I can't complain. And you? I was so sorry to hear about your mom."

"Thank you," replies Kate. "I think of her so much now. I always did, but I do even more now."

"I know how that is."

"I know you do," replies Kate. "Sometimes I'll go to call her and then realize I can't. So I talk to her. Is that crazy?"

"Of course not! You know I talk to my mom and Nana and Pops all the time."

"That's right, you told me that in Kauai," says Kate. "You know something else?"

Olivia raises her eyebrows in interest.

"Before my mom passed, she told me that she would always be around us. Sometimes I can actually feel her. I get a warm feeling, a happiness in my heart . . ." Kate struggles to find the right words.

"I know," Olivia smiles.

"It's a feeling of such peace and contentment," continues Kate. "Strange things seem to be happening, too."

"Like what?"

"I know this sounds a little out there, but the other night the television went on without me turning it on, then last night, the light . . . and other little things. For example, last week I was sitting having tea in my living room, and I just kept seeing some dark shadowy movement out of the corner of my eye. It didn't frighten me, but I noticed."

"So what did you do?"

"I said, 'Hi Mom,'" chuckles Kate.

"I would have done exactly the same thing."

"Really, you think it could be my mother?"

"Look, you're very intuitive and aware of your surroundings. You're connected on a spiritual level to your family and loved ones. Why not? There are so many mysteries to the universe, and I believe that loved ones are with us and around us. So, if it's not frightening to you or disrupting your life, it's actually quite a beautiful affirmation to experience evidence of the afterlife. There are many scientists, experts in quantum physics, who believe that consciousness exists after the body dies, and that it exists outside of the constraints of time and space. I believe that. I also think if you speak to others about your experiences, you'll find they have similar stories."

"You know, after my mother's funeral, on my first train trip back to the city, I had a little time to kill before boarding, so I perused the newsstand. I wasn't planning on buying any books because I have several waiting to be read, but I found myself drawn to the book *Proof of Heaven*, written by a surgeon who had a near-death experience."

"Eben Alexander. Of course I know the book," says Olivia.

"It's quite a read, and I've been seeking out other books with similar subjects—John Edward's *Crossing Over*, James Van Praagh's *Talking to Heaven*, and more recently, *There's More to Life Than This* by Theresa Caputo, the Long Island Medium."

"Oh, she's fantastic. I've actually been meaning to get her on the show," comments Olivia.

"These books have given me such tremendous peace. I find that sometimes at night, I just want to be quiet, to hear myself think, and to read these books. I think I've always been aware of spirit, but my Mom's passing is making me look at life so differently now . . . I feel so much more. I pay attention to my dreams, I listen to my intuition, I'm more conscious of synchronicities . . . I try to process information with all my senses. Her passing has also given me an urgency to do more of what I believe I was put on Earth to do."

"More?"

"More than I'm doing now. More with my creativity, more with my personal life—like actually having one."

"Hmm, that doesn't sound good. What's up with Jason?"

"We broke up right after I got back from Kauai," Kate says, shaking her head. "It's completely over. We haven't been in contact with each other since."

"Oh, Kate, you've really had it rough," Olivia condoles empathetically.

"It's OK," said Kate. "It is what it is. I've come to accept that. I want a deep, meaningful, lasting love with a man who returns my passion and isn't afraid to go the distance. With my mother's passing, this has become even more evident."

"Good. I'm glad."

"I also have one more confession, if you're willing to listen."

"I'm all ears."

"I don't know what's wrong with me, but I'm not that into work lately. I have to give myself pep talks to get out of bed to go into the office. My mind is just elsewhere. I spoke to my sister about it, and she feels the same way. My brother's more practical, and I know he's dealing with things in his own way, but sometimes I feel like I, like I . . ."

"Go on," replies Olivia with anticipation.

"Like I just want to run away!" Kate releases a loud sigh. "There I said it!"

"Well, good for you Ms. Workaholic—and I say that respectfully, from one workaholic to another."

They both laugh.

"Is something wrong with me?"

"Girlfriend, you've been through a lot recently. Hello! A major breakup with the man you thought you were going to spend the rest of your life with, and of course your mom's passing. I think you just really need some time off. Can you take a few weeks to go chill and regroup?"

Kate thinks about it for a few seconds. The idea resonates with her. "I do have about a month's vacation coming."

"Well, then . . ."

"I don't know," Kate starts to waiver.

"Go away. Get out of town, rest, relax, be you—and do it in a place where you can really think about your life and what you want, where you're going, and what's important to you," insists Olivia. "You could be just going through something temporary, but if you're truly finding the need to make some changes, at least give yourself some time to regroup."

"I like it. That sounds good," Kate nods in agreement.

"Hey, I've got an idea!" says Olivia in a lightbulb moment.

"What?"

"I had some friends booked to stay in a furnished rental in Hanalei starting next week. It's already paid for, a done deal, and they just told me they couldn't make it. Why don't you take it as my guest and my gift to you?"

Kate's jaw drops. "What? Are you kidding me?"

"I'm dead serious. It's a cute little cottage in a quiet, private area not too far from the beach. It's fully stocked, so it's just as convenient as a hotel, but much more comfortable."

Olivia watches as the wheels in Kate's head turn.

"I would insist on paying—"

"No way! I said, as my guest!" Olivia says firmly.

"I'm just, I'm overwhelmed," says Kate. "That is just so kind."

"Hey, it's my pleasure," Olivia responds as she pats Kate's arm. "I know we talked about this before and agreed we both felt like we knew each other somehow—even before this lifetime. So I'm chalking it up to a soul connection. Let's just go with it. What do you say?"

Kate nods smiling, "Okay."

"Grant and I will be flying back to the island in about three weeks. I wish we could be there sooner. However, just rest up, and then get ready for some serious partying when we return," adds Olivia.

"I'm taken aback, I really am."

"Well, what do you say?"

"I say, *Aloha Kauai!*"

21

Kate sits next to her father on her sister's backyard porch and sips a glass of iced tea as Carla places crudités of sliced carrots, broccoli tops, radishes, celery, and a bowl of freshly prepared hummus before them.

"The hummus is delicious, Sis," says Carla. "Thanks for making it."

"Sure thing," Kate replies as she dips a radish into the creamy appetizer.

"The weather today can't be beat," says Glen.

"September is always beautiful," Frank chimes in as he flips the salmon on the grill. "Pretty soon we'll have to close up the pool for winter."

"Hey, Dad, when's dinner?" yells Lucas, shooting hoops in the side yard.

"About twenty minutes," Frank yells back. "So, Glen, are you looking forward to going to Florida?"

"You bet. Looking forward to playing golf with some of my buddies. It will be good to get . . ." Glen wipes a tear from his eye.

"Oh, Poppy, it's OK. Let it out," says Kate as she rubs her father's shoulder. Carla goes to his other side and puts her arm around him.

"I'm OK, really girls," he gently assures his daughters.

"Dad, are you sure you want to go to Florida right now?" asks Carla.

"You children all have your daily routines, your work and responsibilities," Glen replies. "I really appreciate how you've included me, and everything else you've been doing for me, but I've got to find ways to keep myself busy and entertained on my own."

Kate and Carla look at one another. They understand how their father feels, but they have concerns and Glen sees this.

"In Florida, I can play golf every day, and the community has all types of events and activities. It's a good climate for my arthritis, and

I'm not isolated, I have a lot of friends there—full-timers and snowbirds. Trust me, I'll be fine."

"Hey, folks!" Derek calls out cheerfully. He and Julie enter through the backyard gate.

"Hey, guys!" Carla greets them. "Glad you could make it. Kiddies coming?"

"Dawn and Ashley will stop by to say hello and grab some appetizers, but they have to leave early for a friend's party. So it's just me and Julie at the moment," Derek replies.

"Hey, Frank, what's cooking?" asks Julie.

"My famous grilled panko salmon!" exclaims Frank with bravado.

"With my famous fresh pesto to go on top," Carla adds, taking Frank's lead.

"And for our appetizer, I made my famous Mediterranean hummus!" Kate follows suit.

"To have with the famous pita chips I personally picked out at the market!" chimes Glen.

The patio erupts with laughter.

"We're a crazy bunch, aren't we?" laughs Carla.

"It's one of the reasons why I married into this family," Julie says happily.

Derek kisses his wife's cheek.

"Well, not to be outdone, I made my famous chocolate chunk brownies for dessert!" adds Julie, holding up the dessert tray. "Where would you like me to put this, Carla?"

"Just on the long table over here," indicates Carla as she tilts her head in the direction of the buffet. "It's no muss, no fuss tonight folks, just enjoy and feel free to take what you want."

"Hi, Glen," Julie says as she plants a kiss on Glen's cheek before dropping off the tray of chocolate treats.

"Hey, there. How was your week Julie?" asks Glen.

"Real estate market is picking up, so I've been busy. Kids are good, and Derek, honey, did you tell your dad about your new client?"

"Oh yeah, got a line on a new West Coast client. They're looking to develop an exclusive chain of health and wellness centers in California and Hawaii."

"Hawaii?" Kate asks, surprised. "Where?"

"The Big Island and Kauai, I believe," says Derek.

"That's fantastic, Derek. I'll keep my fingers crossed. Speaking of Kauai . . ." Kate pauses, a little nervous about revealing her newly conceived plans. "Olivia Larkin offered me a place to stay as her guest for a few weeks."

"Wow!" exclaims Carla. "Are you kidding? That's awesome!"

"That's very generous of her," adds Derek as he munches on a carrot.

"When do you think you'll go, dear?" Glen inquires.

"Well, to tell you the truth, sooner rather than later. I've been feeling the need to just take a little time, regroup a bit."

"Are you OK, hon?" asks Glen.

Kate thinks about sharing, but decides not to. Her dad is fragile right now, and she doesn't want to upset him with the truth.

"I found out I've accrued about a month's vacation, and I really haven't had a proper vacation in years, so when Olivia made the offer, I thought, why not? I could use some time to just chill."

"Well, it sounds like a dream," says Carla.

Later that evening after Derek and Julie leave for home, Glen, Frank, and Lucas talk sports on the patio while Kate and Carla clean up in the kitchen.

"Thanks for helping out, Sis," says Carla, loading the last of the dirty dishes into the dishwasher.

"Of course," Kate replies as she places several Tupperware containers full of leftovers in the fridge before sitting down.

"So Kate, tell me how you've been . . . really."

"What do you mean?"

"It's great Olivia offered you a place to stay, but I know you. Taking off work for a few weeks at once is not your MO. You started to tell Dad something at dinner, then stopped. I noticed."

"Yeah," confesses Kate. "You and I have already talked about it. That feeling of not wanting to work, how things that used to matter seeming so unimportant lately . . . I didn't want to share that with Dad though. I don't want to put more on his plate than he already has to handle."

"I know," says Carla as she puts an arm around her sister. "Some days it's all I can do to get dressed, put on makeup, and go to work. If it wasn't for Lucas and Frank . . . I don't know. They keep me hoppin' for sure. But even so, I know what you mean. I'm not sweating the small stuff. I'm thinking more big picture, enjoying every moment, cherishing everything and everyone I value in my life."

"That's what's important," agrees Kate. "I love my writing, it's wonderful working for Edward and the magazine, but I feel, or actually, *I know,* I'm supposed to be doing more professionally. And then there's my personal life, or lack thereof. I just can't quite get motivated yet. I also feel like I'm changing."

"How so?"

"Looking at life differently, feeling things even more deeply, noticing things more. I feel myself getting more intuitive, more spiritual, more . . . something. Am I making sense?"

"Perfect sense."

"I need to find what that something is," Kate continues. "Just before Mom died, she told me that she would be with us all, always."

"She told me that as well, that she'd watch over us and guide us," says Carla.

"Do you believe that's really possible?" asks Kate, looking for more reassurance, even though she and Carla have had this conversation before.

"I know it to be true. When Frank's mother passed, she appeared at his sister's bedside."

"Really?"

Carla nods.

"Then, remember when I was having a tough time getting pregnant?"

Kate nods.

"Well, one day, when I was going to see the doctor for yet another visit, I saw ladybugs all over the house, and it wasn't even the season."

"Ladybugs?"

"That was Frank's father's pet name for his wife, and she loved ladybugs. So later that day, when we found out I was pregnant, we felt the ladybugs were a sign that Frank's mother was around us, sharing in our good news."

"How come you never told me that story?"

"Well, it's not every day people talk about these things, but I have several friends that have had these types of experiences that can't be explained. Skeptics may try and dispute it, but when these things happen to you, you become a believer. Do you believe it's possible?"

"I've always believed it possible," says Kate. "But now, with Mom's passing, and thanks to everything I've been experiencing, I know with all my heart and being that it's true."

That evening, Kate falls into a deep, restful sleep. This time her dream feels real, and she is completely present, experiencing it with all of her senses.

Kate stands before the pretty white cottage on Weke Road. A warm wind gently glides by and caresses her skin as she marvels at the beautiful mix of tropical foliage that graces either side of the cottage's front entrance, and which seems to vibrate alive with color. The front door begins to open, and Kate expects to see the pretty Hawaiian woman greet her as she has done in the past. Instead, she is stunned to see who answers.

"Kate, sweetheart, come in!" Catherine calls to her, arms wide open. Kate feels a surge of love from her mother that is all encompassing.

Instantly waking from the dream, Kate bolts upright in bed. Her heart beats so fast that to calm herself she takes several deep and deliberate breaths.

The dream felt so real, thinks Kate. *The breeze, standing there in the street looking at the house, Mom's love coming towards me . . . it was as if I was actually there. Why did I wake up so suddenly? I wish I could've had more time with Mom.*

Kate glances at her bedside. The clock reads 3:00 a.m.

Typical, thinks Kate.

Unable to sleep, she stares at the ceiling for about half an hour until she accepts the fact that it's futile. Then she gets up and heads to the kitchen where she quenches her thirst with a glass of water. As she sits at the kitchen table in the moonlight, she powers up her laptop.

Kate navigates to Google and searches, "*The meaning of waking up at three o'clock in the morning.*" Surprised at the pages and pages of results on the topic, Kate finds a recurrent theme on the subject, and tonight her research takes her to a deeper level of understanding.

For one, it's a time when people seem to sense the presence of spirits, of God, angels, and deceased loved ones, in visitations, dreams, and visions. It's also a time known as the "witching" hour, the time where the veil between our world and the next is most thin, and where both good and evil can operate. However, from what she can gleam, the connotations are mostly positive and holy in nature. In the Bible, God spoke to Samuel at 3:00 a.m., Christ also passed from this world to the next somewhere between 3:00 p.m. and 3:30 p.m.

Even more curious now, on a hunch she Googles "the angel number 3" and finds that it's a number that represents the Holy Trinity. It's also a time when guardian angels ask us to use our intuition and inner wisdom to take appropriate action. The number (or symbol) encourages us to follow our life's path and soul mission with enthusiasm and urges us to use our skills and abilities to manifest personal desires that enhance not only our lives, but also the lives of others.

How beautiful, thinks Kate. *I'll definitely have to be aware of these signs and their messages and be more conscious to ask God and his angels for guidance.*

Throughout her life thus far, Kate has always held the desire to embrace life to its fullest—to love and understand deeply, to live her soul mission, and to do her part to make the world a better place. However, since her mother's passing, this need and impulse has become even more intensified.

Part Three

WHEN THE TIDE RECEDES, LOVE AWAITS

Hawaii

22

"You never take any time off," says Edward. "Go with my blessing. It will clear your mind and give you a fresh perspective. If there's anyone that deserves to, it's you!"

Kate still feels a little guilty about taking so much time away from the office, even if she has the vacation days coming to her. Support from Edward, Cindy, and her other friends means a lot to her, and they are of course on board with her decision. So, it's with a feeling of almost complete freedom that Kate finally embarks on her well-deserved respite.

At 7:30 a.m., JFK airport bustles with aggressive drivers honking and a plethora of people buzzing about to check luggage, inquire about flights, and say goodbye to loved ones. Kate feels a keen sense of relief when her bags are finally checked curbside.

"Travel safe, Sis. Love you," Derek says as he kisses his sister on the cheek.

"Love you, too."

"Have a marvelous trip, dear. Love you lots," says Glen as he embraces Kate.

"Love you too, Poppy. To the moon and beyond."

Although Glen smiles, Kate can see the sadness in his eyes as he remembers that's what Catherine always said to their children.

Kate watches as Derek and her father get into Derek's van. After they all wave goodbye to one another and the van leaves the curb, Kate, armed with her preprinted boarding pass in hand, and her two large quilted totes wrapped around each of her shoulders, walks into the airport terminal. She is stylishly dressed in a long floral print skirt with a cami top, a jean jacket, sandals, and a new pretty white wide brimmed hat. She feels a tremendous surge of excitement as she walks towards her plane's gate.

A month in Kauai! How lucky am I? Kate smiles to herself, feeling almost giddy as she finally boards the plane.

Those Amex travel miles are really paying off now, she thinks, when she takes her seat in first class.

"Mimosa, miss?" asks a flight attendant with a tray full of cocktails.

"Yes, please," says Kate as she takes a tall glass of the fizzy orange colored drink and a napkin from the server.

As she lays her head back on the cushioned headrest and sips her morning libation, Kate's mind drifts to some of her finest memories of Kauai—from the beautiful lush greenery, the sultry breezes and fantastic sunsets, to the faces of Olivia and Grant laughing at Elaine and Trevor's funny barbs at the barbecue. She remembers Sukey's fantastic laugh, Malie's friendly face, and Malie's brother Kai . . . Kai's smile and sense of humor, his strong handshake, his sexy, athletic body . . . Kate's eyes fly open at the thought.

Just where is this reverie going, Kate? she asks herself with a smile.

"Aloha, here is your veggie omelette," says another pretty flight attendant, breaking Kate's pleasant daydream. "Would you like me to freshen up your mimosa?"

"Please," Kate answers, holding out her glass. "And a cup of coffee with a little cream too, if you wouldn't mind."

"I'll have that to you in just a minute."

Kate takes another sip of her mimosa and turns toward the window as her thoughts return once again to Kauai—going to the market to buy fresh produce and snorkeling in the calm, blue waters. She wonders where life will lead her on this trip, and what creative ideas may flow. In her daydream, she walks along the shores of Anini Beach. As she does, she thinks of her sweet mother. In her mind's eye, she imagines walking along the water's edge with her mother, and asks her:

Mom, will you walk along Anini Beach with me? Will you go shopping with me to the farmers' market and help me prepare some great dishes to share with my new friends? I love you so much, to the moon and beyond my own, sweet Mommydoo . . .

Lady in the Window

They must have gotten some type of deal on these PT Cruisers, thinks Kate as she loads her suitcases into the trunk of yet another silver car.

As she drives down the lush, green winding road towards from Lihue airport to Hanalei, she feels strangely invigorated, even after the more than thirteen-hour plane ride from New York. The sun shines brightly, and she's happy that she has gained six hours of the day back. She heads for her new home for the next several weeks with excited anticipation.

The GPS on the PT Cruiser leads Kate into Hanalei Town. It looks as sublime and wonderful as she remembers. Kate is suddenly anxious to visit The Plumeria Café and enjoy one of their delicious muffins with a cup of that rich Kona brew. Perhaps Elaine, Olivia's realtor friend who was to meet her at the property to let her in, might like to join her?

The computerized voice on the PT Cruiser's GPS leads her down Weke Road. Kate marvels that this area is the location of the house she'll be staying at for the next few weeks. While she meant to Google Earth the address Elaine emailed her the night before, she got sidetracked. Now that she's close to the house on Weke Road which she loves so much, she feels a surge of excitement.

What are the odds? she happily thinks.

Nothing, however, could prepare her for what she sees next as she parks her car alongside the road's edge in front of her new residence.

"Oh my God!" exclaims Kate, "It's *the* house!"

It's the charming white cottage that Kate discovered on her first walk down this street—the same home from her dreams.

"I just can't believe it!" says Kate out loud as she gets out of the car, her head still reeling with wonder. Mesmerized, she stares at the house for a time, and then starts to mindlessly pace, deep in thought.

A tropical breeze fingers gingerly through Kate's shoulder-length auburn hair, and tiny pebbles alongside the road crunch beneath her sandals as she randomly kicks a stone here and there with the rim of her shoe.

When I first saw this house, I felt there was hope for Jason and me . . . and my mother was still alive. So much has changed in just a few short months, she thinks, now consumed with emotion.

Kate stops her pacing and, filled with an overwhelming sense of loss, bursts into a torrent of tears. With her head in her hands, she falls forward onto the PT Cruiser's hood.

Then something miraculous happens—the grief dissipates almost as quickly as it has consumed her. She feels as if loving arms surround her, bringing her solace. An amazing sense of peace permeates her soul, giving her hope and faith, which transport her from desperation. The sense of calm is so instantaneous that she cannot help but smile and marvel at this strange occurrence. Puzzled, she takes a few minutes to process what just happened. When she glances at her watch, she realizes Elaine is due to arrive momentarily. She doesn't want to see her with a tearstained face, so she digs into her purse to retrieve her compact and makeup necessary to repair the damage.

As she looks into the mirror, she notices some movement—a darkened figure in the cottage's second-story window.

Is someone home?

"Hello! Hello!" Kate turns around and calls out, waving.

Walking onto the stone pathway, she yells out again, "Excuse me, hello. Is anyone home?"

The sun must be playing tricks on her eyes. There is no one home. Elaine told her the house has been empty for some time. Leaning with her back against the PT Cruiser now, she stares up at the vacant window. As she does, she feels another curious surge—a tingling sensation on her bare arms. She hugs herself, and revels in the warm feeling.

23

"Isn't it fabulous?" asks Elaine as she and Kate walk around the cottage's large great room.

The charming living space is light, bright, and decorated in various shades of white, sand, teal, sea greens and blues, with accents of yellow and gold. Strangely, it's the same color palette that Kate chose for her newly renovated Manhattan apartment.

To the room's left, two oversized white slipcovered sofas with decorative tropical-patterned pillows face each other, and a large, rustic wood coffee table sits between them. There's a wall of windows directly in front of the sofas that showcases the front yard lanai and the ocean view just beyond. Adjacent to the sofas, a stone fireplace with a wood mantle takes up the entire wall. The white wood shelves that surround the fireplace hold an assortment of books, shells, pretty tropical artwork, and objets d'art. Just above the fireplace, a flat-screen television peeks out from behind slightly open shutters.

To the right of the great room is a large, open kitchen with white cabinets, slate gray countertops and a large maple butcher-block island with a stainless steel gas cooktop centered between two large prep areas.

"What a great kitchen to cook in!" exclaims Kate as she soaks in every element of the cottage.

A rectangular wooden table that comfortably sits six and boasts a welcoming fresh arrangement of tropical flowers is nestled in a windowed alcove with stunning ocean views.

"I can't believe how charming this house is!"

"If you like what you're seeing so far, then I know you're just going to love the rest of the place," says Elaine.

Kate follows Elaine up a small staircase to a loft landing that's used as a sitting room and a den. On this floor are two spacious bedrooms with a large Jack and Jill bathroom between them.

"Each guest bedroom is beautiful in its own right," Elaine says, as Kate *oohs* and *aahs* over the tastefully decorated rooms that could easily be featured in an interior design magazine. "But wait until you see the downstairs master."

"Oh my!" cries Kate when she views the large, luxurious master bedroom.

The palette for the bedroom includes soothing natural tones of white, green, and beige. Light grass cloth wallpaper covers three of the walls, and another textured wallpaper with a beautiful display of palms and tropical plants graces the wall behind a king-size bed with a plush cloth headboard. An assortment of pillows in fabrics that match the wallpaper rest against the headboard, and on either side of the bed are exquisitely carved koa wood nightstands with matching lamps. Opposite the bed is a large picture window with a stellar view of a gorgeous patio and the glistening ocean in the distance. Adjacent to the sleeping area is a sitting room complete with sofa, lounge chair, wood coffee table, television hutch, and a handsome koa wood writing desk and cushioned chair.

"This place is a dream," Kate murmurs in awe.

"I knew you'd love it."

Elaine opens a pair of dark wood plantation style shuttered doors that lead to a walk-in closet.

"There's plenty of room to hang your clothes, with built in cabinets for your shoes, tops, and sundries."

Kate follows Elaine into the master bath.

"In here, you'll enjoy this jetted soaking tub with garden view."

"I may never leave!" laughs Kate.

"Olivia's so pleased you were able to visit."

"Well, I can assure you and her, the pleasure is going to be all mine!"

"And here," Elaine says as she opens French doors that lead outside, "is your private lanai."

Kate follows Elaine, marveling at the slice of paradise surrounded by lush greens, flowering trees and plants, and enchanting water views. Two cushioned chaise lounges rest in the center of the lanai, and to the side of the outdoor room sits a small, round wood table and two chairs.

"I can definitely see myself out here, with my laptop fired up and iced tea in hand just waiting for inspiration to hit," says Kate. "This is the most wonderful aloha."

"Well, my dear, if you're game, let's bring in your suitcases and then hop into town to grab a spot of tea and maybe a bite."

With the six-hour time change from Manhattan to Kauai, Kate's internal time clock is completely awry, and she finds she's suddenly famished.

"I'm so glad you suggested this place," Kate says as she munches on a piece of bread.

"The food here is fabulous—all local produce and fresh seafood," says Elaine as both she and Kate take in the sights and smells of Postcards, an adorable little café with a quaint, home-style atmosphere in the heart of Hanalei Town.

Kate orders a hearty meal consisting of a mixed green salad and grilled salmon over polenta served with an array of fresh, roasted veggies. Elaine opts for lighter fare, choosing a trio of tapenades—artichoke, mushroom, and roasted eggplant—with house-made crostini. Both complement their repast with large glasses of iced tea.

"Ah, I guess I needed that," Kate laughs as she gestures to her empty plate.

"Would you like dessert?"

"Mahalo, but no. I don't think I could eat another bite."

"Well, this is my treat, a welcome to you on your visit to the Garden Isle."

"Oh, I couldn't . . ."

"Please, Kate, it's my pleasure," says Elaine. "Before I take you home, let's visit the grocery store across the street so you can pick up a few things to tide you over until the weekly farmers' market, which I know you'll love."

At the market, Kate picks up the essentials—bottled water for her excursions and breakfast foods like Greek yogurt, cereal, a selection of fresh fruit, almond milk, coffee, and a few freshly baked pastry treats from the deli. She doesn't want to shop too much, figuring she'll definitely make her way to the local farmers' market soon enough.

"Have a wonderful evening and get some rest," Elaine says as she gives her a big hug before dropping Kate off in front of the cottage. "I'll touch base with you tomorrow to see how you're doing. If you need anything, you have my number."

"Mahalo," waves Kate as Elaine pulls away from the curb.

Once inside the cottage, Kate heads towards the master suite. Exhausted, she looks at the comfy sea of pillows on the king-size bed and just can't resist resting her eyes for a moment. However, no sooner does she lie down than she's fast asleep.

Her dreams are full of beautiful flowering trees and balmy ocean breezes. Suddenly she finds herself walking the shoreline with her mother beside her. They laugh, enjoying one another's company just like they had so many times in her parents' home by the shore in the years before her mother's passing.

On their walk, her mother notices something glistening lying partially beneath the sand. Catherine reaches down slowly and pulls the object up out of the earth. As she brushes the beige grainy particles aside, a pair of white angel wing seashells with two sides delicately attached at the top is revealed.

Catherine places the shell in the palm of Kate's open hand. When she does, Kate can feel a jolt of electric heat enter through her palm and rise up to her heart, filling her with a sense of love and contentment. Mother and daughter smile at each other with joy.

Kate wakes from the dream and knows instantly that it was no ordinary dream. She and her mother have made another soul connection.

Once again, too awake to sleep, Kate walks around the moonlit room and out into the hallway towards the great room and kitchen. As she wanders aimlessly, she looks around the comfortable space.

In the great room, she scans the books and DVDs on shelves in the floor to ceiling media center. From classic films to more modern fare, art books, design books, best-selling fiction, pretty colored vases, and objets d'art, it's an eclectic mix.

It was then Kate noticed *them.* Inside a small, antique white painted wooden frame, mounted on a pastel blue cloth, are two white angel wing seashells, joined at the top—exactly like the ones in her dream earlier that evening.

Kate gasps and her free hand flies up to cover her mouth in surprise. She sets her water glass down on the shelf, picks up the framed wings, and studies them intently. Happy that her dream is now manifest in physical form, Kate looks about the room, half expecting to see someone to share her find.

"Hi, Mom!" she cries out with joy. It feels so good to say hello out loud, she continues.

"I know that you're here, and I love that you're visiting me!" Kate smiles as little tears of happiness form at the corners of her eyes.

Kate sits on the sofa and stares at the angel wings. It's a long time before she returns to bed, but when she does, it's one of the most peaceful sleeps of her life.

24

The next morning sun pours in through the partially open bedroom shutters. It takes Kate a moment to reorient herself and remember where she is. A big smile blooms on her face when she sees the angel wings sitting on the nightstand. After several minutes pass, she slips out of bed and into her silky robe as a craving for freshly brewed Kona coffee hits.

In addition to the coffee, Kate fixes a small bowl of fruit and yogurt and unwraps the banana macadamia-nut scone she purchased from the market the previous evening. She carries her breakfast out to the cottage's lanai and sets it down on a small table next to a large cushioned wicker chair.

Heavenly, thinks Kate as she sits and takes a sip of the rich coffee with a hint of almond milk. She breaks off a piece of the pastry. *Delicious.* The flavors of the banana scone with hints of ginger and lemon swirl in her mouth, and the addition of the crunchy macadamia nuts make the treat sheer perfection.

As she enjoys her breakfast, Kate listens to the happy banter of birds chattering in the trees, and as she does, she begins to think about her family. It would be late afternoon in New York right now. She wonders what her father is doing.

Probably at Carla's or Derek's, or maybe he's out to a movie, thinks Kate, knowing that her father sometimes enjoys taking in a film by himself. She makes a mental note to call Cindy later in the day, and then, unexpectedly, Jason pops into her mind. Her stomach feels instantly queasy at the thought of him. But just as she starts to dwell on the past, a little bird flies right up to the porch and perches itself in front of her on the lanai's wood rail.

The bird's joyful chirping, seemingly in conversation with her, chases thoughts of Jason right out of Kate's mind. She almost wants to burst out laughing at the little bird's boldness, as it dances about twittering and tweeting.

There's something about the bird that causes her to think of her mother and the memory of Catherine's grinning face puts a smile on hers.

"Hi, Mom," she speaks softly aloud to the bird. "Sit here with me, won't you, and enjoy this lovely view?"

The bird cocks its head to each side, unafraid of Kate, and does just that. Kate pictures her mother's presence in her mind's eye, knowing how much she would enjoy sitting here enjoying morning breakfast with her.

I love you, Mom, thinks Kate. A tingly, warm sensation runs up Kate's spine and through her body. It's palpable, but not unpleasant, and Kate immediately takes notice as the electric feeling is followed by a second jolt, and then a third. Kate is in such a pleasant, relaxed state that she goes with the pulsing energies that sweep in small waves throughout her body.

If such sensations happened somewhere else, she probably would have ignored the feelings they evoked. However, sitting here in the cottage on Weke Road, so calm and peaceful, the pulsing waves can't be refuted. Kate instinctively knows that somehow she is connecting to an otherworldly energy. Instead of being frightened, she finds herself actually reveling in the feelings, which last for a few minutes, after which she experiences a heightened sense of well-being.

"Aloha, come back and visit soon," says Kate to the little bird as it flies off the ledge into the nearby foliage.

After breakfast, Kate sits at the kitchen counter checking her emails and sending off quick notes to her father, siblings, and friends. She also does a Google search for local farmers' markets in the area where she can shop for fresh produce and other fare.

OK, so after the farmers' market where shall I go today? Kate thinks as she considers her upcoming day's adventure. Before she finalizes her plans, her cell phone rings.

"Hello, this is Kate."

"Hey girl, it's Olivia. How are you? Did you settle in?"

"Oh, the cottage is just perfect. I love it! After Elaine showed me the lay of the land, we grabbed a bite in town. I really can't thank you enough, Olivia."

"I'm so glad you like it. I'm looking forward to seeing you when I get back, too. We'll have some good times."

"Absolutely!"

"What are you up to today?"

"I'm headed to the farmers' market in town, and then I figured I'd just roam around, take some photos, and maybe stop by The Plumeria Café to say hello to Malie."

"Sounds wonderful. And when you see Malie, she can fill you in on activities around town. FYI—she and her husband are famous for their killer barbecues, and there's usually always something going on at their place on weekends."

Over the phone line, Kate can hear someone call out Olivia's name.

"Oops! Got to run, but I'll touch base with you later. Aloha!"

"Aloha. Speak to you soon."

Kate walks down Weke Road and snaps photos as she journeys into town. The natural sunlight is so magnificent in its ability to make all of the colors in nature's splendor pop that Kate finds herself stopping every few feet to capture close-ups of tropical flowers, unique groupings of foliage, and stunning views of the ocean surrounded by majestic peaks.

A thought comes to mind that she should frame a few of her photos as a thank-you to Olivia. Olivia's generosity is truly a gift, and she wants to show her appreciation with something that she knows Olivia will enjoy.

As she snaps a photo from the road's edge, Kate happens to glance down at the ground. A single, exquisite, iridescent peacock feather lies at her feet, away from any foliage or signs of wildlife.

"Wow!" Kate squeals with excitement.

Immediately mesmerized by the ten-inch long feather's unique hues and intricate patterns in deep sea-green, purple, blue, gold, and white, Kate picks up the unexpected treasure. When she does, a warm tingle of energy surges through her body.

"OK," says Kate aloud, acknowledging the bolt.

She holds the feather up to the sun and notices its beautiful sheen. It's a special find, and Kate feels grateful as she places it in her quilted tote for safekeeping.

Not far from The Plumeria Café, in Hanalei's neighborhood community center off the town's main road, the Saturday farmers' market is overflowing with booths where local farmers and other vendors sell their organic produce and wares to eager shoppers.

Kate picks up a large bag of lettuce mix, tomatoes, onions, garlic, a pineapple, some dried fruit and nuts, broccolini, cauliflower, and apples, all of which she places in a reusable bag. For a time, Kate gets lost in the market, which beyond edible treats, fish, meat, and organic produce, includes sundry items from candles to soap, jewelry, arts and crafts, clothing, and other eclectic fare.

Her hands now full with all she can carry, Kate wishes she had driven her car to town. She makes a mental note to do so for next week's market, and is quite tired by the time she arrives at The Plumeria Café.

"Aloha!" Malie waves to Kate when she sees her walk through the doors.

At noon, the place is abuzz with patrons, and the smell of the brewing coffee and the sights of the delicious pastries on display make Kate's stomach growl.

"Aloha!" Kate waves to Malie.

Even though breakfast was not so long ago, Kate's body clock is still off from traveling, and with a little urging from Malie, she succumbs to a mouthwatering warm panini sandwich oozing with mozzarella, sun-dried tomato, and basil pesto.

"Don't feel like you have to join me if you're busy," says Kate as Malie sits down at her table with a cup of coffee in hand.

"Not at all, Manny can take over the cash register for a bit," Malie replies as she cocks her head towards the front where a handsome guy in his twenties with long, blonde hair pulled back in a ponytail talks to a customer. Like Malie, he wears the café's signature apron over his jeans and t-shirt.

"Olivia mentioned you're staying at the cottage on Weke Road. You all settled?"

"Yup. The place is just charming."

"I'm glad you like it," says Malie, blowing on her hot coffee before taking a sip. "My mother loved that cottage, it was her favorite place."

"Your mother?"

"It was my parents' retirement home," Malie explains.

"Seriously?"

"Yeah, my dad knew my mom wouldn't want us to sell it after she died, but he didn't want to live there either, so now he rents it out."

"Wow! I'm blown away. What a strange synchronicity."

"What do you mean?" asks Malie, taking another sip of her coffee.

"Well, on my first trip here, when I walked by the house, for some reason, I was really taken with it. So much so that when I saw the watercolor of the cottage you sell here at the café, I had to buy it because it reminded me so much of the cottage on Weke Road."

"It is the same cottage, you know," says Malie.

"It is?"

"Yes, and my mom painted it."

Kate's jaw drops. "Now wait, that's just crazy!"

Malie laughs out loud at Kate's amusingly dramatic outburst.

"Not really, but it is interesting, isn't it? I sell a lot of my mom's prints. See over there," Malie motions towards the baskets of prints and wrapped gift cards in the café's pretty wood armoire. "They're all my mom's work."

"Wait a second," Kate says, still processing. "OK, so it was your parents' place that's used as a rental now, your mom was a painter, so she painted the cottage she loved, and you sell her prints. Elaine is a realtor friend, you all know Olivia, OK, I'm beginning to make sense of the interconnections, and I get it, it's a small community and all . . . but still, I was drawn to the house enough to photograph it. *It called to me.* I even see the place in my dreams sometimes! Isn't that a little, you know . . . *woo-woo*?" says Kate, making circular movements with her index fingers.

"Yeah, I know, it is a little cosmic, but that kind of stuff happens all the time," shrugs Malie. "Just enjoy and recognize the connections when they happen. It just means you're on the right path."

Kate feels a familiar chill run up her spine. "Yeah, I will. I know what you mean."

"So, what do you have on your agenda today? Just hanging?"

"I thought I'd take some more photos, maybe get inspired to do some creative writing, and just see what the day brings."

"Well, Aukai and I are having a barbecue at our place tonight, if you'd like to come. Just a few friends. You met Sukey and Kamal at Olivia's. I have to call Elaine and Trevor to see if they can drop by, too. There might also be a few more folks from the neighborhood. It'll start about five o'clock."

"Sounds great, can I bring anything?"

"Whatever you feel like," Malie says, waving the popular Hawaiian shaka sign, extending her thumb and pinky out and curling in her three middle fingers towards the palm of her hand. "It's a 'hang loose' kind of get-together."

Kate nods and takes a sip of her coffee as Malie writes down her address on the back of a business card she takes from her apron.

"Here's where we live," says Malie, handing Kate the card. "You know, Kate, Olivia told me about your mom's passing. I'm sorry for you. My condolences."

"Mahalo."

"Since Kai and I lost our mom, I know how you must feel."

"Sorry for your loss as well, Malie. How long ago did she pass? I mean, if you don't mind me asking."

"A few years now. It was a boating accident. She and Kai were out on the open sea and all of a sudden the weather changed. The waves kicked up, and Mom fell and hit her head. It happened in an instant."

"That's horrible, to lose her so suddenly," Kate says empathetically. "At least we knew my mom was ill and had a little time to ready ourselves—if you ever are ready for something like that. Thankfully, she passed peacefully."

"Yeah, that's a blessing, no doubt about that. The way my mom died was not only a shock; it also caused a real divide in our family."

Kate looks at Malie, her eyes conveying her curiosity.

"My dad didn't want my mom to go out with Kai that day. After the accident, they both said some things to each other that I think they regret. Needless to say, they don't really speak that much anymore. So between that, and their feelings of guilt, pain, and remorse, not to mention the fact that they both have a stubborn streak . . . you get the picture."

"Well, I'll say a prayer, and keep a good thought that they can heal and come back together again."

"Mahalo," says Malie. "I appreciate that, and no offense, but I think it's going to take a lot more than that to bridge their divide."

25

Even though her arms are full of bounty from her farmers' market purchases, on her walk home after lunch, Kate can't resist entering a quaint bookstore she notices along the way.

Once inside, she peruses the shelf of best sellers. Her eye stops at *You Can't Make This Stuff Up: Life-Changing Lessons from Heaven*, authored by Theresa Caputo, the Long Island Medium. She thumbs through the pages and makes up her mind to purchase it, especially in light of her recent experiences.

"Whew!" says Kate as she scurries down the stone pathway to the shelter of the cottage's lanai just as the heavens break open with a light, refreshing afternoon rain.

Once inside, Kate lays back on the great room sofa and sips some apple cinnamon tea as she reads her new book, which explains how spirits of our deceased loved ones and friends can contact the living if they're open to it. In the book, Theresa also explains how she interprets the signs in her readings for people, and how we can attune ourselves to be more aware.

Kate finds tremendous comfort from reading the book, as she believes its message to be true. Her mother's spirit *is* all around her. She knows instinctively that her mother can hear her when she speaks to her, and that her mother can still feel the love Kate has in her heart for her.

Kate believes in God, in the guidance of guardian angels, and that the soul never dies. She believes that her family will one day be together in heaven, just like she had written in the poem for her parents' fiftieth anniversary.

I was so close to Mom when she was alive, how is it possible I feel her almost even closer after her passing? ponders Kate.

As an adult living on her own in New York City, Kate has always thought about her parents daily. Nothing has changed in that regard. However, now it's as if her mother is part of her. She easily envisions Catherine's smiling face in her mind's eye and recalls the sound of her voice, the feel of her touch. Sometimes a thought or a saying of her mother's will just pop into her head, which always makes Kate smile.

Since her mother's passing, while Kate still cries for the physical loss of her dear mother, she also feels Catherine's presence everywhere around her. She is grateful for the peace this feeling brings. When she feels the need to talk to her mother, she does. When she wants to hold and kiss her, she closes her eyes and tells her how much she loves her. She pictures being cheek to cheek with her mom, arms around one another, and feels the love in her heart.

Kate has also become keenly aware of the fact that when she allows herself to be more relaxed, especially now that she's in and around nature, she feels acutely connected to her mother. In Kauai's atmosphere of "ohana," of family, and it being a culture that strongly believes that we are forever joined with our deceased loved ones, Kate is experiencing an even more joyful, palpable connection to her mother and to spirit, and is more intuitively tuned into the world around her. She likes the feeling.

Kate wanders back into the kitchen to heat more water in the teakettle. As she waits for it to boil, she pulls the pretty peacock feather she found earlier that day out from her tote. As she examines the feather's many colors and intricate patterns, she decides to Google the meaning of such a find.

As she navigates the Internet, Kate is led to a host of sites that say feathers are actually very spiritual signs. Supposedly they are signals from the angelic realms to remind us of their presence. To find a feather, particularly in the way Kate did, where it sticks out and isn't easy to explain why it's there in the first place, is a message that tells the person that she or he is on the right path and is being divinely guided.

Kate is surprised to find out that this belief has been held for centuries, and by many different cultures. Further investigation reveals the meaning behind finding a particular color of feather. For example, a white feather indicates spirituality, protection, peace, and that heaven's angels are close; a pink feather signifies unconditional love and romance are in your path; an orange feather portends successful changes are on the horizon; and mixtures of colors, for example, black mixed with purple, represent deep spirituality.

To find a peacock feather, Kate discovers, is significant in many cultures and has a range of meanings which include: spiritual healing energy, renewal, knowledge, integrity, prosperity, love, compassion, soul, peace, and good luck.

I'll take it! thinks Kate, feeling blessed as another energetic wave of calm and well-being wash over her.

"MAHALO," SAYS MALIE as Kate hands her a bouquet of colorful flowers.

"Something smells amazing," Kate says, as she gets a whiff of the aromas emanating into Malie's kitchen from the lanai.

"That's Aukai doing his thing at the grill. I hope you're hungry. I think he bought the store out."

"I've been looking forward to the barbecue all day," Kate grins. "I made a green salad, too," she adds, handing Malie a large, reusable bag with the salad and a side of homemade dressing.

"Mahalo," says Malie.

"Can I help with anything?"

"Only with letting me know what you would like to drink. Everything's pretty much under control. Would you like a glass of Chardonnay?"

"Mahalo," Kate nods.

"Go ahead outside; the gang's all here," says Malie cocking her head in the direction of the lanai. "I'll bring one out to you."

As Kate steps onto the lanai, she waves to Aukai, Elaine, Kamal, and Trevor standing by the grill.

"Aloha, Kate!" everyone greets her enthusiastically.

"Here, sit next to me," Sukey calls to Kate as she pats the chair next to hers at the large, circular wooden table. "How are things going?"

"Just great," answers Kate.

"Taking lots of great photos I presume?"

"Yes, I've been getting some fabulous shots!" gushes Kate enthusiastically.

"Well, I'd really like to see some of them," Sukey replies. "We're always on the lookout for new talent to exhibit. Why don't you drop by our shop this week and show me. You'll get to see our gallery, too. Then maybe we can grab a bite for lunch."

"Sure, that sounds great," says Kate. "I'll call you tomorrow, and we'll set a time."

Sukey nods in agreement as she takes a carrot from the crudité plate and dips it into the cool, creamy tzatziki cucumber yogurt dip. Elaine leaves Trevor, Aukai, and Kamal at the grill.

"Kate, you're glowing tonight," Elaine observes, noticing how beautiful Kate looks.

"Glowing?"

"You do look radiant," chimes Malie.

"Must be the clean air, fresh food, and the much-needed sleep," laughs Kate.

"Whatever it is, keep it up, bottle it, and give me some," quips Elaine. They laugh.

Kate does feel different tonight. Getting ready for the barbecue, she even acknowledged how great she feels—and looks—to herself. However, now that she's at Malie's, she's experiencing an even more heightened, happy energy.

Perhaps it's just the fact that I get to do whatever I want without a care in the world? Or perhaps it's the sensuous island breeze blowing in from the ocean tonight, the joyous sound of birds singing in the trees, or how amazing it is to watch the beginnings of a multicolored sunset emerge on the horizon? Whatever it is, I feel fantastic.

In fact, she can't remember the last time she felt as good. She knows, somehow, that she is on the verge of something wonderful.

"The ahi is ready!" announces Aukai as he places an impressive piece of fish on a large platter.

Within minutes the barbecue guests begin to devour the buffet of fresh tuna, an assortment of grilled garden veggies, baked taro and yams, and the spinach salad prepared by Kate.

"The salad is delicious," Malie notes.

"What's in it?" asks Elaine. "Looks like spinach, strawberries . . ."

"Walnuts, red onion, and goat cheese crumbles," Kate says. "Mixed with my recipe for citrus vinaigrette."

"Fabulous!" adds Elaine.

"To our ohana!" toasts Aukai.

"Here, here!" Trevor calls out as he lifts his wine glass. The others follow suit.

"Here, here!" chimes Kai as he steps out onto the lanai and toasts with a box of goodies from Lei Petite Bakery.

"What happened? I thought you had to work late?" Malie asks as she rushes to give her brother a kiss on the cheek.

Kate immediately perks up at seeing Kai, who she assumed wasn't coming. She notices that he looks extremely handsome in his khaki shorts, sandals, and form fitting t-shirt that shows off his amazing physique.

"I thought so too. There was a mix-up in scheduling at the ER. When I was offered the chance to leave early, I took it as a sign to come to the barbecue."

"Well, we're glad you did!" says Aukai. "Did you eat yet? There's plenty of ahi."

"Great, I'm famished."

"I'll get another plate," Malie says as she takes the bakery box from Kai. "What did you bring?"

"Chocolate macaroons."

"Yum!" cries Malie.

Trevor makes room for Kai at the table, which places him directly opposite Kate. As he sits down, he smiles warmly at her. His eyes sparkle, and his face is open and friendly. The sensual energy Kai exudes makes Kate feel tingly all over.

In an attempt to appear nonchalant, Kate takes a sip of her wine, hoping the thrill she feels at being so close to Kai will go unnoticed by the others.

"Good to see you again, Kate."

"You too."

"I hear you're staying at my parents' old cottage."

"It was an offer from Olivia I couldn't refuse. Apparently, she had it rented for some friends who couldn't make it into town, so she offered it to me instead," replies Kate, hoping Kai won't notice her nervousness.

"Olivia's like that, she's got a big heart."

For the rest of the dinner, Kai and Kate share glances and smiles and chime in on the group conversation. Each time Kai smiles at Kate she feels her insides lurch with excitement.

Later, after dinner, as Malie, Aukai, and some of the others are busy clearing the table and making coffee for dessert, Kai walks up behind Kate who is standing on the lawn, gazing out at the moonlit waters. Kate isn't surprised. Somehow she had a feeling he might reach out to her; indeed, she was consciously waiting for him to approach her.

"Beautiful, isn't it?" asks Kai, his husky voice making Kate's knees weak.

"It is," says Kate, looking up to smile at Kai.

"Kauai is filled with so much beauty, the flowers, the landscapes, and the amazing sunsets. I've lived my life here, and the exquisiteness never fades. There's always something new to appreciate."

"I know what you mean, and I've only been here twice. Even so, every day, I find something new to look at and . . ." Kate pauses, thinking, "to perhaps write about."

"For the magazine?"

"For that, but I'm also toying with some ideas for a novel."

"You're a book author, too?"

"None written yet, but I'd like to go in that direction."

"Well, I'm sure you will. If it's what you truly desire, and you put your mind to it, it will happen."

Kate smiles.

"What's so funny?"

"You sounded like my mother just then. She was a very positive person, always talking about visualizing and thinking positive thoughts in order to manifest your dreams."

"Well, she was right," asserts Kai with conviction, then softening his tone he adds, "I'm very sorry to hear of your loss, Kate. Olivia told Malie and me."

"Mahalo," Kate says, feeling Kai's genuine emotion. "She and I were really close. She wasn't just my mom, she was my best friend."

"I'm sure she was."

Kate and Kai look silently out to sea for several beats before Kai breaks the silence.

"I heard you also like to take photographs."

"Oh, you did?"

"I overheard Malie and Sukey talking earlier."

"Well, I'm not a trained professional, but sometimes the magazine uses my photos. I also like to capture images that speak to me."

"Well, Kauai is a place that will inspire you, that's for sure. The last time you were here, did you get to do much sightseeing?"

"A little," Kate replies. "One place I'd really like to see though is the Na Pali Coast. I hear it's breathtaking."

"It's amazing. I boat and snorkel there all the time. Now, that's a great place to take photos."

"I'm sure."

"If you'd like, I could take you there, and show you around to some other local sweet spots?"

"I'd love that," says Kate.

"Well, I'm off this Wednesday. Will that work for you?"

"Yes, it would!" Kate says, just moments before Aukai bellows, "Dessert time folks! Come and get it!"

It's around midnight when Kate returns to the cottage. As she washes and changes for bed, she realizes that she's way too amped-up to sleep. Instead she takes some of her writing files out onto the bedroom lanai. As she sits at the wooden table, she sifts through the contents of the accordion folder and peruses photos and articles that she has previously cut from magazines and newspapers for future writing inspiration.

In one of the folds, she comes across some of her old writings that she had long since tucked away—the ones her mother gave her months earlier. When her mother handed her the box of writings and keepsakes, Kate had only scanned through the short stories written when she was a young teen. Now, however, in the quiet of the night, she's compelled to read them.

What was it I wrote about then? It will be interesting to see what stories I would think to tell at the tender ages of thirteen and fourteen.

Kate picks up one of the more extensive writings entitled, "Jessica." On the colored cover is a magazine cutout. It's an art rendering of a pretty girl, perhaps about nineteen, with long, flowing golden hair, who wears the look of another time.

For this particular class assignment, Kate was told to write about the Civil War. So, she wrote about Jessica and her family, and their hopes and dreams for the future while they attempted to survive tumultuous, war-torn times. Kate's teacher praised her creativity and gave her an A+ on the paper. Reading the story through adult eyes, Kate feels proud. She is also filled with questions.

Why didn't I pursue writing short stories and novels earlier? The desire to write fiction has always been with her. Even as an adult, her education and journalistic pursuits have never squelched that desire. Kate remembers her mother's words and hears them in her head as if her she were speaking them to her at this very moment: "*You have the talent, Kate. If you want to write fiction, do it.*"

Yes, I will, thinks Kate. In order to set off on this new track, however, Kate knows she must make some changes in her daily routine. Desires and wishes are one thing, but now is the time to make things happen.

Why wait? A tingle of energy runs up and down her spine. Kate chuckles, and says out loud, "Thanks for reminding me, Mom. I obviously need the encouragement to light a fire under my *you know what.*"

Kate continues to read her story about Jessica. Her mouth drops open when she reads the next passage spoken to Jessica by a family friend: "We are all heartbroken about your mother's passing, but she is still with us, you know. She's watching over us, and anytime you ever want to speak to her, whether it's in prayers or out loud, she'll hear."

Kate cannot believe what she is reading. She completely forgot she wrote those words. Now, reading this passage as an adult, the content is astonishing to her.

She continues: "Jessica realized that with each passing day, her mother was still with her. Perhaps she was with her now, even more than in life, because now her mother could be with her everywhere, and in every place, and even though Jessica missed seeing her mother in physical form, when she wanted to 'see' her, all she had to do was to pray or talk to her mother."

Kate sighs deeply, tears forming in the creases of her eyes as she reads on. The story goes into detail about her father's reaction to her mother's passing: "After his wife's death, Jessica's father wasn't the same for a long time. But soon, he too began to believe that his wife's spirit was with him always. Our loved ones never die, they are forever with us."

How could I possibly know this at thirteen? Kate asks herself. In her writings, it was clear. Definite. This belief about our loved ones living on inspired the heroine, giving her comfort and an ongoing connection to her mother. In her own life, Kate can't remember the first time she had ever had this thought, nor could she remember ever telling anyone about this belief. Yet clearly from Jessica's story, she had always believed it.

As Kate continues to flip through her old compositions, she feels as if she is meeting her young self, and in many ways, she is. Her writings are reminders for her to explore her talents and story concepts. If she did it at thirteen, she can certainly do it now! She feels an overwhelming desire to connect with this particular writer-self, and for the first time in a long while, she senses a positive intuitive feeling about her destiny. She will make it happen.

It's past 3:00 a.m. by the time Kate finally puts her writings away. She closes the lanai door behind her as she heads back into the bedroom guided by the light of the full moon. Slipping beneath the silk sheets, her mind takes an active account of the day's events. Several minutes later, she's in a deep sleep.

Out of the darkness a ray of sun breaks through the sky and reveals a most beautiful and magical tropical setting. Majestic waterfalls pour down from high peaks, and the sounds of nature fill the lush jungle.

Kate's eyes focus on a single pink lotus sitting in a calm stream, and as she stares, its leaves begin to slowly open. The beauty and wonder of this magical flower transfix Kate. Then suddenly, just as the lotus appeared out of the darkness, Kate stands in another lush landscape close to the water's edge.

It's dusk, and the peach, pink, and golden rays of the setting sun fill the horizon. In the next instant, Kai is by her side. His vibrant smile is welcoming. Kate feels the powerful connection between their souls. When he reaches for Kate, she feels the warmth of his masculine power as he encircles her hand with his own. They feel so right, so wonderful together.

Kai brings Kate's open hand to his mouth and begins to slowly and tenderly kiss the underside of her wrist and palm, gently pulling her closer. She feels the heat of his breath and moans slightly as his tongue lightly brushes her wrist, once, and then again. His touch creates a sublime longing in her most intimate core.

With her free hand, Kate reaches for Kai's face. She runs her fingers over his cheek, and then through his hair. She holds him as close as possible while he kisses her face, her neck, and then her lips with relish.

The sensuous movements with which his tongue enters in and out of her mouth ignites such a mounting heat within her that Kate's only release is a series of primal moans. No longer in control, Kate feels Kai's excitement also building, yet he continues to control his passion, silently asking her to do the same, as they explore and savor other pleasures.

In the next instant, they lie on a sumptuous, white netted bed in the midst of a tropical paradise. As they embrace with hunger, there is no time, no space, and nothing else but this moment matters.

Kate's fingers run across Kai's muscular shoulders and chest. She revels in his fragrant scent, the taste of his lips, and the weight of him on top of her. She pulls his buttocks closer into her, the heat and the desire inside her becoming unbearable.

"Please, please," Kate moans with urgency.

Kai covers her neck and chest with wet kisses, knowing full well what they both desire as they playfully tease one another. The longing in her eyes speaks to him of the emergent need to be satiated by him, and he smiles knowing her desire. He caresses her face gently before hungrily kissing her lips.

Kate writhes violently in her bed, her sheets tilted at odd angles, pillows strewn about the floor, as she jolts awake with a gasp. It takes her a few seconds to comprehend that she's been dreaming.

Even now that she is wide-awake, both the dream and Kai are still very much with her. She can feel their warmth and the lingering hunger. The intensity of the dream surprises her. After all, she barely knows Kai. Then she recalls the daydream she experienced after meeting him for the first time—the one on the plane.

OK, she thinks. *I get it, he's gorgeous and I'm attracted. So . . . ?*

There is no denying this dream. On some level it was real. She could sense, taste, and feel him. Now there is absolutely no denying the attraction and the obvious, palatable chemistry between them. She instinctively knows Kai feels it too.

Experience has taught her, however, that there is more that she desires besides chemistry. Yes, primal attraction is vital, and she does want it, but she also wants more, something deep and lasting.

She had chemistry with Jason, and look where that road led. If she knows anything now, it's that when she makes love to a man, she bonds emotionally; but it may not be the same for her partner. All the passion in the world isn't worth it if it's going to leave her with a gaping hole in her heart. She also isn't into wasting time having a brief affair or in the futility of carrying on a long-distance relationship. So if her dreams are prophetic, and she and Kai are somehow fated to be, then she is going to have to see what he is made of beyond heat and passion.

26

Wednesday morning arrives, and Kate works through several changes of bathing suits, sundresses, and pairs of shorts and tops before she finally decides on what to wear for her first date with Kai. Extremely anxious, she tortures herself with the concept of opening herself up to someone she's obviously got chemistry with. She knows full well that she has to leave in a few weeks' time.

Am I setting myself up for disaster or heartbreak? Maybe I should call him and cancel our date? A hundred thoughts nag at her until she comes to the realization she'd probably beat herself up even more if she doesn't go.

I'm a grown woman, in control of my emotions. What's there to be afraid of? I know how to say the word, "No." So what if Kai is a handsome, educated, knowledgeable, and genuinely nice person who happens to be a caring doctor and super hunk? I'm leaving in a few weeks. There's nothing to worry about. Right? Oh, puh-lease! Who am I kidding?

Kate knows she is about to step into deep doo-doo with her eyes wide open.

Come on, she gives herself a pep talk, *you know you want to see the Na Pali Coast and this is a generous offer. Be brave, stay centered, and see what unfolds.*

Finally making the choice to stay in a positive mind-set, Kate puts on an attractive Michael Kors bikini in various shades of teal that will be perfect for snorkeling. Next, she slips into a pair of formfitting short shorts in a matching tropical print and a spotless white top to wear over her suit for the day's boating expedition.

Last but not least, she puts on her deck shoes and packs her waterproof camera, sneakers (in case she needs them), flip-flops, and one of her signature floppy hats to match the ensemble.

Once dressed, she paces the cottage living room, until she realizes she's making herself even more nervous. So she stops, takes in several cleansing deep breaths, checks herself in the mirror again, and finally sits on the sofa to wait for Kai.

Kate picks up a magazine and turns the pages without digesting a word. The activity, however, proves to have quite a calming effect, until the phone rings. Kate dives to pick up her cell from the coffee table and, all fingers, winds up juggling it around in the air until she can get a firm grip on it, nearly missing Kai's call.

"Hi! This is Kate," Kate says, trying to sound calm and upbeat.

"For a minute there, I thought the call might go to voice mail," Kai replies cheerily. "I just wanted to give you a heads-up I'm headed your way. Be there in five."

"OK. See you in a few."

Kate breathes deeply as she ends the call and gets up to check herself once more in the hall mirror for good measure. Then, there's a knock at the door. Her stomach lurches up to her throat as she answers it.

"Hi!" says Kai, looking gorgeous in an understated pair of black board shorts, a cobalt blue t-shirt, and a pair of black waterproof deck shoes.

"Come on in," waves Kate.

"Ah, the memories," Kai says nostalgically, giving the place a once over. "Great view from the lanai, too, isn't it?" he adds peering out the glass doors of the living room to the ocean beyond.

"It is. I've already spent quite a lot of time out there!"

"You look beautiful," says Kai.

"Thank you," Kate laughs nervously. "You do too."

OMG! Why did I just say that? thinks Kate.

"Let's get our beautiful selves on the road, shall we?" Kai suggests charmingly, prompting them both to laugh. "It's a fantastic day to be on the water!"

"I couldn't agree more," Kate says, as she reaches to grab her tote from the coffee table.

"Here, let me," offers Kai, as he takes Kate's heavy bag.

"Mahalo," Kate smiles, still a little nervous about what will happen next.

But Kai's easygoing and friendly manner as they make the short drive to Hanalei Pier puts Kate's imagined fears to rest.

"How long have you been rafting and sailing?"

"Since forever," says Kai. "I really can't remember a time when I didn't."

"With your work, do you get to go out regularly?"

"Oh, sure. I work about three to four shifts a week, then the rest of the time is my own. So, when I'm off, I'm either out on the water or playing in the garden."

"You garden?" asks Kate curiously.

"What? I don't look like a gardener?" Kai smiles.

"Well, I don't know," shrugs Kate sweetly. "What do you like to grow?"

"All types of fruits and veggies, tropical flowers and trees."

"Do you cook?"

"Well, I wouldn't exactly say 'cook,' but I grill," announces Kai proudly.

"Typical male," laughs Kate.

"Oh yeah?" Kai is amused. "Must be something primal about cooking over a fire." Kai gives her a delicious smile that makes her want to melt, scream for joy, and call Cindy on the spot.

"You like to cook though, don't you? Those dishes you made for Olivia's and Malie's barbecues were really delicious."

"Mahalo," says Kate. "Yes, I love to. I always have. I grew up helping my mom prepare meals, and we did a lot of entertaining with family and friends. I like playing around in the kitchen after spending most of my waking hours on a computer. I find it really relaxing."

"You're really quite a creative then . . . with your writing, photography, and cooking," observes Kai.

"That's very perceptive of you," Kate returns playfully.

"Well, I like to say that as a physician, between my training, meeting, and treating so many patients, I've become somewhat of an expert in Homo sapiens."

"Oh, really?"

"Well, at least that's what my sister says, although in more condescending terms when I tell her what's what."

Both Kate and Kai laugh out loud.

"I'm glad to see you can laugh at yourself."

"Yes, a little self-deprecation now and then is always a good thing," says Kai as he flashes her one of his devastating smiles.

He's so charming, thinks Kate, *so genuine and completely comfortable in his own skin.* Kate doubts that he fretted over their date like she did. Naturally, she also can't help but compare him to Jason.

Kai's life is focused on healing people, in growing things in his garden, and in exploring the ocean; those are his loves and his passions. Jason's were finding the next windfall deal, closing out the competition, being seen at the right places wearing the right clothes, and presenting the right image. Kate wanted to believe he was good to her and shared a lot with her, however, when it came right down to it, he always put himself first.

Now, with more perspective, Kate realizes that although Jason said he loved her, and perhaps he did in his own way, he also might have said that to control her, to get her to do the things he wanted, the way he wanted. He obviously led her to believe they would someday be married and share a life. But when it came right down to it, he abandoned her without a second thought. He hadn't called her since the night of their official breakup, and she wasn't sure if he knew about her mother's passing. If she had ever meant anything real to him at all, extending his condolences to Kate and her family would've been the least he could've done. And he hadn't.

THE WATERS ARE CALM AND CRYSTAL CLEAR as Kai's 24-foot inflatable, motorized raft propels the pair forward into Hanalei Bay.

Almost immediately, Kate begins to snap shots of the beautiful coastline with its jagged peaks and aquamarine waters.

"This is the most amazing place I've ever seen!"

"That's what I tell myself every day. I've seen many beautiful places around the world, but I always feel blessed to call Kauai home."

"I can see why," says Kate. "You know what I find most fascinating?"

"What?"

"When you're out in nature like this, there are almost no traces of the modern world . . . and you can get really tuned in. Know what I mean?"

"That's precisely what I'm talking about when I say I'm blessed to call it home."

"I can feel the 'mana,' as the Hawaiians call it."

"Well, since it's been around for six million years and it's Hawaii's oldest island, it's no wonder."

"I've been reading that Hawaii's Polynesian founders were very spiritual people, and believed that the gods and spirits of their ancestors controlled the elements of nature."

"That's right," agrees Kai. "The ancient Hawaiians believed in the importance of living in balance with nature, and of honoring Mother Earth and their ohana. In fact, I'm not sure if you know this, they even embraced the idea that their loved ones live on after death, and surround and guide their ohana on Earth."

Kate feels those familiar tingles as she listens to Kai speak. She has a feeling that she suddenly wants to cry, not from sadness, but happiness. She is deeply touched.

"Are you OK?" Kai asks, seeing the emotions registering on her face.

"Yes," says Kate, as she swallows hard. "That was so beautiful, what you just said, and the way you said it."

"We are all connected with a responsibility to one another that transcends the physical into the spiritual realms."

"It's my belief too," states Kate. "And the part about our ancestors always being with us, even when they have passed . . . The other night I read over some short stories I wrote when I was a kid, and I actually mentioned that in one of my stories."

"Well, then, you've got a Hawaiian spirit," Kai says, smiling at Kate fondly.

"Maybe it's why I feel such an affinity to the island."

Kate and Kai are both silent for a moment as they take in the sacred vistas. Kai looks at Kate, as if he is about to speak, but he holds back. Kate notices, but she gives him his space and just smiles sweetly.

"There's a place over there that's great for snorkeling," says Kai, pointing ahead. "Do you like to snorkel? I brought gear for both of us."

"I can't think of anything I'd rather be doing more," beams Kate.

As Kai and Kate explore the colorful sea life beneath the ocean's surface, they point out various beautiful marine creatures to one another. They snorkel at different locales for several hours until their stomachs begin to growl with hunger. Then they take a break and board the raft to partake in the picnic lunch Kai packed.

"Turkey and swiss never tasted so good," Kate declares, as she washes down a bite of the sandwich with a huge gulp of bottled water.

"There are also some fresh cut veggies and apples in the backpack to munch on, so be my guest," says Kai.

"Is everyone in your family into water sports?"

"Well, Malie and Aukai enjoy sailing, and like me, they go in for all types of water sports. Dad and I used to like to sail and fish together . . ." Kai trails off nostalgically.

"Used to?"

"Yeah, well, my dad and I, we really don't see eye to eye anymore."

"I'm sorry."

Kai looks at Kate, unsure if he should share.

"You don't have to tell me why if you don't want to," says Kate, noticing Kai's hesitation.

"No—it's cool. I don't tell a lot of people this, but I can already tell I can trust you," Kai says. "A few years ago my mom and I went sailing, and all of a sudden the weather changed. The ocean got quite turbulent, and she slipped and hit her head hard and . . ." Kai stalls and clears his throat, remembering. "Then she was gone, just like that. There was nothing I could do."

"I'm so sorry, Kai," murmurs Kate. "That must have been especially hard on you, to have her pass so suddenly like that."

"It was."

"Malie had mentioned to me that your mom died in an accident. But what happened between you and your dad?"

"He didn't want her to go out sailing with me that day. I was insistent, so he blames me, and I think we both blame ourselves. I know I do, anyway. We had a huge fight about it after the funeral and said some pretty tough things to each other, and well, I don't know, things have never been quite the same."

"It was an accident. You understand that, right?"

"I do, but it's more complicated than that," sighs Kai with such a sad look on his face. "I miss her, so much," he adds with longing.

"I know exactly how you feel," Kate replies as she places her hand over his, hoping to provide some solace.

"I know you do," says Kai, tightly grabbing hold of her hand.

It's 5:00 p.m. by the time Kai pulls his slate gray Land Rover into the cottage's driveway. Both he and Kate have a healthy glow about them, thanks to the day in the sun.

As they sit there for a minute, not wanting the day to end, Kai takes Kate's hand. His hands feel firm and warm as he gently entwines his fingers with hers.

"I have to get home and get ready for my shift at the ER. Would you like to do this again?"

"Yes, I would."

"There's a slack-key concert in Hanalei this Saturday starting at one o'clock. We could pack a picnic lunch and head over there to listen to some great music. I think Malie and Aukai will be going at some point as well, so maybe you'd like to go out to dinner with them afterward?"

"That sounds like fun," beams Kate. "I'd love it."

"I really had a wonderful time today."

"So did I."

Then, quite naturally, as they hold hands, Kai leans in to kiss Kate. As they touch, they both feel an exciting, warm connection. For a brief moment, their open lips invite their tongues to gingerly mix. The sensation takes Kate's breath away.

"I'll call you tomorrow, and we'll figure out the details for Saturday," says Kai as he gives Kate's hand once last squeeze and kisses it.

"Sounds good," smiles Kate. "Till Saturday then," she adds as she opens the car door and waves good-bye.

27

Saturday is only a few days away, but it feels like a lifetime to Kate. Still, having to wait to see Kai gives her something to really look forward to. Besides, she's got quite a lot to explore as she enjoys the newfound freedom from her customary workday routine.

Kate adds a few more gorgeous color shots from her recent jaunt into Hanalei to her laptop portfolio. She's excited to show it to Sukey today when she visits her at The Princeville Gallery.

The portfolio, which Kate started a few years back, is full of images from Long Island's North Shore. There are stunning photos, both summer and winter shots, of the area's pristine beaches and quaint towns, as well as a plethora of gorgeous culinary shots, sunsets, landscapes, and other vistas and images that have inspired Kate.

As she packs up to head off to the gallery, a wave of doubt washes over Kate, and she begins to wonder if her work will be good enough for Sukey to want to show it. She takes it as a good sign when she pulls up and scores a parking spot right in front of The Princeville Gallery.

Maybe this will be easier than I think, Kate hopes.

"You have a great eye," notes Sukey, clicking through Kate's electronic photo gallery.

"Mahalo. I have to admit, I was a little nervous about sharing my artwork with a professional. Other than the occasional shot I take during one of my interviews that happens to work out for the magazine, usually only family and friends get to see my photos."

"Well, I mean it. You're great with light and composition," says Sukey, as she gazes intently at the on-screen images.

Kate, standing and looking over Sukey's shoulder, decides to give her some space and begins to wander around the gallery, perusing the myriad of paintings and photographs that hang on the walls. Works of local artists, as well as those from around the world, are displayed. The central theme, however, is that all of the images depict island life and scenes from coastal living, from Kauai and the Hawaiian Islands to other tropical areas.

"Kate, I'm seeing some things here that I'd like to showcase in the gallery," Sukey calls out.

"What? Are you serious?"

"I'm dead serious," says Sukey, still looking carefully at the images.

"Well . . . I'm honored," stammers Kate.

"Great. Maybe we can even make prints along with some special edition note cards to sell. We have a vendor that does that for us."

"Seriously? I don't know what to say!"

"We'll have to come up with a price that works," continues Sukey. "Most of our note cards sell for six dollars. Our matte prints vary in price, depending on if they're framed or not. We can think about that and talk more. You keep 75 percent of your sales, and we keep a 25 percent commission."

"Works for me," Kate replies excitedly.

As Sukey continues to view the images, Kate's mind begins to reel. She walks about the gallery viewing her competition in a new light. On the walls are moonlit seascapes, recognizable Kauai landmarks in chalk, oil, and pastels, and portraits, as well as still life paintings. Kate hones in on a beautiful watercolor of the Hanalei Pier.

"Oh my God!" she gasps when she sees the artist's name.

"Everything, OK?" asks Sukey.

"Yes, fine. This painting here . . . it's lovely."

"Ah, yes, that's a local artist, too—one that will always remain very close to my heart."

"I know," answers Kate, staring at the work, overcome with emotion.

"You do?"

"It's Leilani, Kai and Malie's mother. I picked out a print of hers at The Plumeria Café on my first trip to Kauai before I even knew who she was."

"Well, there's that eye of yours again in action."

"Strangely enough, the print was of the cottage where she lived with her husband, and where I'm staying right now . . . and actually, I was drawn to the cottage and took a photo of it before I even got the print!"

"Now, isn't that something? Well, actually, no. I believe in synchronicity. To me something like that means that you're on the right path, so just follow the signs."

"You think so?"

"Absolutely."

"That's how I look at it too," smiles Kate. "It's good to have confirmation from someone else, though. It's just amazing when it happens, isn't it?"

"Amazing *and* affirming," Sukey heartily agrees.

When Kate gets back to the cottage later that afternoon she calls Cindy. "Can you believe it, Cindy? Some of my photos are actually going to be displayed for sale in The Princeville Gallery!"

"When opportunity knocks, open the door girl. Speaking of that, how's the *hunk*? Has he knocked down any of your doors yet?" asks Cindy with a lascivious tone.

"When I get to know him better, I'm going to tell him you called him that," jokes Kate.

"Please do," quips Cindy. "I have the photos to prove it. I especially loved that one where he's shirtless on the raft. Yummy yum yum!" squeals Cindy like a schoolgirl. "Don't tell Vinnie I said so, though. Actually, do tell him, it might get him motivated to go work out."

"You are evil," laughs Kate.

"Speaking of *working out* . . ." Cindy says suggestively.

"Enough! No, we haven't!" exclaims Kate, stopping Cindy in her tracks. "We won't either, unless I know he's serious about me. I don't care how hunky a man is."

"Really?" asks Cindy incredulous.

"Really!" affirms Kate.

"Geez, and I thought I was going to live vicariously through you," Cindy laments. "Truth be told, I hear ya. After Jason, you have to be sure your guy is not just stringing you along, and that he really means business. Make sure his heart and mind are in sync. The rest will follow. Just remember, when it does happen, I want *details*."

"Cindy, I beg your pardon—I don't kiss and tell!" exclaims Kate.

"I don't need a complete blow-by-blow—oops, poor choice of words," howls Cindy with laughter. Kate chimes in, laughing so hard she has to wipe a tear from the corner of her eye.

"But a few tantalizing tidbits would be appreciated," continues Cindy.

"OK, now that I can handle."

On Friday, Kate leisurely sips her morning coffee at the kitchen countertop as she reads and sends emails from her laptop. Every so often, she notices quick movements and bursts of light from the corners of her eyes.

"What the heck?" she says out loud after another swoosh of brightness interrupts her typing.

Kate's cell, sitting beside her computer starts to vibrate and ring its tropical melody.

It's Kai! Kate thrills at seeing his name pop up on her phone's display.

"Hello," she answers nonchalantly.

"Hey, beautiful, how are ya?" Kai asks, breezy and happy.

"Hi Kai, I'm good. How are things in the ER today?"

"Same old, same old. Coughs and colds, a few fractures, nothing major at the moment. Just wanted to check in about tomorrow. OK if I drop by about twelve thirty?"

"Sounds good."

"It will probably be best to park at the cottage, then walk into town. The concert's in the center of Hanalei, and parking will be impossible."

"OK."

"What's on your agenda for today?"

"Well, I thought I'd take a leisurely walk into town, maybe do some window shopping, perhaps pick up some groceries, then walk to the pier and see if I get inspired to take more photos or maybe write some ideas out for a novel."

"Sounds like a great way to spend the day," says Kai. "Might be a good idea to pack an umbrella, too. As I'm sure you know, afternoons here usually bring showers."

"Good thinking, I just barely missed one the other day. At least when it rains here, the sun follows right after. Who knows, maybe I'll get lucky today and snag a shot of a rainbow."

"You just might. I think you've got a lucky star watching over you," Kai says tenderly.

Kate hears Kai's name being paged over the hospital PA system.

"I have to run, but have a beautiful day. Aloha for now!"

"You, too, aloha!"

Kate refreshes her cup of coffee with the hot brew still sitting in the coffee maker and plays back the conversation with Kai in her mind. His voice sounded clear and crisp. She can feel he has a good heart when she talks to him; it comes through not only in his physical presence and how he lives his life, but also in his voice.

Her thoughts then run back to Jason. Had she known then what she knows now, she realizes there were things in Jason's demeanor that would give her pause if she met him today. There was something in his choice of words and actions, as well as the intonations and cadence of his voice that would cue her in to the fact that he could be selfish and not necessarily aboveboard. Experience and retrospect. The important thing is to process, learn, and look ahead.

That is exactly what Kate intends to do, she thinks as she plans her afternoon activities and decides to get organized with a shopping list. On her laptop, she scrolls through a file of personal recipes that she's developed. Inspired by some of the tasty treats at The Plumeria Café, she feels the desire to play in the kitchen and whip up some of her own concoctions—maybe adding in some new tropical ingredients to some of her favorite standards.

She settles on one of her basic whole-wheat muffin recipes to which she'll add in fresh fruit—maybe some banana, pineapple, and macadamia nuts, or even some organic dark chocolate morsels. Yum. She's excited to make something fabulous to bring to the picnic to share with the group tomorrow. Looking through the kitchen cabinets, she finds a food processer.

Perfect for blending ingredients for a sundried tomato hummus appetizer to serve with crudités, thinks Kate. She adds the following to her list, "Garbanzo beans, tahini, garlic, lemons, basil leaves, sundried tomatoes, fresh veggies."

Those treats, and perhaps some fresh pineapple slices for dessert, will be a perfect complement to the grilled chicken and coleslaw that Kai said he'd pick up.

The muffins smell heavenly as Kate pulls them out of the oven with two large quilted mitts. Hungry now from both her shopping expedition and also from skipping lunch earlier, Kate puts a kettle of water on the stovetop and opens the recently purchased box of cinnamon chai tea.

She takes a tea bag out of its clear wrap and places it into a large ceramic coffee mug decorated with colorful tropical blooms. Carefully removing one of the oversized muffins from the tin and placing it onto a matching tropical plate, Kate waits for the kettle to sing.

Minutes later, with her snack in hand, Kate walks through the great room out onto the cottage's front lanai and sits in a large wicker chair. As a gentle rain falls, she revels in her world of cinnamon chai happiness and savors every bite of her heavenly muffin creation.

Later that afternoon, with the rain still falling without sign of letting up, Kate sprawls out comfortably on the great room sofa and begins to jot down potential ideas for her future novel. After an hour or so passes, the rain finally subsides, and beautiful natural light pours in through the windows. Kate grabs her camera in order to snap a few photos of the muffins to record with the recipe. This one's definitely a keeper to add to her ever-expanding database of culinary creations.

Wanting to find just the right lighting to make the muffins look as scrumptious and attractive as possible, Kate stages several on a pretty white plate. She cuts one muffin and places it in front of the others to display the chunks of pineapple, dark chocolate chips, and nuts.

Perfect composition, she thinks.

Kate snaps away at various angles until she is pleased she's got her shot. She then downloads the images to her computer and, satisfied with the results, opens a new Word file to begin documenting the recipe ingredients and preparation instructions.

As she drops the file with the muffin photo and recipe into a larger folder with at least a hundred of her other creations, she has a lightbulb moment. *Why not start a recipe blog?* With a blog she'll be able to share her creations with friends and family, and anyone else that might be interested.

Edward is always looking for added value for the online edition of the magazine, and this blog would undoubtedly incorporate my work influences as well as my photography and cooking passions. Maybe I could approach him with the idea of incorporating it into the online site?

With a knack for design, as well as a the technical skill she's acquired working with *New York View's* digital edition, Kate begins to form ideas for her new blog. The first step is choosing a domain name. Kate plays around with a few ideas, and then finds an available URL, *thewriterspantry.com*.

As Kate spends time perusing the sumptuous photos of delectable dishes, she becomes increasingly aware of her own need for sustenance. Her neck and back are also aching due to the long stretch at the keyboard.

She powers down her computer and heads towards the kitchen. For dinner, it's a simple tuna salad mixed with a little mayo, red onion, and freshly squeezed lemon juice served over a mix of lettuce and sliced carrots, diced tomato, radish, and cucumber.

As Kate sits at the kitchen table enjoying her salad and the view outside the bay window, the microwave turns on, light and all. Kate hears the noisy rumbles of the circular glass microwave dish turning in the empty oven.

"How can that be?" Surprised and shocked, Kate gets up to check the microwave. She presses the "stop" button and opens the oven door. There's nothing inside but the glass dish.

How odd. The microwave was definitely off and it just turned on like that, thinks Kate as she closes the oven door. Kate looks around the kitchen, then the great room.

What am I doing? There's no one here! Physically anyway, she thinks.

"Well, you definitely got my attention," Kate says out loud. "I'm not afraid, and I like the fact that you're around, but don't do anything that will really freak me out, OK? Mom, if that's you, hi! Guardian angel, if that's you, hi too!" Kate chuckles as she unplugs the microwave.

Okaaaay, Kate! Time to finish dinner and get a good night's rest for tomorrow.

28

Kate sleeps peacefully throughout the night and wakes to the sound of light drops of rain on the roof. Huddled beneath the comfortable, silky bed sheets and surrounded by warm, cushy pillows, she knows the precipitation will soon subside, and the sun will come out to reveal yet another glorious day.

Feeling completely rested and refreshed, her body is electric with positive energy, and she's excited that the day of her date with Kai has finally arrived. She swings from beneath the covers and propels herself out of bed to open the bedroom shutters.

In the kitchen, she enjoys her morning ritual, fixing her morning brew and signature yogurt and fruit parfait. As she leisurely goes about her business, her thoughts turn to what a luxury it is not to have to rush into the office and eat breakfast on the run.

Yes, living like this could become very addictive, she thinks.

After breakfast, Kate powers up her computer, full of new ideas for her blog, and wanting to sketch out more ideas for her novel. She laughs when she realizes that even when on vacation, her mind turns to some type of creative work.

Well why not? Vacations are supposed to give pleasure . . . to let you do what you love.

In fact, Kate feels she has plenty of time left on her trip to take part in different adventures. A portion of her delight in being in Kauai stems from the freedom it affords her to do as she wants, when she wants, and to explore—not only physical geographical landscapes and sights, but also her own internal geography.

She now decides that for the rest of the trip and beyond, she will make a commitment to spending at least two hours a day on her creative writing. Furthermore, that will always be her first order of business moving forward, even when she gets back to New York. Her ongoing daily agenda will also include a workout of some kind—a walk, a run, a gym session, *something*—for at least one hour a day. As a writer with long periods of time sitting in front of a computer, physical workouts are essential for health, focus, and stamina.

Then, she determines, after her agenda essentials are completed, and if she feels like it, she'll work on her blog, take photos, or do whatever else inspires her. While three hours a day commitment feels like a tall order, Kate decides it's important—even if it means getting up extra early. She is ready to stake a solid claim in her life and her future.

Glancing up at the wall clock, Kate realizes that in about an hour and a half Kai will be at her door, the thought of which brings a huge smile to her face.

Yes, it's going to be a very good day! She can feel it in her bones.

After her beach run, Kate showers, blow-dries her hair, puts on some understated makeup, and slips into a pretty jersey print sundress with comfortable beige wedge sandals. She packs her oversized tote with sunscreen, a foldable floppy SPF sunhat, sunglasses, sundry makeup items, her wallet, keys, and a small perfume atomizer of Christian Dior's J'adore perfume. Countless friends and colleagues have told her that the scent is irresistible on her—and that is exactly what she wants to be today.

"You smell delicious," says Kai as he gives Kate a quick peck on the lips before they head into Hanalei Town. Kai carries a wicker basket filled with goodies including Kate's delectable additions to their picnic menu.

"I'm really looking forward to the concert," continues Kai. "They have a great lineup in the slack-key guitar department."

"Oh, I love slack-key guitar music! The last time I was here I picked up an album by Paul Togioka, and I love it," Kate says as she rearranges the large blanket she carries for them to lounge on.

"Wow, I'm impressed. If you like his music, you'll love today. They'll have a number of artists and bands playing. It's always a great time."

"I bet. What time will Malie and Aukai be joining us?"

"Around two o'clock. Then after the concert, maybe around six or so, we'll grab dinner."

As Kai predicted, all of the performers are phenomenal. People enjoy the stellar music as they lounge about, eat, drink, converse, and dance on the lawn in the center of the town's marketplace.

At one point, Kai pulls Kate up from their picnic blanket and the two dance to the exotic beat and rhythms. Their bodies naturally blend in harmony together, and they both find it fun and arousing.

"You two are quite something out there," says Malie as she munches on one of Kate's homemade muffins. Aukai is busy conversing with a group of friends that sit on nearby blankets.

"Well, if you got it, flaunt it!" Kai grins, making his point by twisting his body this way and that in a sexy but funny fashion that make both Malie and Kate break out laughing.

"Yeah, you got the moves alright, geez!" kids Malie. Turning to Kate she adds, "Hey girl, these muffins are fab. I mean really yummy. Moist, cakey, almost like dessert. From what I've tasted of the recipes you've made so far, I must say I'm a fan. If you ever decide to stay in Kauai, I might just have to offer you a job behind the counter!"

"Oh, yeah?" Kate asks playfully. "Well you never know, I might just have to accept!"

This date with Kai is amazing! thinks Kate as she watches him interact with some of his friends. She appreciates the fact that she's had an opportunity to witness his funny and playful side, as well as his genuine affection for his sister and brother-in-law. *I feel so at home here. How am I ever going to be able to leave?*

For a second, she becomes nervous, worried about the future. Then she decides not to think too far ahead. She'll live in the moment for right now, appreciate what's happening, and take mental photographs and notes with her mind and senses.

This is what happy is, she thinks. *This is the good stuff.*

It's after 9:00 p.m. by the time Kai walks Kate back to the cottage. At the front door, they sweetly kiss. Before she can invite Kai in for tea, he tells her that he has to be at the ER first thing in the morning.

It's probably better, she thinks, going with the flow. *Let us both have time to process the day and our feelings.*

"Would you like to go to dinner with me Tuesday night?" asks Kai.

"I'd like that," answers Kate without missing a beat.

"I'd ask you out sooner, if it weren't for work," Kai explains. "I've got a busy next few days."

"No need to apologize," smiles Kate.

"I'll look forward to Tuesday," says Kai. "I'm going to take you to a restaurant that has incredible food, especially their fish, and even more spectacular views."

WHAT WAS INITIALLY JUST A SPARK is clearly now a flame. Kai calls Kate every day from the hospital to chat, even if it's just for a few minutes between patients.

When Tuesday night comes, Kate carefully selects her outfit—a simple yet casually elegant maxi halter dress in a silky stretch fabric with a gorgeous green, pink, and blue floral tropical print. It has a plunging neckline that plays up her great shape and clings to her in all the right places. She complements her outfit with a pair of strappy nude wedge sandals that are as comfortable as they are cute.

"You look gorgeous!" says Kai when he sees Kate in her beautiful flowing dress. Her hair cascades onto her shoulders, and her skin has a bronze glow.

"Mahalo, and you look very handsome and very Tommy Bahama, I must say," smiles Kate as she flirts comfortably with Kai. He looks killer in his beige khaki pants and a classy white linen Hawaiian shirt that accents the brilliance of his golden tan.

Kai can't resist Kate. He reaches out for her hand and kisses it, then playfully pulls her to him and they share a delicious kiss.

"Are you hungry?" Kate asks, breaking off the heated embrace.

Kai raises his eyebrows and smiles amusingly.

"For food!" laughs Kate.

"Oh, yeah, *that*," jokes Kai. "I am, let's go!"

For their date, Kai takes Kate to the top-rated Kauai Grill, located inside the luxurious St. Regis Princeville. The restaurant, which offers fresh, eclectic fare, is both romantic and impressive. The modern décor features dark, rich, zebrawood and natural, earthy hues, and is complemented by a dramatic fabric ceiling with a sparkling chandelier descending from its center.

Kate takes note of the spectacular panoramic vistas from the room's wall of circular windows. The skyline, which features unobstructed views of Hanalei Bay, is already turning magnificent shades of peach and purple as the sun slowly sets on the horizon.

An elegantly dressed hostess leads them to a window table.

"The sky is amazing tonight," Kate says.

"Mahalo, I ordered that just for us," smiles Kai as he pulls out Kate's chair.

"Would you like to see a wine list?" the hostess inquires, placing two menus down on the table.

"Thank you," nods Kai as the hostess hands him the wine list.

"Take your time, please. Your waiter will be by shortly."

"Much appreciated," Kai adds as an attentive busboy pours water in their glass goblets.

"White or red?" asks Kai.

"I'm a Chardonnay kind of girl, so I'd prefer white," Kate smiles.

"I noticed that from the barbecues, but I thought I'd ask. French, Californian, or Hawaiian?"

"Hawaiian!" answers Kate.

"You're on."

After they both look over the menu and decide to order the fresh catch of the day—a macadamia nut-crusted mahi mahi with a side of ginger rice and local grilled veggies—Kai orders a signature bottle of Symphony Dry from the Big Island's Volcano Winery.

"What made you decide to make writing your profession?" asks Kai, after listening to Kate talk about life at *New York View Magazine.*

"I always excelled in English and creative writing. In middle school and high school I wrote for the student paper, and journalism just became my thing. In college, I decided to make it my major."

"Always feature stories?"

"I've done a bit of everything—news, lifestyle pieces, women's issues, environmental, food, home and garden, you name it. I like learning about people, places, and things," says Kate, taking a sip of her water. "What was it that inspired you to become a doctor?"

Kai takes a moment to answer.

"My maternal grandfather. He was a doctor, and for birthdays and holidays, he always gave me gifts having to do with science and chemistry. He was in private practice, and sometimes I used to go with him to his office. He had me do all sorts of jobs. He died just after I did my residency, and looking back, I'm really grateful he got to see me graduate."

"I'm sure he was really proud of you. What made you choose to work in an ER versus a specialty?"

"I like the challenge of having to use my expertise to make a diagnosis and do what's necessary to help facilitate a patient's treatment. We see everything—from coughs and colds to water accidents, heart attacks, you name it. Once I leave for the day, though, everything pretty much gets left behind until my next shift."

"So you get to go home and chill without having to take the work home?"

"Something like that. Certain cases stay with you, though, and you find yourself getting more involved."

"How so?"

"A few weeks ago I handled a drowning incident. The little girl was only three, and it was just tragic."

"Oh, no."

"When it was concluded that she was brain-dead, and her parents made the gut-wrenching decision to take her off life support . . ." as he remembers, Kai's eyes get moist.

Instinctively, Kate reaches out to comfort him, and places her hand over his.

"Let's just say, I had a hard time sleeping that night, and I wound up going to the wake and funeral, which is not something we ER doctors normally do." Kai intertwines his fingers with Kate's.

"That must be rough. Some of the things you see."

"It is, and we train for them, but there are those times when it just really gets to you."

"That family was lucky to have you for their doctor," says Kate.

"Thanks. I always do try my hardest for the best outcome," Kai says, smiling so broadly at Kate, his eyes attentive and sparkling, that she almost feels like swooning.

He's divine, she thinks.

The waiter returns to the table with a bucket of ice and uncorks the Symphony wine, interrupting their connection momentarily and allowing their kinetic energy to slow. The waiter pours some wine in a glass for Kai to approve.

Kai sniffs the wine's aromatic bouquet and then takes a sip.

"Delicious."

The waiter proceeds to pour them each a glass.

"Huli pau!" says Kai as he lifts his glass in a toast to Kate.

"What's that you just said?"

"*Huli pau*," pronounces Kai slowly, "It means cheers!"

"*Huuli paau*," Kate repeats, drawing out the vowels, making sure to pronounce the words correctly as she touches her glass to Kai's.

Over an appetizer of crispy crab cakes and a green salad followed by their mahi mahi entrées, Kai and Kate talk about many things—from family and work, to their hopes and dreams for having their own families someday. All the while, the soft sensuous music and romantic candlelight add to the magic of the evening.

After dinner, Kai asks Kate to join him at his place for a nightcap on his oceanfront lanai. In another instance, Kate might have taken this opportunity to bow out of such an extended date, however, she feels that she and Kai are on the same wavelength.

She feels so comfortable with him, like she has known him forever, and the feeling is mutual. There's scintillating chemistry, and Kai's relaxed, easy manner puts her at ease in a way she hasn't been in a very long time—including her years with Jason.

He feels good, thinks Kate. *More than that, he feels right.*

For perhaps the first time in her life, Kate decides not to stress out about what she's doing or where things will lead. She feels a sense of well-being and peacefulness, and she tells herself, *That's what matters right now.*

Kai's handsome modern plantation style home is in Princeville, and like The Westin where she stayed on her first trip, it's perched on a cliff that overlooks the Pacific.

"Your place looks like a pictorial for a design magazine," says Kate as she peruses the large open floor plan, which showcases a long, glass retractable wall that overlooks the lanai to reveal a stunning water view.

"Thanks to Malie and my mom," Kai smiles. "I'm afraid I can't take any credit. If I decorated it myself, it would've been college male dorm chic instead of *Coastal Living*."

Kate laughs aloud.

Kai opens the retractable wall to the lanai and a welcome balmy breeze flows in.

"Ahh, it's just lovely tonight."

"Can I get you anything? Water? Juice? Some Cognac, perhaps?"

"I'm good for now," smiles Kate.

"Well then, how about a little walk along the shore?"

"Sure."

Kai and Kate slowly make their way down the cliff's steep staircase to the beach floor guided by the moon's rays and the soft lights that twinkle from homes that dot the hillside. Walking along the water's edge, they hold hands and talk until Kai pauses to gently brush several strands of Kate's windblown hair from her face.

Kate's heart skips a beat as she looks into Kai's soulful eyes. With their bodies close and their faces perfectly aligned, a passionate embrace follows naturally.

Kai's lips are tender and moist. Even though he probably shaved that morning, Kate can feel the slight, soft stubble of his beard, and that, combined with his warm kisses and the heat from his breath on her neck and ears, proves intoxicating.

"Now you're the one that smells delicious," says Kate as she breathes in Kai's cologne, which teases with a hint of sandalwood.

"Mmm," Kai moans as he grazes her bare shoulders with his fingers and lips. "You smell of, what is it now, plumeria?" he asks.

"That's my body lotion," Kate softly laughs as her excitement builds.

"You taste good too," he adds as he sensually kisses her shoulders.

"You're so beautiful Kate, inside and out," says Kai as he looks deep into Kate's eyes before they kiss again.

Kai pulls Kate gently to the sand, and they take their time as their hands and mouths continue to explore each other's bodies.

"Kate, I hope I don't sound corny saying this, but I feel like I've known you forever," Kai says, stopping for a minute to take a deep, lingering look into Kate's eyes.

"I feel the same way about you."

Kai reaches for Kate's hands, brings them to his lips, and covers them with kisses. "I want to spend as much time with you as possible. I don't want to see anyone else . . . only you. Can we do that, and see where it leads?"

Once again Kate feels his heart, and she knows he is sincere. She swallows hard before she speaks, and looks up to the full, gorgeous moon hanging low in the dark sky. She thinks of her mother's words then, and remembering her sage advice, she musters the courage to dare to speak her truth.

"Kai, I need to tell you . . . a few months ago, I was in a long-term relationship that ended because I thought we were on the same page, but it turns out we never really were."

"Tell me more."

"My boyfriend at the time told me he was interested in marriage and having a family, and that should things work out between us, we would be headed down that road in the not too distant future. One year led to another, and then another, and as it turns out, unbeknownst to me until recently, we actually were never on the same page."

"Kate, let me tell you something about me. There was a time when I just wanted to date . . . and I did. I've had my share of flirtations and aimless relationships. I'm not into that either. I've changed a lot since I first started dating, and I look deeper now—especially since my mom died. I know we've only known each other for a short time, but I do share that same vision of marriage and family for my life, and I'm interested in *you* that way, Kate. The only way we'll know, though, is to take a chance on each other. But I'm willing . . . if you are."

"What about the fact I'm only here for a few weeks?"

"We'll figure that part out together," says Kai.

"I'm not really a fan of long-distance relationships . . ."

"I agree, and I don't want any physical distance between us, but I have a feeling we'll find a way," smiles Kai as he notices the wheels turning in Kate's head.

Kate believes Kai, but there is a part of her that's beginning to wonder about her good fortune.

Can this amazing man be for real and be feeling the same things I'm feeling? Is this really happening to me? she thinks. She almost pinches herself to make sure she isn't dreaming.

"That guy, whoever he was, was a real jerk," says Kai.

Kate gives Kai a questioning glance.

"Yeah, he's a jerk because he let you go."

Kai rubs Kate's back and shoulders as they both look at the full moon in the sky.

"I love you, Kate . . . to the moon and beyond."

"What? What did you just say?" exclaims Kate, her mouth open in shock as she bolts upright.

Kai smiles at Kate's theatrical outburst.

"I love you to the moon and beyond. Even if you are a little clumsy and goofy," Kai laughs out loud.

"Clumsy and goofy?"

"Yeah, that day at the pier, when you stubbed your toe."

"You knew I was *that girl* when you saw me at Olivia's party?" asks Kate, incredulous.

Kai nods.

"And you didn't say anything?"

"I didn't want to embarrass you if you didn't want to bring it up. I figured we'd get around to talking about it, anyway."

"You are a gentleman," Kate says with a grin.

Kai smiles.

"Kai, what you said about the moon . . ." suddenly Kate swallows hard and becomes a little teary. "I'm sorry, I . . ."

"What is it?" asks Kai, as he grabs hold of her hand and pulls her close to him again.

"I love you to the moon and beyond is what my parents, and my mom and I used to say to each other."

"And do you then?"

"Do I what?"

"Love me that way like I love you?" he asks.

"I do, *to the moon and beyond*."

"Well, your mother must approve of me, then."

"Definitely," says Kate with a big smile, finally allowing herself to completely relax and revel in the delicious sensations and feelings as she surrenders herself to an ecstasy that she previously only imagined could really exist.

29

Later that night, a cool, gentle breeze flows through Kai's open bedroom window, through the white mesh curtains, causing them to dance about the room.

Kai lies awake next to Kate and watches her sleep. Her body and essence are so delicious to him, that he can't resist the urge to touch her. He gently plays his fingers over her bare shoulders; then, with the desire to embrace her so strong, he begins to plant a row of tiny kisses all the way up her back from her waist to her neck, and finally to her lips.

Waking up to this sweet aloha, Kate moans with pleasure. Kai slips his tongue gingerly through Kate's parted lips while his hands caress her arms and the sides of her body, and she returns the favor, rubbing Kai's strong, muscular arms and back.

"I'm sooo happy," she says softly into his ear.

"So am I," says Kai. "I love you."

"I love you, too."

Kai interlaces his hands and fingers with Kate's as he looks at her with unbridled desire. Kate lifts her body to his, mouth open, without words, asking for his lips again. Their bodies entwine harmoniously.

"Let's savor every moment," says Kai, teasing her with his mouth, tongue, and fingers, until they can no longer bear to be apart.

As they make love, Kate can't help but feel grateful for this gift, this pleasure. Both their hearts are full. Their passion, ignited now to the point of no return, mounts until its sweet orgasmic release. Afterward the two lovers, wrapped in each other's arms, lie still, relishing the lingering sensations of their lovemaking, and their love for one another, until they drift into a sweet sleep.

Kate is the first to wake the next morning. She slips out of bed without Kai being the wiser, pulling on his Tommy Bahama shirt from the previous evening that lies on a nearby chaise. It fits her perfectly, like a robe, falling just a few inches above her knees.

Some twenty minutes later, Kai wakes to kitchen noises, and sees that Kate is no longer next to him. He slips into his khakis and joins her in the kitchen.

"Aloha kakahiaka e ku'u ipo," says Kai as he kisses the back of Kate's neck.

"If you say so," grins Kate.

"It means, aloha or good morning, my love."

"So teach me, say that again."

"Aloha kakahiaka—"

"Aloha ka . . . kahiaka," repeats Kate.

"Good. Now the rest, e ku'u ipo," continues Kai.

"E ku'u ipo," pronounces Kate slowly.

"Now altogether, aloha kakahiaka e ku'u ipo."

"Aloha kakahiaka . . ." Kate pauses unsure, then without prompting, continues, "e ku'u ipo."

"Excellent. Say 'ipo' again, and slowly."

"Iiipooo," Kate puckers her lips in a round "o."

Kai, unable to resist Kate's pucker, kisses her lips.

"Hey, I'm trying to speak!"

"I like it when you try to speak Hawaiian."

"Oh, you do, do you? You'll have to continue to teach me."

"Whaddya makin'?" asks Kai looking into a large bowl of what appears to be cake batter.

"Buttermilk pancakes. I thought we could have them with some yogurt and fresh fruit."

"Mmmm. Yum."

"Help yourself to a cup of coffee," says Kate, who's clearly made herself at home.

"Don't mind if I do," chuckles Kai. "Can I help with anything?"

"Nothing really to help with," Kate replies. "But you can keep me company while I make 'em."

"Deal." Kai pulls up a chair to the center island. "You've been here three weeks now, right?" asks Kai as he sips on his coffee.

"Mmmhmm," nods Kate, flipping the pancakes with a spatula.

"So, if my calculations are right, you're only scheduled to stay for one more week."

Kate nods.

"Why don't you move in with me?"

Kate looks at him in shock.

"Since you're an editor and writer, maybe you could work something out with your magazine so you could do your job from here? If that doesn't fly, I can take care of things financially and maybe you can work freelance and start to write your novel. You wouldn't have to do anything or take just any job if it wasn't exactly what you wanted . . . but I guess if you really wanted to live in New York, I could take the medical boards . . ."

"Wow, you've really been thinking about this, haven't you?"

"I've been thinking about it since our first date."

"You have?" Kate asks as she places the pancakes onto a nearby dish.

"I felt you were the one for me from day one," he smiles affectionately.

Kate beams.

"Well, first, I really do love it here," smiles Kate. "I've been thinking too, and I think I might be able to work out something with the magazine . . . and as far as my novel writing, I've already put myself on a daily schedule."

"So?" Kai is hopeful.

Kate looks pensive.

"Tell me what's on your mind."

"I don't believe in living together before marriage. It's something that I don't feel is a good fit for me."

Kai runs his fingers through his hair trying to figure out how to put into words what he's thinking.

"I'm not just asking you to live with me," says Kai. "I, I . . ." Kate watches as Kai gets off his chair and walks around the island next to her.

He gets down on one knee and takes her hand, "Marry me, Kate. Let's get engaged, and take it from there."

Kate's mouth falls open. A million thoughts zip around her head. She's not prepared for this, and she's a bundle of emotions rolled into one—shocked, nervous, scared, thrilled, and overwhelmingly happy. For the first time in her life, words escape her.

"I love you to the moon and beyond. So one more time for the record, Kate, will you marry me?" asks Kai with such love and conviction it brings her back down to Earth.

"Yes, I will," she yelps, jumping into Kai's arms.

If she's honest with herself, she's known it from the moment they met, too. This is her moment. This is her man. This is her future, her husband-to-be. Nothing and no one has ever felt as right. Her mother had always told her "you will know," and now she did.

After breakfast, while Kai showers, Kate calls to share the good news with her sister Carla, and fills her in on every detail.

"He sounds amazing!" says Carla to her sister on FaceTime. "I'm so happy for you, Sis. I really am, and I don't want to rain on your parade, but you just met. Are you sure you're sure?"

"Yes," Kate replies. Her conviction quiets her sister's concern.

"Okay," says Carla. "I must say, I'm a little sad, though, that you'll be living so far away from us."

"I know," Kate responds empathetically. "I'm not going to become a stranger, you can rest assured. As a matter of fact, I'm going to talk to Edward. I think I can work out an arrangement with him for freelance work, and that will bring me to New York a few times a year at least. And then you, Frank, and Lucas can visit us in the summers and holidays and stay as long as you like. We'll FaceTime all the time, too. Don't worry; we'll work something out. It's too important for us not to."

"I love you, Sis."

"I love you, too," beams Kate.

"Well, in a total change of subject . . . you're not the only one who's moving out of town."

"What do you mean? Who else is moving?"

"Dad," says Carla.

"To Florida for a few months, he said that before I left."

"Well, actually . . ." Carla stalls.

"Carla, tell me," demands Kate. "What's going on?"

"I think Dad has found someone, too. He's already talking about . . . in the abstract . . . about maybe getting married again."

"*What?* You've got to be kidding, married again?" Kate is both shocked and disturbed. Kai notices immediately as he enters the kitchen. He rubs his wet hair with a towel.

"Kai, this is my sister Carla in New York," says Kate, introducing the two.

"Congratulations, Kai, nice to meet you."

"Aloha, Carla. Glad to know you, and I'm looking forward to meeting you in person," Kai says warmly. "You and Kate seemed to be involved in something important, so let me give you your space, and we'll talk more later." Kai mouths to Kate that he'll be in the great room.

Carla gives Kate a devilish smile when Kai is out of earshot and whispers, "Very nice, Sis. Well done."

Kate smiles, but then gets back to business. "So Dad's already dating someone? Mom only just passed away a few months ago. How can he move on so quickly? She was the love of his life."

"I hear this sometimes happens with men, especially after long, happy marriages. They just don't know what to do with their grief. I think he's just struggling and trying to find his way," says Carla.

"I can't help it, I'm upset. Maybe he just needs counseling?"

"Sis, I feel the same way. But you know how he is when he's got his mind set on something."

"Who is this lady? Does anyone know anything about her?"

"It's a sister of one of Dad's good friends. Her name is Peggy Montgomery. She's a year younger than Dad and lost her husband to cancer about four years ago. She lives on Long Island, but has a house in West Palm Beach, too."

Kate starts to rub her head, processing.

"Dad already asked Frank and me to meet her," Carla says.

"Really?"

"I'm sorry, Kate. I didn't want to tell you over the phone . . . and I certainly don't want to spoil your good news. I was going to tell you first thing when you got back."

"Maybe this thing with Dad will burn itself out?"

"Maybe, I'm trying to encourage him to take things slow. Try not to worry too much, Sis."

"I just don't want him to make any rash moves and get hurt."

"Neither do Derek and I."

"OK, I'll talk to you later, Carla. Call or text me if you hear more. Love you."

"Love you too, Sissy," says Carla, ending the call.

"AHHH!" Kate moans loud enough for the entire neighborhood to hear.

"Wow! That conversation sounded intense," Kai remarks. "I think I overheard that your dad is thinking about getting remarried?"

"I can't believe it."

"He's still in shock, Kate. After fifty years, he's grieving big time. Probably any Band-Aid will suffice at the moment. Give it some time. Whatever's meant to be, will be. He needs to find his own way through this, and no one else can do it for him."

"You think? That's what Carla said, too."

Kai feels Kate's pain and kisses her forehead. He wraps his arms around her, allowing her to sink into the comfort of his strong arms.

After Kai drops Kate off at the cottage, she immediately starts leaving phone messages for family and friends indicating she has some "good news" to share.

Derek calls back first and is stoked to learn not only about Kate's engagement, but also to tell her that his company has officially landed the Hawaiian Islands account, and he'll actually be visiting Kauai and the Big Island on a regular basis going forward.

Within a few hours, Kate has even worked out the details with Edward to continue with the magazine in a newly created position; writing feature lifestyle content, most of which will be stories focused on the Hawaiian Islands that will satisfy some of the magazine's new advertising sponsors. Once a quarter she'll also travel to New York to meet with staff, but most of her work will be done virtually. Her hours, no longer the usual nine to five, will be much more flexible, and that also works well for Kate. She'll make use of the gift of flexibility to work on her novel, and who knows, she might even take Malie up on doing some baking at The Plumeria Café to get a break from the computer.

"Way to go," says Cindy after she sheds a few tears upon hearing the news that Kate will be living in Kauai full-time.

"Don't cry," Kate chides.

"I can't help it, I'm gonna miss your face at work every day."

"Hey, we can talk by FaceTime every day, and Edward said he's going to have me fly in a few times a year. And then you and Vinnie can also visit anytime and stay as long as you want."

"Well, you better have that guesthouse done in my colors. I plan to crash often."

"Promise?"

"You bet. I love you kiddo, and I'm so happy for you. If anyone deserves happiness, it's you. You'll make a great wife."

As soon as Kate hangs up the phone with Cindy, Olivia returns her call.

"Hey, girlfriend. Sorry I didn't get back to you earlier, but things have been crazy around here. How are you? Are you having fun?"

"Ooooh yeah," says Kate, full of innuendo.

"OMG! Tell me, tell me," exclaims Olivia her voice now a few octaves higher.

"First, I want to thank you," Kate starts.

"Thank me?"

"For inviting me to stay in this amazing cottage and . . ." Kate hesitates looking for the right words in her excitement.

"Spill it girl, I'm getting gray hairs waiting for you already!" chuckles Olivia.

"For introducing me to Kai."

"Oh, my . . . Aaaah!" Olivia cries so loudly that Kate has to remove the cell phone from her ear. "You guys are a thing?"

"Yes."

Olivia continues to scream, until Kate flips the phone to speaker and puts it down on the kitchen table, far from her ear.

"I thought you'd react that way," Kate laughs.

"That is awesome!"

"It's more awesome than you know. I'm staying in Kauai . . . and we're engaged."

"Engaged?" asks Olivia, shocked and elated.

"These past few weeks, we've really gotten to know one another on a deep level, and well . . . we want to share our lives together. I love him so much, Olivia."

"I am sooo happy for you both. You are such dear people, and I'm so glad you found each other."

"I know," says Kate, so emotional now she starts to cry. "Mahalo."

Kate hears Olivia blow her nose on the other end, and through her tears, can't help but smile. It is wonderful to share such an emotional moment with her incredible friend.

"You don't have to thank me, Kate," Olivia says. "Let's just give thanks for this blessing."

"I am and I will, every day."

"I hope you know that I must insist on throwing you and Kai an engagement party at my house."

"Oh, no, we couldn't ask that of—"

"I insist! You met him at my home after all. Malie and Kai have been my friends forever, they're my ohana, and now you are too. We'll invite the usual suspects, and of course you can invite your family and friends. We'll talk more about it when I get back and plan to do it at a time that works best."

"Olivia—"

"I insist. After all, I feel like the fairy godmother here and I can't shirk my responsibilities. We'll make it a beautiful, festive, and intimate affair."

"Mahalo," says Kate. "You're the best."

Things were really coming together; her only concern now was in the dad department. They had been playing a game of phone tag all day. Finally, Kate sees Glen's number pop up on her cell's display.

"Dad! I've been trying to reach you. Where have you been?"

"Out, dear. I have a lot of spare time on my hands now, and I have to keep busy. Can't sit around waiting to die."

"Daddy!"

"Well, I could die tomorrow. I have to live for today. I may not have many years, you know."

"None of us know how long we're going to live. You should enjoy life, but shouldn't you give yourself the time to grieve?"

Glen falls silent for a minute, processing Kate's inference. Finally he says, "Your sister told you about Peggy, didn't she?"

"Dad . . ." Kate searches for the right words. She loves her father, and wants to be respectful, but she needs to express her feelings and her concern.

"You know how much I love you, Dad," she begins, "I just think a person can get into trouble rushing into something too quickly without the proper time to mourn, especially after such a long and happy marriage. Grief counseling can be a very—"

"I'm not going to any counselors," Glen states emphatically. "Never have and never will. The silence and memories in this house are enough to kill me," Glen adds as he starts to sob.

"Oh, Poppy, don't cry. Please, I don't want to upset you. You do what you need to. I know you were never one for hobbies, but maybe you could join a reading club, or a local group that dines and goes to the theatre. There are a million—"

"I'm not joining any senior groups," states Glen firmly. "They just sit around playing cards and moan about their ailments. They're all just a bunch of old fuddy-duddies."

"And after everything you had with Mom, you think this woman could be the one *too*?"

When Glen pauses, Kate doesn't quite know how to interpret the silence.

"Dear, no one can ever replace your mom. She was my life."

"Poppy, you know she is with you still, only now in spirit?"

"I guess."

"*She is*, and when you miss her, when you feel sad, talk to her, and she can hear you."

"You think so?"

"I know so."

30

"Kate, I heard on the news a bad storm is headed our way," comes Kai's voice over the phone.

"I heard that on TV, too."

"I should be at the cottage early evening before the heavy rain's expected. Might be a good idea not to go out if you don't have to. Need me to pick up anything on my way home from the hospital?"

"Nope, the fridge is pretty full."

"OK then, see you later. Love you."

"Love you, too."

The downpour and the heavy gales acting in unison cause a number of trees to drop their branches, and as a result, their limbs scatter haphazardly across the streets and landscapes.

Inside the warmth and protection of the cottage, Kate barely notices the menacing activity that takes place outside the kitchen window as she puts the finishing touches on a delicious Bolognese sauce to serve over penne pasta later that evening. She sighs with delight as she contemplates a romantic candlelit dinner with Kai in the cozy cocoon of the cottage.

Now that her work in the kitchen is complete, she removes her apron and sets it aside. She looks forward to spending the rest of the afternoon until Kai gets home curled up on the great room sofa with a mug of steaming apple cinnamon tea and her Kindle.

A BEAUTIFUL SPRAY OF RED ROSES sits in a tall glass vase by the bedside; the sweet floral scent permeates the room as do little beams of light that shoot through the bedroom's white wooden shutters and curtains.

Kate wakes with a feeling of peace and serenity. For a time, she lingers in bed, watching Kai sleep soundly next to her. As she listens to his rhythmic breathing, she remembers last night's lovemaking and the warm nest they created afterward as the rain pounded on the rooftop and windows. She feels blessed and thanks heaven for this gift.

Curious to see for herself what's happening with the weather outside, she gingerly slips out of bed and, careful not to wake Kai, puts on her robe. She walks over to the window and spreads the curtains a tad for a quick peek, and notices that yesterday's storm has vanished completely and the early morning's warmth is already drying the wet earth.

Knowing that Kai likes to sleep in as long as possible before rousing himself for work, Kate decides to go for a quick beachside morning run. Slipping into her jogging pants and baseball cap, she then straps on her waist pack with her cell phone and keys inside, and leaves the cottage as quietly as possible. As she walks across the lawn towards the shore, she sees tree branches, leaves, and other debris strewn about the still-wet landscape—more evidence of last night's imposing storm.

Towards the end of her beach run, Kate sees something sparkling protruding from the beige sand. She bends down and pulls the shiny object out of its resting place. Dusting the sand aside, Kate sees it's an antique locket that's missing its chain.

The face of the locket is magnificent. The exquisite marcasite cover has an intricate lotus flower blooming at the center. Kate opens the small clasp, and inside is a black and white picture of a man and a woman, which clearly must have been taken many years ago.

The man is a handsome, light-haired youth wearing a tailored suit. The lady in the photo is a beautiful young Hawaiian woman, who wears a lacy dress and floral headpiece. It is easy to see that this photo is a wedding photo, and the people in it are very much in love. Kate is drawn to their happy expressions. She takes note of the familiar tingly sensation that runs up and down her spine and places the locket into her waist pack.

When Kate returns from her run Kai is still sound asleep. She showers and changes in the guest bathroom. Once dressed, she heads into the kitchen to make breakfast. All the while, she keeps seeing swooshes of light out of the corner of her eyes.

Now that Kate is consciously aware of such unusual happenings, she has come to accept them as regular occurrences, and validation of the existence of life—and spirit—from beyond. Sometimes the meaning of these metaphysical intrusions are clear, other times they are not, but the one thing Kate knows for sure is that she is always fascinated by them. If there is a meaning to be found, she tries to ascertain it.

"Morning, sweet," says Kai as he comes up behind Kate and kisses her neck.

"Morning, sleepyhead," smiles Kate as she cuts up chunks of melon and pineapple. "Want some breakfast?"

"OK, maybe some of that fresh fruit and some toast," Kai says, looking at his watch. "I've got to get into the ER within the next hour. I'll be off around 7:00 p.m. though. Take you to dinner tonight?"

"It's a date," smiles Kate.

Later that morning, Kate carefully polishes the locket she found on the beach. Then she threads one of her silver necklace chains through the loop at the top. She clasps the locket around her neck and admires her reflection in the bathroom mirror. A surge of warm energy fills her heart, and once again, she sees a flash of light out of the corner of her eye.

"OK," Kate acknowledges out loud, "lots of energetic activity today."

"Hello!" she calls out. "You like my necklace do you? Well so do I," she chuckles.

Kate hears her cell phone ring in the bedroom and goes to answer it.

"Kate . . . I, um . . ."

Of course Kate saw his name on her cell as she answered it, but the voice on the other end of the line certainly doesn't sound like her love.

"You sound horrible, is everything OK?"

"It's my father. He had an accident in the rain last night, his car spun out of control . . ."

Kate's mouth falls open; she's almost unable to speak.

"Is he . . . ?"

"No, but he's in the hospital and going for tests."

"Oh, my. Is Malie there?"

"Yes, and Aukai's here too. Will you come?"

"Of course!"

"Meet me in room 332."

"I'm on my way."

Kate can't get to the hospital soon enough. "Thank you!" she says out loud as she slips into an empty visitor parking space directly in front of the emergency room entrance.

Kate runs into the hospital and frantically searches for room number 332. When she enters the small, private room she sees Kai. He sits alone in the back of the room, and looks extremely pale, as if he's about to be sick.

"Kai, is your dad . . . ?"

"No. He's going to be fine. It's me. I don't know why . . ." Kai chokes out as he tries not to cry. His efforts are futile, however, and his tears begin to flow freely. "I'm sorry."

"Don't be," says Kate, giving him a hug. "We're here to help one another."

"I'm a mess," he says. "I know you think I'm brave, but today I've been anything but."

"What do you mean?" Kate asks, pulling up a chair next to Kai.

"I've been helping out from behind the scenes, but I just can't seem to look my dad in the eye ever since my mom . . . well, you know the story."

Kate covers Kai's hand with hers.

"Kai, I respect your choices," begins Kate. "However, we both believe that we have an eternal soul connection to our ohana, and because of that, aren't we also bound to love, honor, and forgive? Isn't it our responsibility to find ways to make amends?"

As Kai considers what Kate says, he suddenly notices the locket around her neck.

"That locket—!"

"Oh, I found it on my beach run this morning. It was sticking out of the sand."

"Can I see it for a minute?"

"Sure," says Kate as she unclasps it and hands it to Kai.

Kai examines the outside of the piece and when he unclasps it to look at the photo inside, he gasps.

"Oh, my God!" he cries.

"What?" asks Kate, alarmed by Kai's response.

"I can't believe it," Kai says tearfully.

Kate looks at him, shocked and surprised.

"Kai, I don't understand . . . ?"

"This locket . . . it was *my mother's*."

"Your mom's?" Kate tries to wrap her head around this information.

"I can't believe you found it. My father had it custom made for her, and she never took it off. But *that day*, she lost it somehow in all the turbulence. We looked in every part of the boat, but couldn't find it."

Kai and Kate stare at the locket in silence for a time.

"I wonder if it's a sign?" Kai finally asks.

"It sure seems that way," nods Kate.

Kai starts to tear up again, and he and Kate embrace.

"Let's go see my father," Kai says. Taking a deep breath, and still clutching the necklace, he heads out the door.

As Kai and Kate walk down the hospital corridor, they see Malie and Aukai walking out of Kai's father's hospital room.

"He's resting," says Malie as she hugs Kai, then Kate.

"Is he still awake?" asks Kai.

Malie nods.

"I want to speak to him for a minute."

"You do?" Malie asks, a little surprised.

"Yes, with Kate."

"Okay," says Malie tentatively, but hopeful, as she looks at Kai, and then her husband. "Aukai and I were just going to grab a coffee in the cafeteria. We'll give you guys some privacy."

Kai nods, and taking Kate's hand, walks towards his dad's room.

"Are you sure you want me to be in the room with you?" asks Kate.

"Yes. There's nothing I plan on saying to my father that I can't say in front of you. Besides, I want him to meet you. Okay?"

"Of course."

Kai swallows as he gently opens the door. He and Kate step into the room, and Kai gently closes the door behind him. Bradford Stevens, a handsome, dignified man about the same age as Kate's father, lies in the hospital bed, his eyes closed.

Kai walks up to his father's bed, and Kate stands back watching. Seconds later, as if feeling his son's presence beside him, Bradford stirs in his hospital bed, and slowly opens his eyes.

"Hi, Dad," Kai says quietly, a little unsure of what his father's reaction might be at seeing him.

Surprised, Bradford blinks, wondering if he's seeing things or if his son is really there.

"Kai?"

"Yeah, Dad, it's me. How you feeling?"

"I've been better," answers Bradford tentatively.

"When I heard you had the accident. It sounded really bad at first. I . . . I just really wanted to see you," Kai says softly.

"I'm okay," Bradford replies, with a light smile blooming on his face. He's clearly touched, and glad to see his son.

There is silence between the men as they look at one another, not sure of exactly what to say to each other or how to say it.

"Dad, I'm so sorry for everything," says Kai after a few moments of silence. "I'm sorry I insisted mom come out with me on the boat that day and . . ." Kai wipes tears from his eyes. "I'm also sorry for some of the angry things I said."

Bradford nods slowly, accepting the apology.

"And I'm sorry I acted as though I thought you were to blame for your mother's death," Bradford says. "It wasn't your fault, Kai. Deep down, I knew it could've happened with anyone at the helm. You were right; there was nothing you could've done differently to prevent it. It was an accident."

"You tried to tell me that a number of times, but I was so stubborn and angry," says Kai. "At myself mostly."

"Sometimes in the heat of the moment, when we're upset or in grief, we can say things we don't really mean," Bradford remarks. "It's the anger, the frustration, and the devastation that comes out. Come here." Bradford holds out his arms to Kai. "I'm sorry."

"I'm sorry, too," says Kai, going to his father.

"I love you, son."

"I love you too, Dad."

The men embrace for a moment or two before Kai looks up at Kate, who is clearly touched by what she has witnessed between father and son.

"Dad, I want to introduce you to someone special," Kai adds, as he motions for Kate to come over to the bed. "Meet my fiancé, Kate."

"Your fiancé?" asks Bradford, surprised. "You're getting married?"

Kai nods.

"Aloha," Bradford smiles at Kate.

"Aloha," says Kate sweetly with a smile.

"Look," Kai shows his father the locket he holds in his hand.

Bradford takes the locket.

"What? Where did you find this?" Bradford asks incredulously as he examines the outside of the locket and then opens the clasp. Bradford sees the photo of himself and his wife on their wedding day. He bites his lip, his face emotional.

"Kate's the one who found the locket this morning when she was running on the beach. When she showed it to me, I told her it was Mom's."

As Kate watches Kai and Bradford, she begins to feel a sense of tremendous calm and peace infiltrate the room. Suddenly, she feels a hand touch her shoulder ever so slightly. She turns, but no one is there and the hospital room door is closed. Then she hears it.

"Kate! Kate!" an ethereal voice whispers into her ear. It's the same voice that spoke to her the very first time she saw the cottage on Weke Road. In the next instant, she hears another voice, and she knows immediately that it's her mother's, *"To the moon and beyond."*

Kate gasps, which causes Kai to turn in her direction. He motions for Kate to come closer.

"You OK?" Kai whispers.

Kate nods, too emotional for words. In another beat, Bradford starts to smile, then chuckle.

"Dad?" asks Kai questioningly.

"I'm chuckling because don't you think this would be just like your mother, finding a way to bring us back together *and* deliver a beautiful bride to you at the same time? She always loved a happy ending."

Kai nods, smiling nostalgically.

"What do you think, Kate?" asks Bradford.

"Makes sense to me," answers Kate, still processing everything that has transpired in this room. "I think our mothers are looking down on us from heaven, and they're very happy right now."

"Welcome, my dear, to our ohana," says Bradford as he places the locket back into Kate's hand, then pulls her in for a heartfelt hug.

31

"You look gorgeous!" exclaims Olivia as Kate primps in Olivia's dressing room.

"You really like it?"

"It's stunning."

Kate wears a gorgeous white jersey halter dress. A delicate tropical pattern in teal blue adorns the bottom of the skirt, which rests just above her ankles, showcasing a pair of sexy, strappy sandals. Her hair flows in a cascade of curls about her shoulders, and a white plumeria with a sunburst yellow center is tucked behind her left ear in a traditional Hawaiian sign to indicate that she is "taken."

Olivia also looks phenomenal. She wears a stunning silk emerald green dress adorned with sparkling silver jewelry and strappy silver sandals.

"Come, let's get you outside. Kai wanted to grab some time with you alone before the guests arrive."

"Just a few more minutes. I have something for you."

"For me?"

"Yes, for all you've done. You've been so kind and generous; now it's my turn to make you smile. I had Sukey help me custom frame some of my photos that you said you loved. I hope you like them," says Kate as she undrapes the pile of framed photos in various shapes and sizes. She proceeds to show Olivia each exquisitely framed and mounted photo. The first picture showcases exquisite and dramatic lighting on the majestic mountains surrounding the pier at Hanalei Bay.

"Ooh!" exclaims Olivia with delight.

The second is a shot of the cottage on Weke Road, where the sun's rays peek through the trees and foliage and cast a heavenly golden hue, surrounding the cottage and accentuating the vibrant colors in an ethereal glow.

"I'm speechless!" Olivia says, as she gazes at the magnificent photo.

Other photos feature several exotic florals bursting with color taken at the Princeville Botanical Gardens and the Na Pali Coast's jagged, dramatic cliffs and aquamarine waters. All in all, there are nine images framed in woods and colors to match Olivia's home and office.

"I am so completely blown away!" exclaims Olivia. "They're gorgeous, and now I see why you asked me which ones were my favorites. Mahalo!"

Kate and Olivia embrace.

"Come, let's go, Kai's waiting," says Olivia as she leads Kate out into the great room.

Olivia's house is beautifully decorated for the evening's engagement party. Fresh cut tropical flower arrangements are placed in strategic points around the great room and atmospheric, tiny white lights give off a magical, romantic glow.

"Hey, beautiful!" Kai says when he sees Kate. "You look stunning."

They kiss briefly.

"And very sexy I might add," he whispers huskily in her ear.

"Mahalo," murmurs Kate in a sultry voice, admiring Kai as well. "You look very handsome," she smiles seductively.

Kai looks absolutely gorgeous in his white linen pants and fabulous white Tommy Bahama shirt with a tropical pastel print. Kai smiles and takes Kate's hand as he leads her out onto the lawn close to the ocean's edge, where the sun, low on the darkening horizon, casts off magnificent rays of color over the still waters.

"I wanted to do this in the place that's special to us, and where I first officially met you," says Kai as he pulls out a little red velvet box from his pants pocket.

"Kai!" Kate gasps with delight, knowing full well what's inside.

Kai opens the lid to reveal an exquisite engagement ring. The custom white gold stunner has a diamond center surrounded by a circle of smaller diamonds. The band also displays an intricate diamond encrusted pattern.

"It's gorgeous!" Kate exclaims excitedly as Kai places the ring on her left finger. "It looks like the design on your mother's locket."

"It is. I had a Na Hoku jeweler create it. The design represents 'lani' or 'heaven' and the continuous flow of life and love."

"I love it!" exclaims Kate joyously.

"I'm glad you like the Weke cottage, Poppy. I knew you would," says Kate.

Glen, the first of the guests to arrive for the engagement party, sports a slight tan, having arrived in Kauai a few days ago. He looks handsome in his navy linen shirt and white pants.

"I'm really enjoying staying there, hon. It's a very special place," Glen says. "I hope you guys will always have it for your family to enjoy—it's a keeper."

Kate and Kai share a smile before Kai responds, "Actually, we both agree. In fact, Kate and I had a talk with my father, Malie, and Aukai, and we've decided that my home in Princeville will be used as a rental, and Kate and I will make Weke Road our new home. The paperwork is already in process."

"Well, you two may just have to build an extra wing," says Glen. "If this week is any indication, I'm sure you're going to have a constant stream of family and friends visiting."

"Actually, Kate and I are already talking about how we could add on to the cottage," said Kai. "The more, the merrier. Ohana is always welcome!"

"I'll remind you that you said that," chuckles Glen.

Kate's father, brother, sister, and their families, as well as Cindy and her husband Vinnie, and Edward and his wife, Meredith, have all flown into Kauai for the weeklong celebration of preplanned activities. With the exception of Edward, who was given a complimentary villa from one of the magazine's advertisers to enjoy, family and friends' accommodations are split between the Weke cottage and Kai's home in Princeville.

"Do you mind if I take my beautiful daughter for a brief walk before the other guests arrive?" asks Glen.

"Not a problem. I'll go inside and see if there's anything I can do to help Olivia and Grant."

Glen takes Kate's arm as they walk towards the ocean.

"You look stunning my dear," he kisses her cheek.

"Thanks, Poppy."

"You've got a good man in Kai. Your mother would be so happy."

"I know . . ." pauses Kate. "Poppy, I believe she's around. I feel her all the time. I even get little signs."

"You do?"

"There's no question. That's one of the reasons I love it here. I can feel her. I can feel all our relatives that have passed. I seem to feel them here more than anywhere else. Maybe it's because we really live in nature here? I don't know."

Glen begins to look a little sad. He misses his wife.

"Don't be down, Poppy. You can talk to Mom anytime, anywhere, and she'll hear you."

"You've told me that before. You really believe it?"

"Yes. I know it to be true."

"A few times when I've sat reading and thinking or listening to music in the afternoons, I've actually heard her call my name, or at least I think I have."

Kate smiles. "You too? So have I, on several occasions," she says. "I think Kai's mother is here with us too."

"What makes you say that?"

"See this locket? It belonged to Kai's mother. I found it after a storm on the beach, and it had been lost at sea for many years. What are the odds of that? Kai took it as a sign to mend fences with his dad. It's that type of synchronicity I'm talking about. There have been so many other examples, too."

"Ah, the ways of heaven are a mystery, aren't they?"

Kate nods.

"I'm sorry, honey, if you were hurt when I started to date so soon after your mother passed."

Kate swallows hard.

"I loved your mother so much. She was everything to me. I guess I'm just a foolish old man looking for comfort, and perhaps I'm a little afraid of being alone. I'm getting stronger though, and I promise I won't do anything rash."

Kate looks at her sweet Poppy. Still a strong, handsome man, but now that she is an adult, he appears to her to be more vulnerable, with human frailties. His eyes hold deep sadness and pain, which he is unable to mask. He tugs at her heartstrings. She grips his arm more tightly.

"Dad, I know you're just trying to find your way through the pain. Each of us has our own process, our own journey. I have to admit, your being single takes some getting used to, but I love you, and I support you. Just take your time, learn to enjoy your life. Find joy in the little things, so that whatever you do, or whatever choices you make, you do what's really right for you."

"Who sounds like the parent now?"

They both laugh. As Kate looks at her father, she realizes how comforting it is to have him close. What a blessing that they can share this time and place together, and she hopes that she will have him by her side for many years to come.

Life holds many journeys, no matter what our age, she thinks as she reaches for her father's hand. Her dear sweet Poppy, who is now looking for solace as he navigates new, unexplored horizons . . . much like she had done until she found her direction, her home, and her love.

THE NEXT MORNING AFTER the engagement party festivities, Kai, Bradford, and Glen hang a beautiful hand-painted oval plaque next to the Weke cottage's front door. On it the name "Marisol" is written in beautiful calligraphy. The word appeared to Kate in a recent dream, which prompted her to look up its meaning. She discovered that it's Spanish and is a shortened form of Maria de la Soledad ("Mary of the Solitude"), another name given to the Blessed Mother.

Both Kate and Kai love the meaning, as well as the symbolism and spiritual mana as it relates to their own beloved mothers. So, with "aloha," known as a greeting given with love and affection, and all the other wonderful meanings the word encompasses, and "hale" meaning house, the plaque reads *"Aloha,"* above a spray of tropical blooms, under which the words *"Hale Marisol"* is written. It is an affectionate, loving welcome to all who visit this house of the blessed mothers.

"It's gorgeous!" exclaims Kate when she sees the pretty sign hanging by the front door. "I'm so glad it was ready in time for the dedication today."

Kate and Kai are hosting a fête to celebrate the dedication of two plumeria trees recently planted in the backyard; one in honor of Catherine, and the other in honor of Leilani. The trees sit next to a beautiful, newly installed meditation garden, complete with exquisite and unique tropical foliage, fountains, and inviting garden spaces to sit and dine.

Visiting family members scurry about getting the house and yard ready for the celebration and breakfast that follows.

"Kate, do you want me to put these dishes out on the buffet table in the garden?" asks Carla, holding some white plates as she peeks out the front door.

"Yes, those are the ones. I'm coming in now to help with the set up outside. How do you like the sign?"

"Oh, Kate, Mom definitely must have had a hand in that!" chuckles Carla.

"You know it," beams Kate. "Come on, we've only got an hour until everyone gets here."

Today, much like the previous evening, the gathering consists of family members and extended ohana—fathers, brothers, sisters, spouses, nieces and nephews, Olivia and Grant, Elaine and Trevor, Sukey and Kamal, Cindy and Vinnie, Edward and Meredith, and a few of Kai's close friends.

"Please, if you would, let's form a circle holding hands," calls out Haku Kamaka, one of Kai's friends and a Hawaiian minister. He wears a traditional dress for the dedication. All the guests, dressed in casual celebratory attire with leis around their necks, do what they have been asked and form a circle in the center between the two newly planted plumeria trees.

"Aloha, friends and loved ones, mahalo for joining us today," says Haku as he lifts a large seashell up for all to see.

"For those of you who are unfamiliar with the Hawaiian *pu* shell, this conch, which is blown at sacred ceremonies, is used to summon the heavenly powers and can be heard from miles away. So we will start by invoking spirit, and then I will ask you to join me in prayer."

Haku lifts the large shell to his mouth like a trumpet and, facing north, brings forth a low, long, primal note from the conch. He repeats the call once again to the south, east, and west, and the sacred dedication begins.

"We are gathered here today to dedicate these two plumerias to two loving members of our ohana, Catherine Grace and Leilani Stevens," continues Haku. "Let us pray in honor of their lives here on earth, and for their souls now in heaven, which, eternally connected to us, help to give us strength, guide us, and protect us. *E hānai ʻawa a ikaika ka makani.*

"It is with great love that we dedicate the planting of these trees, in their names, into this fertile soil, to grow, thrive, and blossom. Let the fragrant sweetness of their blooms remind us of our sweet mothers who watch over us with their tender love. With these trees, we honor our bond and eternal ties, as they are our personal guardian angels who assist us in this life, and to whom we will be rejoined in the next. Repeat after me this simple prayer of love and thanks to our Heavenly Father."

As they watch the ceremony unfold, the ladies in the window, Leilani and Catherine, stand beside each other and smile with pride. With a deep understanding of what they will do next, they reach for each other's hands and hold tight to increase their energies. The passionate love they hold in their souls for their families bursts forth into a beautiful, white, energetic light, which pours out through the open window blowing the curtains this way and that.

As Kate holds Kai's hand, she senses movement coming toward her from behind, and then feels it envelope her. She sees swishes of light out of the corners of her eyes, which causes her to look over her shoulder. When Kate notices that the cottage curtains blow about as if in a joyous dance—despite the fact that elsewhere the air is still—a familiar tingle runs up and down her spine . . . *and then she sees them.*

Two birds in flight overhead make themselves known to the gathering with their sweet song. They fly close to the ohana circle and remain above, as if they harbor a desire to be a part of it. Haku pauses, as does everyone, in awe, as they watch the birds' beautiful choreographed flight.

Kate squeezes Kai's hand hard, and he nods, aware of the magic. Both Glen and Bradford, standing on either side of their children and holding their hands, also silently acknowledge the dance and song of the circling birds.

"Let's pray together," Haku continues, as the birds continue to hover, more quietly now, as if following in suit with the rest of those gathered.

The minister speaks in Hawaiian first, and then in English, and after every phrase spoken, the members gathered repeat in the same fashion.

"Ho'onani i ka Makua mau,
Praise God from whom all blessings flow;
Ke Keiki me ka 'Uhane nō,
Praise him, all creatures here below;
Ke Akua mau ho'omaika'i pū,
Praise him above, ye heavenly host;
Kō kēia ao, kō kēlā ao,
Praise Father, Son, and Holy Ghost."
'Āmene.
"Amen."

As Kate holds Kai's hand on one side, and her father's on the other, she looks out onto the loving faces of her family and friends. Then she looks to the two birds that hover about this pulsating circle of love and thanks God for all her blessings. She knows with all her being that *ohana is where happiness lives.*

About the Author

Photo by Marie Gregorio-Oviedo

Maryann Ridini Spencer is an award-winning screenwriter, producer, author, journalist, TV host, and president of Ridini Entertainment Corporation, a content creation, public relations, and marketing, and TV and film production company. A winner of several scholarships, she received her degree in communications from New York's Hofstra University and soon afterward became a producer/writer for Cable News Network in Los Angeles, later serving as senior vice president at several Hollywood studios and firms.

A member of the Producers Guild of America and the Writers Guild West, Maryann has executive produced/produced movies and series for such networks as Showtime, SyFy, TMC, USA Networks, Time Warner Cable, and the foreign theatrical market, and is celebrated for coproducing and writing the teleplay for the Hallmark Hall of Fame CBS-TV World Premiere of *The Lost Valentine* (based on the novel by James Michael Pratt), starring Betty White and Jennifer Love Hewitt. Upon its CBS-TV debut in 2011, the award-winning film was the evening's highest rated film, with over fifteen million peopled tuning in, and it became Hallmark Hall of Fame's highest-rated film in four years. Now considered a Hallmark Classic, the film airs each year on the Hallmark Channel and is part of Hallmark's Gold Crown DVD Collector's Edition. Maryann is also the creator, writer, producer, and host of the award-winning healthy living TV cooking series (and cookbook), *Simply Delicious Living with Maryann®*, which is broadcast on the PBS-TV station KVCR in Southern California, DirecTV, DishTV, and to a global audience on Roku, YouTube and Maryann's blog at www.SimplyDeliciousLiving.com.

Throughout her career Maryann has worked as a freelance writer and/or contributing editor for such publications as *Los Angeles Magazine, Palm Springs Life* and *Desert Magazine.* Her "Simply Delicious Living" print and video column as well as the environmental news program she created, produces, writes, and reports, *Sustainable Ventura News,* is broadcast on local television in Ventura County, CA, and on the news and lifestyle pages at VenturaCountyStar.com. Maryann lives with her husband, Dr. Christopher Scott Spencer, between Southern California and Hawaii, where she is at work penning the screenplay and sequel book to *Lady in the Window.*

You can visit her online at: www.maryannridinispencer.com.